LES MISÉRABLES

An Engaging Visual Journey

VISIT TYNDALE ONLINE AT TYNDALE.COM

TYNDALE and Tyndale's quill logo are registered trademarks of Tyndale House Ministries.

Living Expressions and Visual Journey are trademarks of Tyndale House Ministries.

Les Misérables: An Engaging Visual Journey

Copyright © 2021 by Tyndale House Ministries. All rights reserved.

Condensed from an abridgement by Douglas Gordon Crawford.

Cover and interior illustrations of hand-lettered quotes and spot embellishments copyright © Jill De Haan. All rights reserved.

Interior illustrations of graphite artwork copyright © Margaret Ferrec. All rights reserved.

Interior full-page color illustrations by Chiara Fedele. Copyright © Tyndale House Ministries. All rights reserved.

Unless otherwise noted, interior photographs are from Wikimedia Commons and in the public domain. Jean Louis Bagot letters © Archives municipales de Saint-Brieuc; rue de Birague © Sanaa78; décret © Département du Rhône; pont de l'Archevêché © Mbzt, 2012; château de Walzin by Victor Hugo © Domergue; château fort sur une colline by Victor Hugo © GilPe.

Designed by Jennifer L. Phelps

Edited by Caleb Sjogren

Scripture quotations are taken from the *Holy Bible*, New Living Translation, copyright © 1996, 2004, 2015 by Tyndale House Foundation. Used by permission of Tyndale House Publishers, Carol Stream, Illinois 60188. All rights reserved.

Les Misérables: An Engaging Visual Journey is a work of fiction. Where real people, events, establishments, organizations, or locales appear, they are used fictitiously. All other elements of the novel are drawn from the author's imagination.

For information about special discounts for bulk purchases, please contact Tyndale House Publishers at csresponse@tyndale.com, or call 1-800-323-9400.

ISBN 978-1-4964-4296-3

Printed in China

27 26 25 24 23 22 21
7 6 5 4 3 2 1

AN ENGAGING VISUAL JOURNEY

The Lord is good
to everyone.
He showers compassion
on all his creation.

PSALM 145:9

INTRODUCTION

In the early morning hours of 5 June 1832, a throng of mourners merged with crowds of students, workers, and others with a political agenda in the streets of Paris, all gathered to redirect the hearse bearing the body of General Jean Maximilien Lamarque to the PLACE DE LA BASTILLE before it took him to his native home in the south of France. Lamarque had been a beloved friend of and advocate for the poor and downtrodden, and the throng numbered in the tens of thousands. Because the people were infuriated by their economic hardships, food shortages, and the callous attitudes of the upper classes, Paris was like a powder keg waiting to go off.

The story is told that on that day, thirty-year-old Victor Hugo was writing a play in the nearby Tuileries Garden on the banks of the River Seine when he heard gunfire from the direction of the Les Halles market, where meagerly equipped rebels and the government's formidable military had begun to clash in a bloody battle. Hugo called the park keeper to open the gates of the garden, now locked because of the impending uprising, and instead of going home to safety, he followed the sounds of gunfire through the deserted streets, unaware that the mob had taken half of Paris. Barricades were everywhere in the Les Halles area, but he headed to the RUE DU BOUT DU MONDE, an alley-like street. The grilles at either end were slammed shut, and all the shops and stores had been tightly closed. As bullets whizzed past him, he flung himself against a wall, finding shelter between some columns, as the rebels exchanged fire with French soldiers from behind a makeshift barricade.

The uprising did not end well for the rebels. Their hoped-for reinforcements did not arrive, and both sides suffered casualties: 166 killed, of which 93 were rebels, with 635 wounded.

Three decades later, Victor Hugo would publish his masterpiece, *Les Misérables*, written mostly on the Isle of Guernsey, where he lived for fifteen years after being exiled in 1851 due to his outspoken opposition to Napoleon. He had begun planning a major novel about social misery and injustice as early as the 1830s, but a full seventeen years were needed for *Les Misérables* to be realized and finally published in 1862. While unpopular at the time because of its fire-and-brimstone-like commentary, it would become his most famous work.

The book is inspired by his unforgettable experience on the day that is known as the June Rebellion. It is one of the few literary works that depict the suffering and misery of the impoverished Parisian underclass, who had little voice in society during this time period. Victor Hugo provides that voice, portraying many of the small revolutionary groups of the time. The June Rebellion was a historic event largely forgotten until 8 October 1985, when the astoundingly popular musical production of *Les Misérables* opened on a London stage.

The book begins in 1815 and tells the fictional story of Jean Valjean, a man who has been cruelly condemned to nearly two decades of prison—hard labor in the galleys—for stealing a loaf of bread to save his widowed sister's starving children. Upon his release, he finds that he is treated like an outcast everywhere he goes and loses all hope until the good Bishop Myriel takes him in and, with the love of God, blesses him. The bishop's Christlike compassion causes Jean Valjean to desire a new life for himself. But for decades, after breaking parole, he is hunted by Inspector Javert, the ruthless policeman obsessively devoted to enforcing the letter of the law. Valjean, who has been miraculously saved for God's work, rather than just securing this gift for himself, then agrees to care for Fantine, a desperate, dying factory worker who has been forced into prostitution, and later her orphaned daughter, Cosette. These decisions change their lives forever. It is a moving story of the transforming power of grace, how God's mercy can redirect one's life, and how striving for salvation through works can break a person. In the original text, Hugo uses the word *transfiguration*—a complete change of form or appearance into a more beautiful or spiritual state—to describe the complete transformation of Jean Valjean through the power of the gospel.

When Victor Hugo returned to Paris in 1870, the country hailed him as a national hero. He died in 1885 at the age of eighty-three. His home in Paris on the PLACE DES VOSGES now houses a museum commemorating his life. He was not only a novelist but also a statesman, activist, poet, dramatist, and artist of more than four thousand drawings. Well over a thousand musical compositions have been inspired by his works from the nineteenth century to the present day.

We first experienced the *Les Misérables* musical by the original national cast at the Auditorium Theatre in Chicago, then celebrating the historic venue's centennial anniversary, in the spring of 1989. Thus began our love for and deep appreciation of the Christian themes of this unforgettable story. While millions have seen the stage production internationally, relatively few people have read the original novel, consisting of five volumes and more than half a million words. Most currently available abridgements were made more than one hundred years ago. In this abridgement, we have sought to capture the essence of the story, the human drama, and the rich spiritual awakening of the characters while maintaining the integrity of Victor Hugo's original work.

What an amazing honor and privilege it has been to be entrusted with the abridgement of this epic novel for the beautiful book you now have in your hands, which we hope will cause you to love the captivating, compelling, and inspiring story of *Les Misérables* as much as we do.

Terri and Jim Kraus

PARIS, RUE DE BIRAGUE • ARTIST & DATE UNKNOWN

Love is a portion of the soul itself,
and it is of the same nature as the celestial
breathing of the atmosphere of paradise.

In all heavens, beauty reigns,
Its beings possess much of divinity.
Peace and harmony rule these realms,
Their beings know not the word war.

VICTOR HUGO

JEAN VALJEAN

After nineteen years in prison, Jean Valjean emerges a hardened man. But when a bishop shows him undeserved grace, Valjean breaks from his parole, leaving behind his old identity and undertaking a life of generosity in which he seeks to live out the truth of his redemption. To begin afresh, he adopts pseudonyms, always hiding from his past. Valjean gives selflessly, expecting nothing in return. He tends to a dying mother, rescues an orphaned girl, visits the sick and needy, and on more than one occasion exposes and implicates himself to save another. Jean Valjean is a character who exhibits both freedom of new life in Jesus Christ and great fear that his past will catch up with him. He loves deeply, for he has experienced deep love, forgiveness, and restoration. In the end, he blissfully enters his final reward, not for anything he has done, but for the great work of salvation that has been done on his behalf.

FANTINE

Abandoned by her lover, Fantine leaves their child with a family she encounters as she travels to look for work. She finds a position at a factory, working diligently and sending regular payments to care for her daughter. But when the other workers learn of Fantine's daughter, she loses her job in the scandal. She keeps receiving letters demanding more money for Cosette's care, forcing her to sell her hair, her teeth, and finally her very body. After Javert arrests Fantine, the mayor of the town—Valjean—intervenes and takes pity on her, earning Javert's scorn. Fantine's sickness takes her life, but not before Valjean promises to care for the child. Fantine is a picture of the desperation and misery that come from a cycle of poverty. Even in her life of misery, her love for Cosette is pure.

JAVERT

A police officer unwaveringly dedicated to justice, with no shades of gray, Javert is uncompromising in upholding the law. Having been stationed at the facility where Valjean was imprisoned, Javert takes a new appointment as a police chief and soon comes to suspect the mayor is not who he appears. Valjean, under a false name, has become the wealthy and successful benefactor of the town. Javert uncovers Valjean's true identity, but Valjean escapes from the law until the two again cross paths in Paris years later. Javert is rigid and unbending, qualities that eventually lead to his downfall when he can neither conceive nor abide a world of ambiguity, in which mercy and grace may be as valid as justice and punishment. Javert is the personification of the rigid law, written on cold tablets of stone.

COSETTE

When Cosette is only a baby, her mother, Fantine, leaves her in the care of an innkeeper and his wife. Unbeknownst to Cosette's mother, the husband and wife are cruel and hardened people. Cosette's keepers work the young girl mercilessly, forcing her to labor with little food and no care or affection. But while her mistreatment scars her, it does not embitter the child. On Fantine's deathbed, Jean Valjean swears to care for the girl. He risks recapture to see that she is safe, and he adopts her as his own daughter, the recipient of his great love. But as Cosette nears adulthood, she longs for more than the cloistered life she's experienced. Cosette is an image of sweetness and innocence, and yet in going behind her father's back to court Marius, Cosette demonstrates a willfulness of her own. Her character shows how even a bruised flower can flourish with the love and care it craves.

MARIUS

Marius is raised by his grandfather, who teaches him to hate his absent father. But when Marius learns that his father has been deliberately kept from him, he denounces his grandfather's household. Three crucial points converge upon him nearly at the same time: the simmering call for revolution, the young woman he comes to love, and the discovery of the man who saved his father's life. Marius is earnest and idealistic, wanting to believe in love and honor. Even confronted with treachery and cruelty, he does not become jaded. When faced with loss, he casts himself into the cause of revolution, heedless of the danger, but he is saved, carried from death to life by the man he thought had destroyed him. In Marius, Jean Valjean passes on the undeserved grace he received many years before.

THE THÉNARDIERS

The innkeeper and his wife are cruel, greedy, and unscrupulous. They agree to care for Cosette, but then use her for forced labor and extort Fantine, driving her deeper into desperation and despair. Years later, M. Thénardier leads a band of cutthroats, luring generous people to his lair to rob and murder them. The two enlist their daughters in their criminal activity, but their youngest, a son, they hardly acknowledge, leaving him to roam the streets and fend for himself. After the revolution is quelled, M. Thénardier lurks in the sewers, robbing the dead of any valuables. These two characters are depictions of humanity sinking into depravity, ever deeper in vice and cruelty. They seem nearly incapable of love, even for their own family, caring only for self-preservation.

ÉPONINE

The Thénardiers' daughter Éponine is party to her family's criminal schemes, but unlike her parents, she demonstrates genuine affection and care for others. She expresses an infatuation with Marius, who seems entirely oblivious to it. Yet despite her unrequited feelings, she cares for Marius enough to protect the ones he loves and to give her own life to save him. Éponine is robbed of her childhood and her innocence. She never has the opportunity to achieve her potential, and still her life is heroic, though tragic.

GAVROCHE

The Thénardiers reject Gavroche, their son, and leave him to roam the streets of Paris and make his own way. His character demonstrates the resilience of the human heart. Though Gavroche's life has been one of hardship and want, he is generous, self-sacrificing, and fearless. He exhibits unparalleled loyalty and bravery during the siege of the barricade by identifying the spy among them and daring the tasks that others fear to attempt. Sadly, his life is cut short, yet another of the miserable poor of France who live only a fraction of the life they were created for.

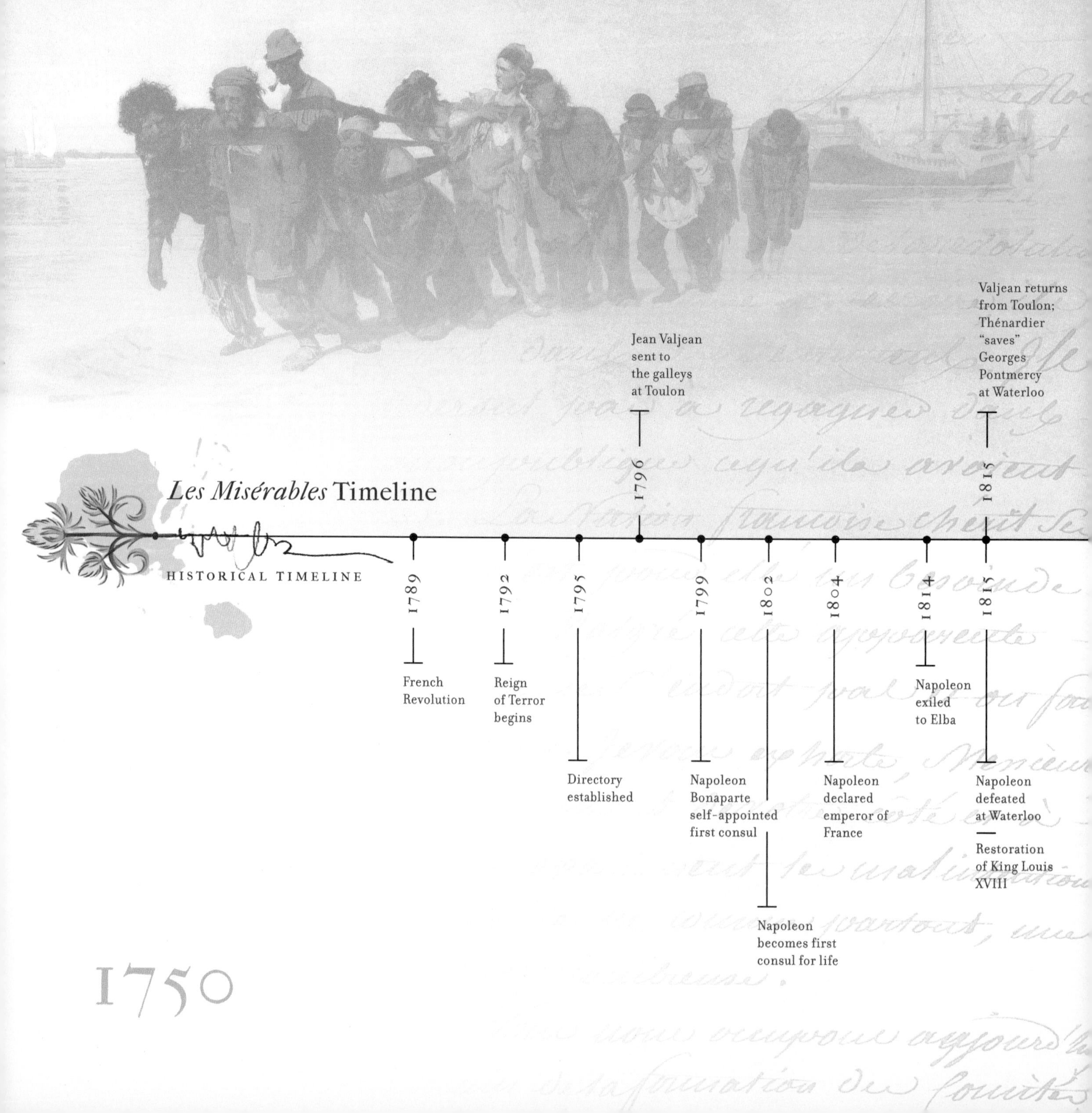
Les Misérables Timeline
HISTORICAL TIMELINE
1750
1789
French Revolution
1792
Reign of Terror begins
1795
Directory established
1796
Jean Valjean sent to the galleys at Toulon
1799
Napoleon Bonaparte self-appointed first consul
1802
Napoleon becomes first consul for life
1804
Napoleon declared emperor of France
1814
Napoleon exiled to Elba
1815
Valjean returns from Toulon; Thénardier "saves" Georges Pontmercy at Waterloo
1815
Napoleon defeated at Waterloo
Restoration of King Louis XVIII

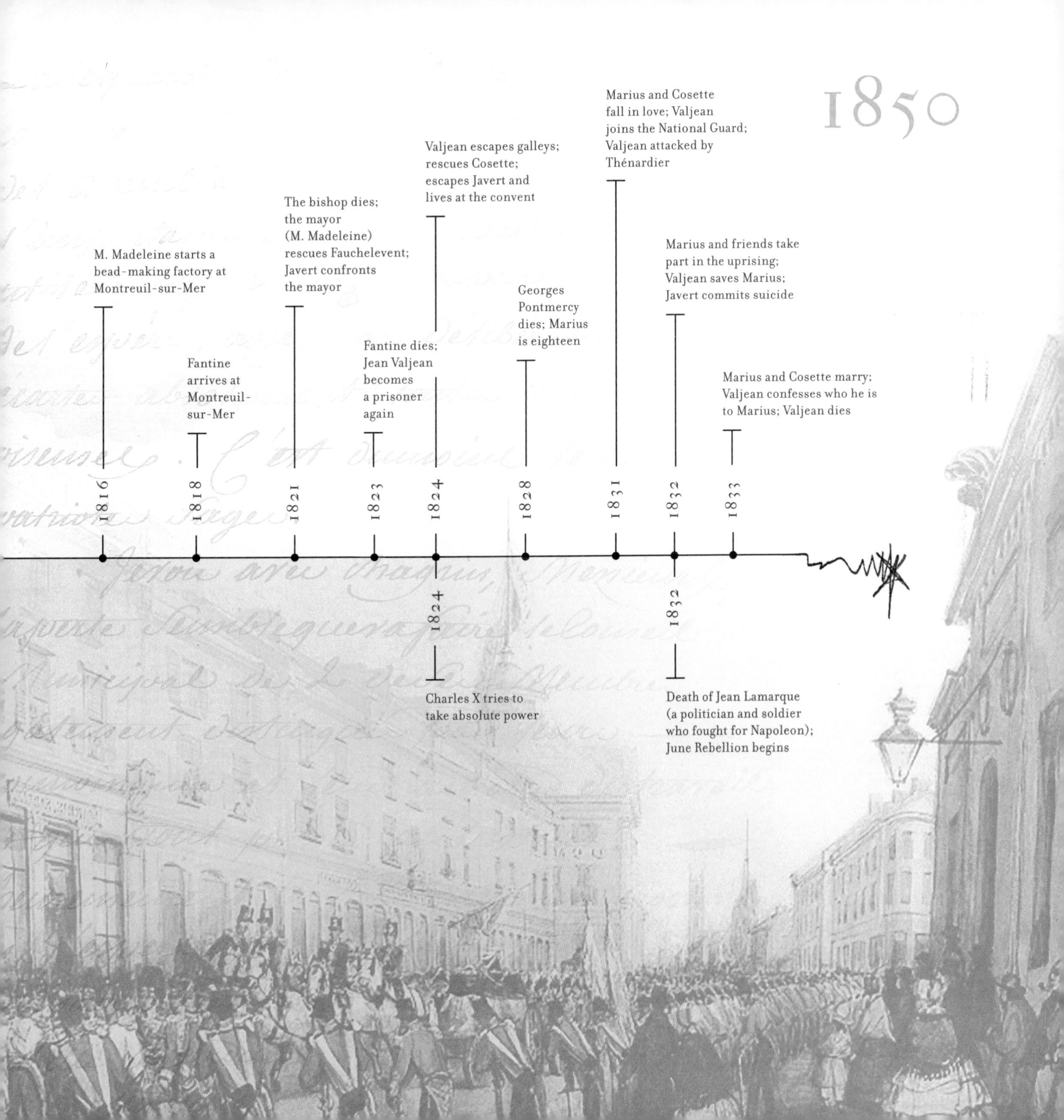
1850
M. Madeleine starts a bead-making factory at Montreuil-sur-Mer
1816
Fantine arrives at Montreuil-sur-Mer
1818
The bishop dies; the mayor (M. Madeleine) rescues Fauchelevent; Javert confronts the mayor
1821
Fantine dies; Jean Valjean becomes a prisoner again
1823
Valjean escapes galleys; rescues Cosette; escapes Javert and lives at the convent
1824
1824
Charles X tries to take absolute power
Georges Pontmercy dies; Marius is eighteen
1828
Marius and Cosette fall in love; Valjean joins the National Guard; Valjean attacked by Thénardier
1831
Marius and friends take part in the uprising; Valjean saves Marius; Javert commits suicide
1832
1832
Death of Jean Lamarque (a politician and soldier who fought for Napoleon); June Rebellion begins
Marius and Cosette marry; Valjean confesses who he is to Marius; Valjean dies
1833

Chapter I

In 1815, M. Charles François-Bienvenu Myriel was bishop of Digne. At age seventy-five, he had occupied the bishopric since 1806. His person was admirably molded; although of slight figure, he was elegant and graceful.

The bishop's palace was contiguous to a hospital. The palace itself was a spacious and beautiful edifice built of stone, with an air of grandeur about everything: the apartments of the bishop, the chambers, the court of honor, with arched walks and a garden planted with magnificent trees. The hospital was a low, narrow two-story building with a small garden.

The bishop invited the hospital director to the palace.

"Monsieur," he said to the director of the hospital, "how many patients have you?"

"Twenty-six, monseigneur. And the beds are very much crowded. The wards are but small chambers, not easily ventilated. And when the sun does shine, the garden is very small for the convalescents."

"That was what I was thinking."

"What can we do, monseigneur?" said the director.

The bishop was silent a few moments, then turned suddenly toward the director.

"Monsieur," he said, "how many beds do you think this hall alone would contain?"

"The dining hall of monseigneur!" exclaimed the director, stupefied.

The bishop looked over the hall, as if taking measure and making calculations. "It will hold twenty beds." Then raising his voice, he said, "Listen, Monsieur Director, there is evidently a mistake here. There are twenty-six of you in five or six small rooms; there are only three of us, and space for sixty. There is a mistake, I tell you. You have my house, and I have yours. Restore mine to me; you are at home."

Next day the twenty-six poor invalids were installed in the bishop's palace, and the bishop was in the hospital.

The bishop had no property, and he resolved to give his salary of fifteen thousand francs* to charity, reserving for himself only one thousand francs.

M. Myriel could be called at all hours to the bedsides of the sick and the dying. He well knew that there was his highest duty and his greatest work. Oh, admirable consoler! He did not seek to drown grief in oblivion, but to exalt and to dignify it by hope. He would say, "Be careful of the way in which you think of the dead. Think not of what might have been. Look steadfastly and you shall see the living glory of your well-beloved dead in the depths of heaven."

It was the custom that all bishops should put their baptismal names at the head of their orders and pastoral letters. The poor people of the district had chosen an affectionate name for the bishop—Monseigneur Bienvenu—which means "welcome." This pleased him. "I like this name," said he. "*Bienvenu* counterbalances *monseigneur*."

The bishop regularly made his visits, and in the diocese of Digne this was a wearisome task. The land was mountainous, with hardly any roads, but the bishop went joyfully.

In his visits he was indulgent and gentle, and preached less than he talked. He would talk, gravely and paternally; he would invent parables, going straight to his object, with few phrases and many images, which was the very eloquence of Jesus Christ, convincing and persuasive.

franc : worth 20 cents in 1815 (worth approximately $3.70 today) *

Chapter 2

A tragic event occurred at Digne. A man had been condemned to death for murder. The bishop went to the prison, into the dungeon of the mountebank,* called him by his name, took him by the hand, and talked with him. He passed the whole day with him, forgetful of food and sleep, praying to God for the soul of the condemned and exhorting the condemned to join with him. He spoke to him the truth. He was father, brother, friend; bishop for blessing only. He encouraged and consoled him. This man would have died in despair. Death, for him, was like an abyss. The terrible shock of his condemnation had broken that wall which separates us from the mystery of things beyond, and which we call life. Through these breaches, he looked beyond this world and could see nothing but darkness, yet the bishop showed him the light.

When the jailers came for the poor man, the bishop was with him. He followed him, in his violet hood, with his bishop's cross about his neck, side by side with the condemned, who was bound with cords.

He ascended the scaffold with him. The sufferer, once horror-stricken, was now radiant with hope. His soul was reconciled, and he trusted in God. The bishop embraced him, and at the moment when the ax was about to fall, he said to him, "Whom man kills, him God restoreth to life; whom his brethren put away, he findeth the Father. Pray, believe, enter into life! The Father is there."

The impression of the scaffold was horrible and deep; for many days, the bishop appeared to be overwhelmed. He, who ordinarily looked back upon all his actions with a satisfaction so radiant, now seemed distraught. One evening his only sister overheard him saying, "I did not believe it could be so monstrous. It is wrong to be so absorbed in the divine law as not to perceive the human law. Death belongs to God alone. By what right do men touch that unknown thing?"

The house which the bishop occupied consisted of three rooms on the ground floor, three on a second story, and an attic above.

Two women—his sister, Mademoiselle Baptistine, and his housekeeper, Madame Magloire—occupied the upper floor; the bishop lived below. The first room, which opened upon the street, was his dining room, the second was his bedroom, and the third his oratory*.

Nothing could be plainer in its arrangements than the bishop's bedchamber. A window, which was also a door, opened upon the garden. Facing this was the bed; two doors, one leading into the oratory, the other into the dining room. A bookcase, with glass doors, was filled with books. Above the fireplace was a copper crucifix, from which the silver was worn off, fixed upon black velvet in a wooden frame; near the window stood a large table with an inkstand, covered with papers and heavy volumes. In front of the table was an armchair.

The bishop still retained, of what he had formerly, six silver dishes and a silver soup ladle which Madame Magloire contemplated every day with new joy as they shone on the coarse white linen tablecloth. He had said, more than once, "It would be difficult for me to give up eating from silver."

mountebank : a person who deceives others, especially in order to trick them out of their money; a charlatan, criminal

oratory : a small chapel, especially for private worship *

THE
SUFFERER,
ONCE HORROR-STRICKEN,
WAS NOW
RADIANT WITH HOPE.
HIS SOUL WAS
RECONCILED,
AND HE TRUSTED IN
GOD.
VICTOR HUGO

With this silverware should be counted two massive silver candlesticks which he inherited from a great-aunt. When he had guests, Madame Magloire lighted the two candles and moved the two candlesticks from the mantel to the table.

There was in the bishop's chamber, at the head of his bed, a small cupboard in which Madame Magloire placed the six silver dishes and the great ladle every evening. But the key was never taken out of it.

Not a door in the house had a lock. The door of the dining room, which opened into the cathedral grounds, was formerly loaded with bars and bolts like the door of a prison. The bishop had had all this ironwork taken off, and the door, by night as well as by day, was closed only with a latch. Any passerby could open it with a simple push.

The bishop had written in the margin of a Bible:

This is the shade of meaning: the door of a physician should never be closed; the door of a priest should always be open.

CHAPTER 3

One evening in October, a man traveling afoot entered the little town of Digne. The few persons who at this time were at their windows or doors regarded this traveler with distrust. He was of middle height, stout and hardy, in the strength of maturity; he might have been forty-six or forty-seven. A leather cap half hid his face, which was bronzed by the sun and wind and dripping with sweat. He wore a coarse yellow shirt fastened at the neck by a small silver anchor, a cravat* twisted like a rope, coarse blue trousers, worn and shabby, and an old ragged gray blouse, patched on one side. Upon his back was a well-filled knapsack. In his hand he carried an enormous knotted stick; his stockingless feet were in hobnailed* shoes; his hair was cropped and his beard long.

When he reached the corner of RUE POICHEVERT he went to the mayor's office. After a quarter of an hour he came out. The man raised his cap humbly and saluted a gendarme* who was seated near the door. Without returning his salutation, the gendarme watched him for some distance and then went into the city hall.

There was then in Digne a good inn. The traveler turned toward this inn and went at once into the kitchen. All the ranges were fuming, and a great fire was burning briskly in the fireplace. The host was busy superintending an excellent dinner for some wagoners in the next room. Hearing the door open and a newcomer enter, the proprietor said, without raising his eyes from his ranges, "What will monsieur have?"

"Something to eat and lodging."

"Nothing more easy," said the host, but on turning and seeing the traveler, he added, "for pay."

The man drew from his pocket a large leather purse and answered, "I have money."

"Then," said the host, "I am at your service."

The man put his purse back into his pocket, took off his knapsack, and, holding his stick in his hand, sat down on a low stool by the fire.

While the newcomer was warming himself with his back turned, the innkeeper took a pencil from his pocket and then tore off the corner of an old paper. He wrote a line or two and handed the scrap of paper to a child, who appeared to serve him. The innkeeper whispered a word to the boy, and he ran off in the direction of the mayor's office.

In a few moments, the boy came back with the paper. The host unfolded it hurriedly. He read with attention, then took a step toward the traveler, who seemed drowned in troublous thought.

"Monsieur," said he, "I cannot receive you."

"Why? Are you afraid I shall not pay you, or do you want me to pay in advance?"

"It is not that."

"What then?"

"I have no room."

"Well," responded the man, "a corner in the garret*, or even a truss* of straw."

"And I cannot give you any dinner."

This declaration was made in a measured but firm tone.

"But I am dying with hunger. I have walked since sunrise; I have traveled twelve leagues*. I will pay." The man settled himself and said, without raising his voice, "I am at an inn. I am hungry, and I shall stay."

The host bent down to his ear and said in a stern voice, "Go away!"

At these words the traveler turned suddenly around and opened his mouth, as if to reply, when the host, looking steadily at him, added in the same low tone, "Stop. Shall I tell you your name? Your name is Jean Valjean. When I saw you enter, I suspected something. I sent to the mayor's office, and here is the reply. Can you read?"

The man bowed his head, picked up his knapsack, and went out. He took the principal street; he walked at random, slinking near the houses like a sad and humiliated man; he did not once turn around. If he had turned, he would have seen the innkeeper standing in his doorway with all his guests and the passersby gathered about him, speaking excitedly and pointing him out.

He walked along in this way some time, going by chance down streets unknown to him. He entered another inn, but once again he was suspected and forced out into the cold. Some children, who had followed him and seemed to be waiting for him, threw stones at him. He turned angrily and threatened them with his stick, and they scattered like a flock of birds.

He passed the prison; an iron chain hung from the door attached to a bell. He rang. The grating opened.

"Monsieur Turnkey*," said he, taking off his cap respectfully, "will you open and let me stay here tonight?"

A voice answered, "A prison is not a tavern. Get yourself arrested and we will open."

He then tried various houses along the street, but his appearance raised suspicion and he was repulsed at every door. On passing by the cathedral square, he shook his fist at the church. Then, exhausted with fatigue and losing hope, he lay down on a stone bench in front of the printing office.

cravat : a short, wide strip of fabric worn by men around the neck and tucked inside an open-necked shirt

hobnailed : describes a work boot or shoe with hobnails in the sole to make it last longer and to provide grip

gendarme : a French armed police officer

garret : a room or unfinished part of a house just under the roof

truss : a tight bundle of straw used for bedding

league : a distance from about 2.4 to 4.6 statute miles (3.9 to 7.4 kilometers)

turnkey : a jailer

*

Just then an old woman came out of the church. She saw the man lying there in the dark and said, "What are you doing there, my friend?"

He replied harshly, and with anger in his tone, "You see, my good woman, I am going to sleep."

"Upon the bench?" said she.

"For nineteen years I have had a wooden mattress," said the man. "Tonight I have a stone one."

"You cannot find lodging in an inn? But have you tried? You cannot pass the night so. You must be cold and hungry. They should give you lodging for charity."

"I have knocked at every door. Everybody has driven me away."

The good woman touched the man's arm and pointed out to him, on the other side of the square, a little low house beside the bishop's palace.

"Have you knocked at that one there?"

"No."

"Knock there."

Chapter 4

That evening, after his walk in the town, the bishop of Digne remained in his room. At eight o'clock he was still at work, writing with some inconvenience on little slips of paper, a large book open on his knees.

At this moment there was a loud knock on the door.

"Come in!"

The door opened quickly, as if pushed by someone boldly. A man entered. It was the traveler. He came in, took one step, and paused, leaving the door open behind him. He had his knapsack on his back, his stick in his hand, and a rough, hard, tired, and fierce look in his eyes, as seen by the firelight.

The bishop looked upon the man with a tranquil eye.

Without waiting for the bishop to speak, the man said in a loud voice, "My name is Jean Valjean. I am a convict; I have been nineteen years in the galleys*. Four days ago, I was set free and started for Pontarlier. Today, I have walked twelve leagues. When I reached this place I went to an inn, and they sent me away on account of my yellow passport*, which I had shown at the mayor's office, as was necessary. I went to another inn; they said, 'Get out!' Nobody would have me. I went to the prison, and the jailer would not let me in. In the square, I lay down upon a stone; a good woman showed me your house and said, 'Knock there.' I have knocked. What is this place? Are you an inn? I have money: my savings, 109 francs and fifteen sous*, which I have earned in the galleys by my work for nineteen years. I will pay. I am very tired—twelve leagues on foot, and I am so hungry. Can I stay?"

"Madame Magloire," said the bishop to his housekeeper, "put on another plate."

The man took three steps and came near the lamp which stood on the table. He exclaimed, "Did you understand me? I am a galley slave, a convict. I am just from the galleys." He drew from his pocket a large sheet of yellow paper, which he unfolded. "There is my passport—enough to have me kicked out wherever I go. See, here is what they have put in the passport: 'Jean Valjean, a liberated convict; has been nineteen years in the galleys: five years for burglary; fourteen years for having attempted four times to escape. This man is very dangerous.' There you have it! Everybody has thrust me out; will you receive me? Is this an inn? Can you give me something to eat, and a place to sleep? Have you a stable?"

"Madame Magloire," said the bishop, "put some sheets on the bed in the alcove."

Madame Magloire went out to fulfill her orders. The

bishop turned to the man. "Monsieur, sit down and warm yourself. We are going to take supper presently, and your bed will be made ready while you eat."

At last the man quite understood; his face, the expression of which till then had been gloomy and hard, now expressed stupefaction, doubt, and joy, and became absolutely wonderful.

"True? What! You will keep me? You won't drive me away? A convict! You call me *monsieur* and don't say 'Get out, dog!' as everybody else does. I thought that you would send me away, so I told you just who I am. Oh, the fine woman who sent me here! I shall have a supper, and a bed like other people with mattress and sheets—a bed! It is nineteen years that I have not slept on a bed. You are really willing that I should stay? You are good people! Besides I have money; I will pay well. I beg your pardon, Monsieur Innkeeper, what is your name? You are a fine man. You are an innkeeper, aren't you?"

"I am a priest who lives here," said the bishop.

"A priest!" said the man. "Oh, noble priest! Then you do not ask any money? You are the curé*, aren't you? The curé of this big church? Yes, that's it. How stupid I am; I didn't notice your cap."

While speaking, he had deposited his knapsack and stick in the corner, replaced his passport in his pocket, and sat down. He continued, "You are humane, Monsieur Curé; you don't despise me. A good priest is a good thing. Then you don't want me to pay you?"

"No," said the bishop, "keep your money. How much have you? You said 109 francs, I think."

"And fifteen sous," added the man.

"One hundred and nine francs and fifteen sous. And how long did it take you to earn that?"

"Nineteen years."

"Nineteen years!" The bishop sighed deeply.

The man continued, "I have all my money yet. In four days I have spent only twenty-five sous, which I earned by unloading wagons at Grasse. As you are an abbé*, I must tell you, we have a chaplain in the galleys. One day I saw a bishop; Monseigneur, they called him, the bishop of Majore from Marseilles. He said Mass in the center of the place on an altar; he had a pointed gold thing on his head that shone in the sun. He spoke to us, but we could not see him well nor understand him. That is what a bishop is."

While he was talking, the bishop shut the wide-open door. Madame Magloire brought in a plate and set it on the table.

"Madame Magloire," said the bishop, "put this plate as near the fire as you can." Then, turning toward his guest, he added, "The night wind is raw in the Alps; you must be cold, monsieur."

Every time he said this word *monsieur*, with his gently solemn and heartily hospitable voice, the man's countenance lighted up. *Monsieur* to a convict is a glass of water to a man dying of thirst at sea. Ignominy thirsts for respect.

"The lamp," said the bishop, "gives a very poor light."

Madame Magloire understood him and, going to his bedchamber, took from the mantel the two silver candlesticks, lighted the candles, and placed them on the table.

galley : a long, narrow boat where prisoners sentenced to forced labor were sent to work

yellow passport : a document issued to a convict upon release from prison; the former convict was required to carry it at all times or risk violation of his parole

sous : copper coins; cent pieces

curé : a parish priest; pastor of a parish

abbé : the French word for *abbot*, a lower-ranking Catholic clergyman in France, literally meaning *father*

"Monsieur Curé," said the man, "you are good; you don't despise me. You take me into your house, you light your candles for me, and I haven't kept from you where I come from and how miserable I am."

The bishop, sitting near him, touched his hand gently and said, "You need not tell me who you are. This is not my house; it is the house of Christ. It does not ask any comer whether he has a name, but whether he has an affliction. You are suffering; you are hungry and thirsty; be welcome. And do not thank me; do not tell me that I take you into my house. This is the home of no man, except him who needs an asylum. I tell you, who are a traveler, that you are more at home here than I; whatever is here is yours. What need have I to know your name? Besides, before you told me, I knew it."

The man opened his eyes in astonishment. "Really? You knew my name?"

"Yes," answered the bishop. "Your name is My Brother."

"Stop, stop, Monsieur Curé!" exclaimed the man. "I was famished when I came in, but you are so kind that now I don't know what I am; that is all gone."

The bishop looked at him again and said, "You have seen much suffering?"

"Oh, the red blouse*, the ball and chain, the plank to sleep on, the heat, the cold, the galley's crew, the lash, the double chain for nothing, the dungeon for a word, even when sick in bed, the chain. Nineteen years! I am forty-six, and now a yellow passport. That is all."

"Yes," answered the bishop, "you have left a place of suffering. But listen, if you are leaving that sorrowful place with hate and anger against men, you are worthy of compassion. If you leave it with goodwill, gentleness, and peace, you are better than any of us."

Meantime Madame Magloire had served up supper. The bishop's countenance was lighted up with an expression of pleasure, peculiar to hospitable natures. "To supper!" he said briskly, as was his habit. The bishop said the blessing and then served the soup himself, according to his usual custom. The man fell to eating greedily.

Toward the end, at dessert, the man appeared to be very tired. The bishop said grace, after which he turned toward this man and said, "You must be in great need of sleep." Madame Magloire quickly removed the tablecloth. Monseigneur Bienvenu took one of the silver candlesticks from the table, handed the other to his guest, and said to him, "Monsieur, I will show you to your room." The man followed him.

The house was so arranged that one could reach the alcove in the oratory only by passing through the bishop's sleeping chamber. Just as they were passing through this room, Madame Magloire was putting up the silver in the cupboard at the head of the bed. It was the last thing she did every night before going to bed.

The bishop left his guest in the alcove, before a clean white bed. The man set down the candlestick upon a small table.

"Come," said the bishop, "a good night's rest to you.

Tomorrow morning, before you go, you shall have a cup of warm milk from our cows."

"Thank you, Monsieur l'Abbé," said the traveler. "Have you reflected upon it? Who tells you that I am not a murderer?"

The bishop responded, "God will take care of that."

Then with gravity, moving his lips like one praying or talking to himself, he raised two fingers of his right hand and blessed the man, who, however, did not bow; and without turning his head or looking behind him, went into his chamber.

When the alcove was occupied, a heavy serge* curtain was drawn in the oratory, concealing the altar. Before this curtain the bishop knelt as he exited and offered a short prayer. A moment afterward he was walking in the garden, surrendering mind and soul to the grand and mysterious works of God, which night makes visible to the eye.

As to the man, he was so completely exhausted that he did not even avail himself of the clean white sheets; he blew out the candle and fell on the bed, dressed as he was, into a sound sleep.

Midnight struck as the bishop came back to his chamber. A few moments afterward, all in the little house slept.

Chapter 5

Born of a poor peasant family, Jean Valjean had not been taught to read. When he was grown, he chose the occupation of a pruner at Faverolles. His mother's name was Jeanne Mathieu, his father's Jean Valjean. He had lost his parents when very young. His mother died of fever; his father, a pruner before him, was killed by a fall from a tree. Jean Valjean now had but one relative left, his sister, a widow with seven children, girls and boys. This sister had brought up Jean Valjean, and, as long as her husband lived, she had taken care of her young brother. Her husband died, leaving the eldest of these children at eight and the youngest at one year old. Jean Valjean had just reached his twenty-fifth year; he took the father's place and, in his turn, supported the sister who reared him. This he did naturally, as a duty. His youth was spent in rough and ill-recompensed labor. He had not time to be in love.

He earned in the pruning season eighteen sous a day; after that he hired out as a reaper, workman, teamster, or laborer. He did whatever he could find to do. His sister worked, but what could she do with seven little children? It was a sad group, which misery was grasping and closing upon, little by little. There was a very severe winter; Jean had no work, and the family had no bread—literally, no bread, and seven children.

red blouse: The predominate color of the galley prisoners' uniforms was red. These uniforms consisted of a white shirt, yellow trousers, red vest and smock, and a cap. Those sentenced to life imprisonment wore green caps; all the others wore red caps.

serge: a durable twilled woolen or worsted fabric

One night Maubert Isabeau, the baker in Faverolles, was just going to bed when he heard a violent crash at the barred window of his shop. He got down in time to see an arm thrust through the aperture made by the blow of a fist on the glass. The arm seized a loaf of bread and took it out. Isabeau rushed out and pursued him and caught him. The thief had thrown away the bread, but his arm was still bleeding. It was Jean Valjean.

All that happened in 1795. Jean Valjean was brought before the tribunal* of the time for "burglary at night in an inhabited house" and was found guilty. There are fearful words; such are those when the criminal law pronounces shipwreck upon a man. Jean Valjean was sentenced to five years in the galleys.

On 22 April 1796, a great chain was riveted at the Bicêtre* prison. Jean Valjean was a part of this chain. Sitting on the ground like the rest, he seemed to comprehend nothing of his position except its horror. As they riveted the bolt of his iron collar with heavy hammer strokes behind his head, he wept. The tears choked his words, and he only succeeded in saying from time to time, "I was a pruner at Faverolles."

He was taken to Toulon*, the chain still about his neck. He was dressed in a red blouse; all his past life was effaced, even to his name. He was no longer Jean Valjean. He was number 24601.

What became of the sister and the seven children? What becomes of the handful of leaves of the young tree when it is sawn at the trunk? These poor little lives, these creatures of God, henceforth without support, or guide, or asylum; they passed away wherever chance led, who knows even?

Near the end of his fourth year, a chance of liberty came to Jean Valjean. His comrades helped him, as they always do in that dreary place, and he escaped. He wandered two days in freedom through the fields, if it is freedom to be hunted, to turn your head each moment, to tremble at the least noise, to be afraid of everything, of the smoke of a chimney, the passing of a man, the baying of a dog, the gallop of a horse, the striking of a clock, of the day because you see, and of the night because you do not; of the road, of the path, of the bush, of sleep. During the evening of the second day he was retaken; he had neither eaten nor slept for thirty-six hours. The tribunal extended his sentence three years for this attempt, which made eight. In the sixth year his turn of escape came again; he tried, but failed again. He did not answer at roll call, and the alarm cannon was fired. At night he was discovered hidden beneath the keel* of a vessel. He resisted the guards who seized him. Escape and resistance were punished by an addition of five years, two with the double chain. Thirteen years. The tenth year his turn came around again; he made another attempt with no better success. Three years for this new attempt. Sixteen years. And finally, in the thirteenth year, he tried again and was retaken after an absence of only four hours. Three years for these four hours. Nineteen years for having broken a pane of glass and taken a loaf of bread.

Jean Valjean entered the galleys sobbing, he went out hardened; he entered in despair, he went out sullen. In physical strength he far surpassed all the other inmates. At hard work, at twisting a cable or turning a windlass*, Jean Valjean was equal to four men. He would sometimes lift and hold enormous weights on his back. His suppleness surpassed his strength. Certain convicts have developed a veritable science of strength and skill combined, the science of the muscles. To scale a wall, and to find a foothold where you could hardly see a projection, was play for Jean Valjean. Given an angle in a wall, with the tension of his back and his knees, with elbows and hands braced against the rough face of the stone, he would ascend, as if by magic, to a third story. Sometimes he climbed up in this manner to the roof of the galleys.

He talked but little, and never laughed. To those who saw him, he seemed to be absorbed in continually looking upon something terrible. From year to year his soul had withered more and more, slowly, but fatally. With this withered heart, he had a dry eye. When he left the galleys, he had not shed a tear for nearly two decades.

As the cathedral clock struck two, Jean Valjean awoke. He had slept only four hours. What awakened him was too good a bed. For nearly twenty years he had not slept in a bed. His fatigue had passed away. He was not accustomed to give many hours to repose. He opened his eyes; then he closed them to go to sleep again. But he could not, and so he began to think.

Those silver plates took possession of him. There they were, within a few steps. He had marked that cupboard well. They were solid, crafted of old silver. With the big ladle, they would bring at least two hundred francs, double what he had got for nineteen years' labor.

His mind wavered a whole hour in struggle. The clock struck three. He opened his eyes, rose up hastily in bed, reached out his arm, and felt for his haversack*; then he thrust out his legs and placed his feet on the ground.

He remained for some time lost in thought and would perhaps have remained there until daybreak if the clock had not struck the quarter or the half hour. The clock seemed to say to him, "Come along!"

All was still in the house. He walked straight and cautiously toward the window. The night was not very dark; there was a full moon, across which clouds were driving before the wind. The window had no bars, opened into the garden, and was fastened with a little wedge only. The garden was enclosed with a low wall and readily scaled.

Observing this, he turned like a man whose mind is made up, went to his alcove, took his haversack, swung it upon his shoulders, put on his cap, and pulled the visor down over his eyes, felt for his stick, and went and put it in the corner of the window, then returned to the bed holding his breath. With stealthy steps, he moved toward the door of the bishop's bedchamber. He found it unlatched. The bishop had not closed it.

Jean Valjean listened. Not a sound. He pushed the door, waited a moment, and then pushed the door again. It yielded gradually and silently. He took one step and was in the room.

A deep calm filled the chamber. Jean Valjean advanced, carefully avoiding the furniture. At the further end of the room he could hear the quiet breathing of the bishop. Suddenly he stopped.

For nearly a half hour a great cloud had darkened the sky. At the moment when Jean Valjean paused before the bed, the cloud broke as if purposely, and a ray of moonlight crossing the high window suddenly lighted up the bishop's pale face. Over the side of the bed hung his hand, which had done so many good deeds, so many pious acts. His entire countenance

tribunal : a judge; a member of a court of justice

Bicêtre : a former prison located in the southern suburbs of Paris

Toulon (the Bagne of Toulon) : an infamous French prison on the Mediterranean Sea in the south of France from 1748 to 1873

keel : a flat blade sticking down into the water from a sailboat's bottom

windlass : a type of winch used especially on ships to hoist anchors and haul on mooring lines and to lower buckets into and hoist them up from wells

haversack : a small pack or bag similar to a backpack, but with a single shoulder strap *

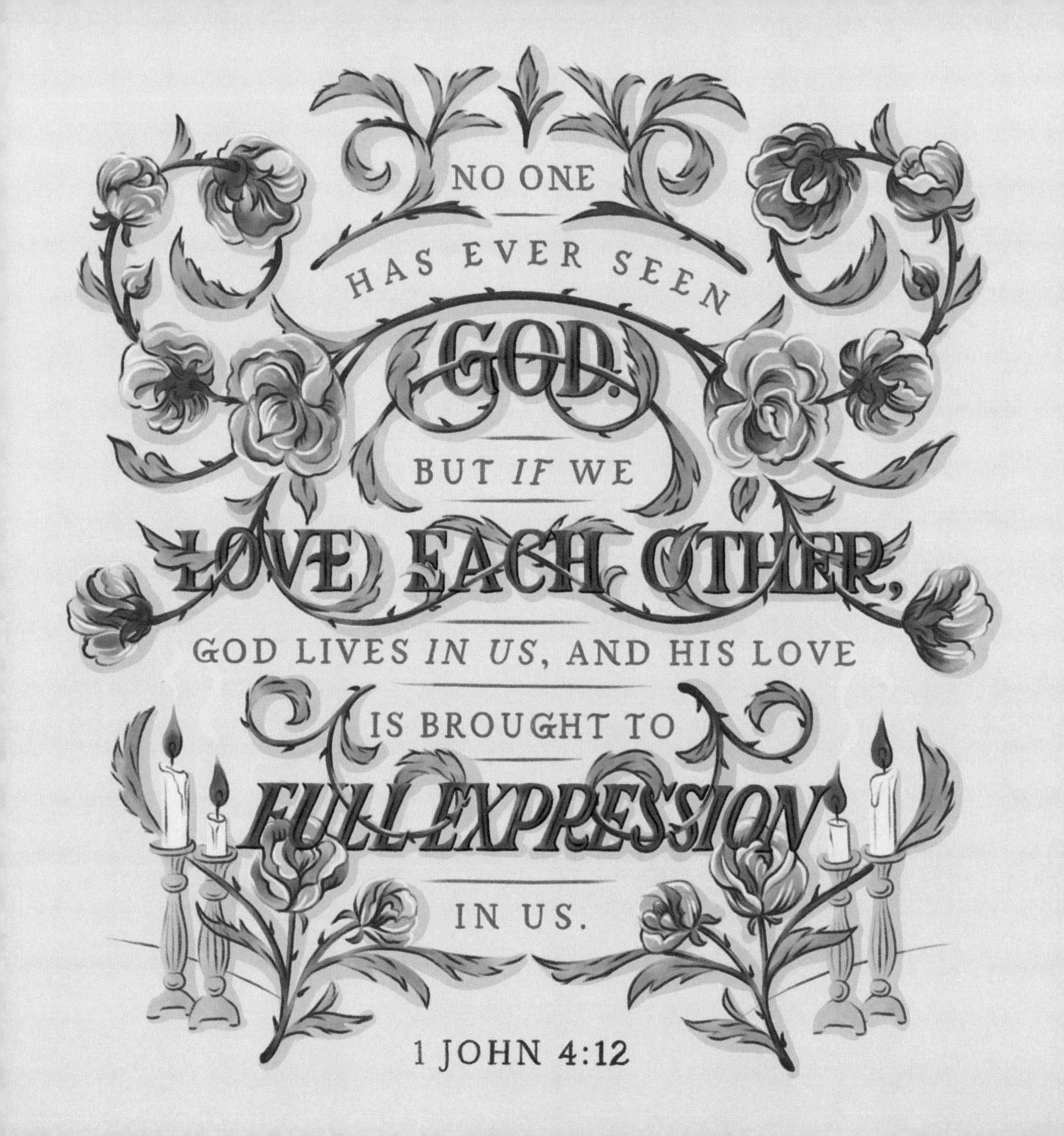
NO ONE
HAS EVER SEEN
GOD.
BUT IF WE
LOVE EACH OTHER,
GOD LIVES IN US, AND HIS LOVE
IS BROUGHT TO
FULL EXPRESSION
IN US.
1 JOHN 4:12

was lit up with an expression of contentment, hope, and happiness. It was more than a smile and almost a radiance.

Jean Valjean did not remove his eyes from the old man. It appeared that he was hesitating between two realms, that of the doomed and that of the saved. He appeared ready either to cleave* this skull or to kiss his hand. In a few moments he raised his left hand slowly to his forehead and took off his hat; then, letting his hand fall with the same slowness, Jean Valjean resumed his contemplations, his cap in his left hand, his club in his right.

Under this frightful gaze the bishop still slept in profoundest peace. The crucifix above the mantelpiece was dimly visible in the moonlight, apparently extending its arms toward both, with a benediction for one and a pardon for the other.

Suddenly Jean Valjean put on his cap, then passed quickly, without looking at the bishop, along the bed, straight to the cupboard. The key was in it. He opened it. The first thing he saw was the basket of silver; he took it, then crossed the room with hasty stride. Careless of noise, he retrieved his stick from the oratory, stepped out, and put the silver in his knapsack. Throwing away the basket, he ran across the garden, leaped over the wall like a tiger, and fled.

The next day at sunrise, Monseigneur Bienvenu was walking in the garden. Madame Magloire ran toward him quite beside herself.

"Monseigneur, monseigneur," cried she, "does Your Excellency know where the silver basket is?"

"Yes."

The bishop had just found the basket on a flower bed. He gave it to Madame Magloire and said, "There it is."

"Yes," said she, "but there is nothing in it. The silver?"

"Ah!" said the bishop, "it is the silver then that troubles you. I do not know where that is."

"Good heavens! That man who came last night stole it. Monseigneur, the man has gone! The silver is stolen!"

She saw that a capstone* of the wall had been thrown down.

"See, there is where he got out; he jumped into COCHEFILET LANE."

The bishop was silent for a moment; then, raising his eyes, he said, "I have for a long time wrongfully withheld this silver; it belonged to the poor. Who was this man? A poor man evidently."

"Alas! Alas!" returned Madame Magloire. "It is not on my account or mademoiselle's; it is all the same to us. But it is on yours, monseigneur. What is monsieur going to eat from now?"

"Well," said the bishop, "wooden plates."

In a few minutes, while breakfasting at the same table at which Jean Valjean sat the night before, Monseigneur Bienvenu pleasantly remarked that there was really no need even of a wooden spoon or fork to dip a piece of bread into a cup of milk.

Just as the brother and sister were rising from the table, there was a knock at the door.

"Come in," said the bishop.

The door opened. A strange, fierce group appeared on the threshold. Three men were holding a fourth by the collar.

The three men were gendarmes; the fourth, Jean Valjean. A brigadier of gendarmes was near the door. He advanced toward the bishop, giving a military salute. "Monseigneur," he said.

At this word Jean Valjean, who was sullen and seemed entirely cast down, raised his head.

cleave : split or sever (something), especially along a natural line or grain

capstone : one of the finishing or protective stones that form the top of an exterior masonry wall

*

"Monseigneur," he murmured. "Then he is not merely the curé!"

"Silence," said the gendarme. "It is monseigneur the bishop."

Monseigneur Bienvenu approached quickly.

"Ah, there you are," said he, looking toward Jean Valjean. "I am glad to see you. But! I gave you the candlesticks also, which are silver like the rest, and would bring two hundred francs. Why did you not take them along with your plates?"

Jean Valjean opened his eyes and looked at the bishop with an expression which no human tongue could describe.

"Monseigneur," said the brigadier, "then what this man said was true? We met him, going like a man who was running away, and we arrested him. He had this silver."

"And he told you," interrupted the bishop, with a smile, "that it had been given him by a good old priest with whom he had passed the night. And you brought him back here? It is all a mistake."

"If that is so," said the brigadier, "we can let him go."

"Certainly," replied the bishop.

The gendarmes released Jean Valjean.

"Is it true that they let me go?" he said, as if he were speaking in his sleep.

"Yes! You can go. Do you not understand?" said a gendarme.

"My friend," said the bishop, "before you go away, here are your candlesticks; take them."

He went to the mantelpiece, took the two candlesticks, and brought them to Jean Valjean, who was trembling. He took the two candlesticks mechanically.

"Now," said the bishop, "go in peace. By the way, my friend, when you come again, you need not come through the garden. You can always come in and go out by the front door. It is closed only with a latch, day or night."

Then, turning to the gendarmes, he said, "Messieurs, you can retire." The gendarmes withdrew.

Jean Valjean felt like a man who is just about to faint. The bishop approached him and said, in a low voice, "Forget not—never forget—that you have promised me to use this silver to become an honest man."

Jean Valjean stood confounded. The bishop had laid much stress upon these words as he uttered them. He continued, solemnly, "Jean Valjean, my brother, you belong no longer to evil, but to good. It is your soul that I am buying for you. I withdraw it from dark thoughts and from the spirit of perdition, and I give it to God."

Chapter 7

Jean Valjean went as if he were escaping. He hastened to get into the open country, taking the first lanes and paths. He wandered thus all the morning. He had eaten nothing, but he felt no hunger. He felt angry, he knew not against whom. He could not have told whether he were touched or humiliated. There came over him, at times, a strange struggle with giving up the hardening of his past twenty years.

He heard a joyous sound. He turned his head and saw coming along the path a little boy, a Savoyard*, a dozen years old, singing. He was one of those pleasant and merry youngsters who go from place to place, with their knees sticking through their trousers.

Always singing, the boy stopped from time to time and played at tossing up some pieces of money that he had in his hand, probably his whole fortune. Among them there was one forty-sous piece.

The boy stopped by the side of the thicket without seeing Jean Valjean and tossed up his handful of sous until he had skillfully caught them

upon the back of his hand. But this time the forty-sous piece escaped him and rolled toward the thicket, near Jean Valjean. Jean Valjean put his foot upon it. The boy, however, had followed the piece with his eye and had seen where it went. He was not frightened and walked straight to the man.

It was an entirely solitary place. Far as the eye could reach, there was no one on the plain or in the path. Nothing could be heard but the faint cries of a flock of birds of passage flying across the sky. The child turned his back to the sun, which made his hair like threads of gold and flushed the savage face of Jean Valjean with a lurid glow.

"Monsieur," said the little Savoyard, with that childish confidence which is made up of ignorance and innocence, "my piece?"

"What is your name?" said Jean Valjean.

"Petit Gervais, monsieur."

"Get out of here," said Jean Valjean.

"Monsieur," continued the boy, "give me my piece."

Jean Valjean dropped his head and did not answer. The child began again.

"I want my piece! My forty-sous piece!"

The child began to cry. Jean Valjean raised his head. Rising hastily to his feet, without releasing the piece of money, he added, "You'd better take care of yourself!"

The boy looked at him in terror and, after a few seconds, took to flight and ran with all his might without daring to turn his head or to utter a cry. At a little distance, however, he stopped for want of breath, and Jean Valjean in his reverie heard him sobbing. Then the boy was gone.

The sun had gone down. The shadows were deepening. He had not changed his attitude since the child fled. His breathing was at long and unequal intervals. His eyes were fixed. All at once he shivered; he began to feel the cold night air.

At that instant he perceived the forty-sous piece which his foot had half buried in the ground, and which glistened among the pebbles. It was like an electric shock. "What is that?" said he, between his teeth. He drew back a step or two, then stopped without the power to withdraw his gaze from the thing that glistened there like an open eye fixed upon him. After a few minutes, he sprang convulsively toward the piece of money, seized it, and, rising, looked away over the plain, straining his eyes toward all points of the horizon.

He saw nothing. Night was falling; the plain was cold and bare; thick purple mists were rising in the glimmering twilight. He began to walk rapidly in the direction in which the child had gone. After some thirty steps, he stopped, looked about, then called with all his might, "Petit Gervais! Petit Gervais!"

He listened. There was no answer.

He began to walk again, then quickened his pace to a run, and from time to time stopped and called out, in a most desolate voice, "Petit Gervais! Petit Gervais!"

The moon had risen. He strained his eyes in the distance, and called out once more, "Petit Gervais! Petit Gervais!" His cries died away into the mist, without even awakening an echo. Again, he murmured, "Petit Gervais!" but with a feeble and almost inarticulate voice. That was his last effort; his knees suddenly bent under him as if an invisible power overwhelmed him at a blow with the weight of his bad conscience; he fell exhausted upon a great stone, his hands clenched in his hair and his face on his knees, and exclaimed, "What a wretch I am!"

Then his heart swelled, and he burst into tears. It was the first time he had wept for nineteen years.

Savoyard : a person from the mountainous Savoy region of France

Chapter 8

In the year 1817, Félix Tholomyès began courting a young woman in Paris who was called Fantine. She loved the dashing Félix. All of Paris became their playground, and the city had become both beautiful and exciting.

Fantine was one of those beings which are brought forth from the heart of the people. Sprung from the most unfathomable depths of social darkness, she bore on her brow the mark of the anonymous and unknown. She was born at Montreuil-sur-Mer. Who were her parents? None could tell; she had never known either father or mother. She was called "little Fantine." She could have no family name, for she had no family, a mere infant, straying barefoot in the streets. Nobody knew anything more of her. Such was the manner in which this human being had come into life. At the age of ten, Fantine left the city and went to service among the farmers of the suburbs. At fifteen, she came to Paris to "seek her fortune." Fantine remained pure as long as she could. She was blonde, pretty, with fine teeth. She had gold and pearls for her dowry, but the gold was on her head and the pearls in her mouth.

She worked to live; then, also to live, for the heart, too, has its hunger, she loved. She loved Félix for nearly a year. The streets of the Latin Quarter, which swarmed with students and grisettes*, saw the beginning of this dream.

They went to Saint Cloud by the coach. Fantine was joy itself. Her splendid teeth had evidently been endowed by God with one function—that of laughing. Her rosy lips babbled with enchantment. Fantine was beautiful without being too conscious of it. She possessed both types of beauty—style and rhythm. Style is the force of the ideal; rhythm is its movement.

Fantine was joy; Fantine also was modesty. Any observer would have found through all this intoxication of age, of season, and of love an unconquerable expression of reserve and modesty. Although she would have refused nothing to Tholomyès, her face was in the highest degree maidenly. Love is a fault. Fantine was innocence floating upon the surface of this fault.

That day was all sunshine, in concert with the flowers, the fields, and the trees. But, abruptly, and without any warning, Félix left Paris and abandoned Fantine in order to return to his home and parents, returning as a prodigal son. He left only a note, leaving Fantine bereft. She wept.

Félix was her first love, as we have said; she had given herself to this young man as to a husband, and the poor girl had a child.

Chapter 9

There was at Montfermeil, near Paris, a sort of chophouse, kept by a man and his wife named Thénardier. Above the door, nailed flat against the wall, was a board, upon which was painted what looked like a man carrying on his back another man wearing the heavy epaulets* of a general, gilt and with large silver stars; red blotches typified blood; the remainder of the picture was smoke, and probably represented a battle. Beneath was this inscription: *TO THE SERGEANT OF WATERLOO**.

grisettes : young working-class Frenchwomen

epaulet : an ornamental shoulder piece on an item of clothing, especially on the coat or jacket of a military uniform

Waterloo : a battle fought on 18 June 1815 near Waterloo, Belgium, when a French army under the command of Napoleon was defeated, marking the end of the Napoleonic Wars

In the courtyard of the inn, the wife of Thénardier sang to her children as they played.

She did not hear or see what was passing in the street. Someone, however, had approached her, and suddenly she heard a voice say quite near her ear, "You have two pretty children there, madame."

A woman was before her at a little distance; she also had a child, which she bore in her arms. She was carrying in addition a large, heavy carpetbag. This woman's child was one of the divinest beings—a little girl of two or three years. She was sleeping in the absolutely confiding slumber peculiar to an innocent child. Mothers' arms are made of tenderness, and sweet sleep blesses the child who lies therein.

The mother appeared as a working woman, a peasant. She was young, and perhaps pretty, but in her garb, her beauty could not be displayed. Her eyes seemed not to have been tearless for a long time. She was pale and looked very weary and ill. She gazed upon her child, sleeping in her arms, with a look which only a mother possesses. Her forefinger had been hardened and pricked with the needle since she was a seamstress; she wore a coarse brown mantle, a calico dress, and large heavy shoes. It was Fantine. Ten months had slipped away since Félix had abandoned her.

"You have two pretty children there, madame." The mother raised her head and thanked her, and made the stranger sit down on the stone step, she herself being on the doorsill. The two women began to talk together.

"My name is Madame Thénardier," said the mother of the two girls. "We keep this inn."

The traveler told her story. She was a working woman, and her husband was dead. Not being able to procure work in Paris, she was going in search of it elsewhere. She had left Paris that morning on foot to Montfermeil, and carrying her child; she had become tired. The child had walked a little, but not much—so young that her mother was compelled to carry her, and the jewel had fallen asleep.

And at these words she gave her daughter a passionate kiss, which wakened her. All at once she perceived the two others. Mother Thénardier said, "Play together, all three of you."

At that age, acquaintance is easy, and in a moment the little Thénardiers were playing with the newcomer, to their intense delight. The two women continued to chat.

"What do you call your child?"

"Cosette."

"How old is she?"

"Going on three years."

"The age of my oldest. See them! One would swear they were three sisters."

These words were the spark which the other mother was probably awaiting. She seized the hand of Madame Thénardier and said, "Will you keep my child for me?"

Madame Thénardier looked surprised, offering neither consent nor refusal. Cosette's mother continued, "You see, I cannot take my child into the country. Work forbids it. With a child I could not find a place there. It is God who has led me before your inn. The sight of your little ones, so pretty, and clean, and happy, has overwhelmed me. I said, 'There is a good mother; they will be like three sisters, and then it will not be long before I come back.' Will you keep my child for me?"

"I must think it over," said Madame Thénardier.

"I will give six francs a month."

Here a man's voice was heard from within: "Not less than seven francs, and six months paid in advance. Six times seven is forty-two."

"I will give it," said the mother.

"And fifteen francs extra for the first expenses," added the man.

"I will give it," said the mother.

The bargain was concluded. The mother passed the night at the inn, gave her money, and left her child.

That morning a neighbor of the Thénardiers met this mother on her way, and came in, saying, "I have just met a woman in the street, who was crying as if her heart would break."

When Cosette's mother had gone, the man said to his wife, "You have proved a good mousetrap with your little ones."

"Without knowing it," said the woman.

A year passed, and then another. People in the village said, "What good people these Thénardiers are! They are not rich, and yet they bring up a poor child who has been left with them." They thought Cosette was forgotten by her mother.

From year to year the child grew, and her misery also. So long as Cosette was very small, she was the scapegoat of the two other children; before she was five years old, she became the servant of the house.

Cosette was made to run errands, sweep the rooms, the yard, the street, wash the dishes, and even carry burdens. Had her mother returned to Montfermeil, at the end of these three years, she would not have known her child. Cosette, so fresh and pretty when she came to that house, was now thin and wan.

Only her fine eyes remained to her, and they were painful to look at, for, large as they were, they seemed to increase the sadness! It was a harrowing sight to see in the wintertime the poor child, not yet six years old, shivering under the tatters of what was once a calico dress, sweeping the street before daylight with an enormous broom in her little red hands and tears in her large eyes.

In the place she was called the Lark, not larger than a bird, trembling, frightened, and shivering, awake every morning first of all in the house and the village, always in the street or in the fields before dawn. Only this poor lark never sang.

Chapter 10

After leaving her little Cosette with the Thénardiers, Fantine went on her way and arrived at Montreuil-sur-Mer. She had left the province some twelve years before, and Montreuil had greatly changed in appearance. While Fantine had been slowly sinking deeper and deeper into misery, her native village had been prosperous. Within about two years there had been accomplished there one of those industrial changes which are the great events of small communities.

The occupation of the inhabitants of Montreuil had been producing imitations of English and German black glass trinkets. The business had always been hard due to the high price of the raw material. At the time of Fantine's return to Montreuil, a transformation had occurred in the production of these goods. Toward the end of the year 1815, an unknown man had established himself in the city, and had conceived the idea of substituting gum-lac* for resin in the manufacture; and for bracelets he made the clasps by simply bending the ends of the metal together instead of soldering them.

This very slight change had worked a revolution; it had reduced the price of the raw material enormously and had rendered it possible to raise the wages of the laborer, improve the quality of the goods, and sell them at a lower price even while making three times the profit.

gum-lac : a resin-like substance secreted by certain insects; used in varnishes and sealing wax *

In less than three years, the inventor of this process had become rich and had made all around him rich. Nothing was known of his birth and but little of his early history.

When the stranger first entered the city on a December evening, with his bundle on his back and a thorn stick in his hand, a great fire had broken out in a town house. This man rushed into the fire and saved, at the peril of his life, two children, who proved to be those of the captain of the gendarmerie*, and in the hurry and gratitude of the moment no one thought to ask him for his passport. He was known from that time by the name of Father Madeleine. He was a man of about fifty who always appeared to be preoccupied in mind and who was good-natured; this was all that could be said about him.

The profits of Father Madeleine were so great that by the end of the second year he was able to build a large factory in which there were two immense workshops, one for men and one for women. Whoever was needy could go there and be sure of finding work and wages. Father Madeleine required the men to be willing and the women to be of good morals.

Before the arrival of Father Madeleine, the whole region was languishing; now it was all alive with the healthy strength of labor. Idleness and misery were unknown.

Father Madeleine employed everybody; he had only one condition: "Be an honest man! Be an honest woman!"

Father Madeleine had made his fortune, but, very strangely for a mere man of business, the business did not seem to be his principal concern. It seemed that he thought much for others and little for himself. It was known that he had 630,000 francs standing to his credit in the banking house of Laffitte; but before setting aside this large sum for himself, he had expended more than a million for the city and for the poor.

Five years after his arrival at Montreuil-sur-Mer, the services that he had rendered to the region were so brilliant, and the wish of the population was so unanimous, that the king appointed him mayor of the city. He refused, but the citizens urged him to accept. The people in the streets begged him to do so, and at last he yielded.

Nevertheless, he remained as simple as at first. He had gray hair, a serious eye, the tanned complexion of a laborer, and the thoughtful countenance of a philosopher. He fulfilled his duties as mayor, but beyond that his life was isolated. He talked with very few persons. He shrank from compliments and with a touch of the hat walked on rapidly; he smiled to avoid talking, and avoided smiling. He always took his meals alone with a book open before him. He loved books. As his growing fortune gave him more leisure, it seemed that he profited by it to cultivate his mind. Since he had been at Montreuil it was remarked from year to year that his language became more polished, choicer, and more gentle.

Although he was no longer young, it was reported that he was of prodigious strength. He would offer a helping hand to anyone who needed it, help up a fallen horse, push at a stalled wheel, or seize by the horns a bull that had broken loose. He always had his pockets full of money when he went out, and empty when he returned. When he passed through a village, the ragged little youngsters would run after him with joy.

When he saw the door of a church shrouded with black, he entered. He sought out a funeral as others seek out a christening. The bereavement of others attracted him; because of his great gentleness, he mingled with those who were in mourning, with families dressed in black, with the priests who were sighing around a corpse. He seemed glad to take as a text for his thoughts these funereal psalms, full of the vision of another world. With his eyes raised to heaven, he listened with a sort of aspiration toward all the mysteries of the infinite, to these sad voices, which sang upon the brink of the dark abyss of death.

He did a multitude of good deeds as secretly as bad ones are usually done. He would steal into houses in the evening and furtively mount the stairs. A poor devil, on returning to his garret, would find that his door had been opened, sometimes even forced, during his absence. He would cry out, "Some thief has been here!" But the first thing that he would see would be a piece of gold lying on the table. The thief was Father Madeleine.

Near the beginning of the year 1821, the journals announced the decease of Monsieur Myriel, bishop of Digne, surnamed "Monseigneur Bienvenu," at the age of eighty-two. The announcement of his death appeared in the local paper. Monsieur Madeleine appeared next morning dressed in black with crepe on his hat.

This mourning was noticed and talked about all over the town. It appeared to throw some light upon the origin of Monsieur Madeleine. The conclusion was that he was in some way related to the venerable bishop.

When one of the dowagers of the village ventured to ask him, "The mayor is a relative of the late bishop of Digne?" he said, "No, madame. In my youth I was a servant in his family."

It was also remarked that whenever there passed through the city a young Savoyard who was tramping about the country in search of chimneys to sweep, the mayor would send for him, ask his name, and give him money. The little Savoyards told each other, and many of them passed that way.

Chapter II

People came from miles around to consult Monsieur Madeleine. He settled differences, prevented lawsuits, reconciled enemies. Everybody, of his own will, chose him for judge. He seemed to have the book of the natural law by heart.

Whatever Father Madeleine did, he remained unchangeable and imperturbable. Often, when he passed along the street, calm, affectionate, followed by the benedictions of all, it happened that a tall man, wearing a flat hat and an iron-gray coat and armed with a stout cane, would turn around abruptly behind him and follow him with his eyes until he disappeared. This personage, grave with an almost-threatening gravity, was one who, even in a hurried interview, commanded the attention of the observer. His name was Javert, and he was one of the police.

Javert was born in a prison. His mother was a fortune-teller whose husband was in the galleys. He grew up to think himself outside the pale of society, and despaired of ever entering it. He noticed that society closes its doors, without pity, on two classes of men—those who attack it and those who guard it. He entered the police. He succeeded. At forty he was an inspector. As a young man, he had been stationed in the galleys.

This man was a compound of two sentiments, very simple and very good in themselves, but he almost made them evil by his exaggeration of them: respect for authority and hatred of rebellion. His stare was as cold and piercing as a corkscrew. His whole life was contained in these two words: *waking* and *watching*. He marked out a straight path through the most tortuous thing in the world; his conscience was bound up in his

gendarmerie : armed police force *

utility, his religion in his duties, and he was a spy as others are priests. Woe to him who should fall into his hands!

Javert was like an eye always fixed on Monsieur Madeleine, an eye full of suspicion and conjecture. Monsieur Madeleine finally noticed it but seemed to consider it of no consequence. He asked no question of Javert. He neither sought him nor shunned him; he endured this unpleasant and annoying stare without appearing to pay any attention to it. He treated Javert as he did everybody else, at ease and with kindness.

It was guessed that Javert had secretly hunted up all the traces of his previous life which Father Madeleine had left elsewhere.

Monsieur Madeleine was walking one morning along one of the unpaved alleys of Montreuil-sur-Mer; he heard shouting and saw a crowd at a little distance. He went to the spot. An old man named Father Fauchelevent had fallen under his cart, his horse being thrown down. The horse had his thighs broken and could not stir. The old man was caught between the wheels. The cart was heavily loaded, and unluckily the whole weight rested upon his breast. Father Fauchelevent was uttering doleful groans. They had tried to pull him out, but in vain. An unlucky effort, inexpert help, or a false push might crush him. It was impossible to extricate him otherwise than by raising the wagon from beneath. Javert, who came up at the moment of the accident, had sent for a jack.

Monsieur Madeleine came. The crowd fell back with respect.

"Help!" cried old Fauchelevent.

Monsieur Madeleine turned toward the bystanders.

"Has anybody a jack?"

"We will have one in a quarter of an hour."

"We cannot wait a quarter of an hour," said Madeleine. "It will be too late! Don't you see that the wagon is sinking all the while?"

No one spoke.

"Listen," resumed Madeleine, "there is room enough

still under the wagon for a man to crawl in and lift it with his back. In half a minute we will have the poor man out. Is there nobody here who has strength and courage? Five louis d'or* for him!"

Nobody stirred in the crowd.

"Ten louis," said Madeleine.

The bystanders dropped their eyes. One of them muttered, "He'd have to be devilish stout. And then he would risk getting crushed."

"Come," said Madeleine, "twenty louis."

The same silence.

"It is not willingness which they lack," said a voice.

Monsieur Madeleine turned and saw Javert. He had not noticed him when he came. Javert continued, "It is strength. He must be a terrible man who can raise a wagon like that on his back."

Then, looking fixedly at Monsieur Madeleine, he went on, emphasizing every word that he uttered. "Monsieur Madeleine, I have known but one man capable of doing what you call for."

Madeleine shuddered.

Javert added, with an air of indifference but without taking his eyes from Madeleine, "He was a convict."

"Ah!" said Madeleine.

"In the galleys at Toulon."

Madeleine became pale.

Meanwhile the cart was slowly settling down. Father Fauchelevent screamed. “I am dying! My ribs are breaking.”

Madeleine looked around.

“Is there nobody, then, who wants to earn twenty louis and save this poor old man’s life?”

None of the bystanders moved.

Javert resumed. “I have known but one man who could take the place of a jack. That convict.”

Madeleine raised his head, met the falcon eye of Javert still fixed upon him, looked at the immovable peasants, and smiled sadly. Then, without saying a word, he fell on his knees, and even before the crowd had time to utter a cry, he was under the cart.

There was an awful moment of suspense and of silence. Madeleine, lying almost flat under the fearful weight, was twice seen to try in vain to bring his elbows and knees nearer together. They cried out to him, “Father Madeleine! Come out from there!” Old Fauchelevent himself said, “Monsieur Madeleine! Go away! I must die, you see that; leave me! You will be crushed too.” Madeleine made no answer. The bystanders held their breath. The wheels were still sinking, and it had now become almost impossible for Madeleine to extricate himself.

All at once the enormous cart rose slowly. The wheels came half out of the ruts. A smothered voice was heard, crying, “Quick! Help!” It was Madeleine, who had just made a final effort. They all rushed to help. The devotion of one man had given strength and courage to all. The cart was lifted by twenty arms. Old Fauchelevent was safe.

Madeleine arose. He was very pale, though dripping with sweat. His clothes were torn and covered with mud. The old man kissed Madeleine’s knees and called him the good God. Madeleine himself wore on his face an expression of joyous and celestial suffering, and he looked with tranquil eye upon Javert, who was still watching him.

Father Madeleine had Fauchelevent carried to an infirmary that he had established for his workmen in the same building as his factory. The next morning the old man found a thousand-franc bill upon the stand by the side of the bed, with this note in the handwriting of Father Madeleine: *I have purchased your horse and cart. You shall not worry.*

Chapter 12

Fantine returned to this prosperous town of Montreuil-sur-Mer. No one remembered her. Luckily the door of Monsieur Madeleine’s factory was like the face of a friend. She was admitted into the workshop for women. The business was entirely new to Fantine. She could not be very expert in it and consequently did not receive much for her day’s work. But that little was enough; the problem was solved. She was earning her living.

When Fantine realized how she was living, she had a moment of joy. To live honestly by her own labor—what a heavenly boon! The taste for labor returned to her. She bought a mirror, delighted herself with the sight of her youth, her fine hair and her fine teeth, thought of nothing but

louis d’or : a French gold coin first minted in 1640; replaced by the franc during the French Revolution * to save Cosette and the possibilities of the future, and was almost happy. She hired a small room and furnished it on the credit of her future labor.

Not being able to say that she was married, she took good care not to speak of her little girl. At first, she paid the Thénardiers punctually. As she only knew how to sign her name, she was obliged to write through a public letter writer. She wrote often, and that was noticed.

It was reported by the rest around her that in the shop, she often turned aside to wipe away a tear. Those were moments when she thought of her child, perhaps also of the man whom she had loved. It is a mournful task to break the somber attachments of the past.

She wrote at least twice a month, and always to the same address. The busybodies in town succeeded in learning the address. In short, it became known that Fantine had a child. And there was one old gossip who went to Montfermeil, talked with the Thénardiers, and said on her return, "For my thirty-five francs, I have found out all about it. I have seen the child!" The busybody was called Madame Victurnien, keeper and guardian of everybody's virtue. She was dry, rough, sour, sharp, crabbed, almost venomous.

All this took time. Fantine had been more than a year at the factory, when one morning the overseer of the workshop handed her, claiming to act on behalf of the mayor, fifty francs, saying that she was no longer wanted in the shop and enjoining her to leave the city. This was the very same month in which the Thénardiers, after having asked twelve francs instead of six, had demanded fifteen francs instead of twelve.

Fantine was thunderstruck. She could not leave the city; she was in debt for her lodging and furniture. Fifty francs was not enough to clear that debt. She faltered out some suppliant words. The overseer gave her to understand that she must leave the shop instantly. Overwhelmed with shame even more than with despair, she left the shop and returned to her room. Her fault then was now known to all!

Monsieur Madeleine knew nothing of all this; it was his habit scarcely ever to enter the women's workshop. He had placed at the head of it an old spinster whom the curé had recommended to him, and he had entire confidence in this overseer, a very respectable person, firm, just, upright, full of charity. Monsieur Madeleine left everything to her.

Fantine offered herself as a servant in the neighborhood. She went from one house to another. Nobody wanted her. She could not leave the city. She divided the fifty francs between the landlord and the furniture dealer, returned to the latter three-quarters of his goods, kept only what was necessary, and found herself without work, without position, having nothing but her bed and owing still about a hundred francs. She began to make coarse shirts for the soldiers of the garrison* and earned twelve sous a day. Her daughter cost her ten. It was at this time that she began to get behind with the Thénardiers.

At first, Fantine was so much ashamed that she did not dare to go out. When she was in the street, she imagined that people turned behind her and pointed at her; everybody looked at her and no one greeted her; the sharp and cold disdain of the passersby penetrated her, body and soul, like a north wind.

She became accustomed to disrespect as she had to poverty. Little by little she learned her part. After two or three months she shook off her shame. She went and came, holding her head up and wearing a bitter smile, and felt that she was becoming shameless. Madame Victurnien sometimes saw her pass her window, noticed the distress of "that creature," thanks to her "put back to her place," and congratulated herself. The malicious have a dark happiness.

Excessive work fatigued Fantine, and the slight dry cough that she had increased. She had been discharged toward the end of winter; summer passed away, but winter returned. Short days, less work. Fantine earned too little. Her debts had increased. The Thénardiers, being poorly paid, were constantly writing letters to her. One day they wrote that her little Cosette was entirely destitute of clothing for the cold weather, that she needed a woolen skirt, and that her mother must send at least ten francs for that. Fantine crushed the letter in her hand for a whole day. In the evening she went into a barber's shop at the corner of the street and pulled out her comb. Her beautiful fair hair fell below her waist.

"What lovely hair!" exclaimed the barber.

"How much will you give me for it?" said she.

"Ten francs."

"Cut it off."

She bought a knit skirt and sent it to the Thénardiers.

Another day she received from the Thénardiers a letter with these words:

Cosette is sick of a miliary fever. The drugs necessary are dear. It is ruining us, and we can no longer pay for them. Unless you send us forty francs within a week, the little one will die.w*

She burst out in bitter laughing and then went downstairs and out of doors. As she passed through the square, she saw many people gathered about an odd-looking carriage on the top of which stood a man in red clothes, declaiming*. He was a juggler and a traveling dentist.

Fantine joined the crowd and began to laugh with the rest. The puller of teeth saw this beautiful girl laughing and suddenly called out, "You have pretty teeth, you girl who are laughing there. If you will sell me your two incisors, I will give you a gold napoleon* for each of them."

"What is that? What are my incisors?" asked Fantine.

"The incisors," resumed the professor of dentistry, "are the front teeth, the two upper ones."

Fantine fled away and stopped her ears not to hear the shrill voice of the man who called after her, "Consider, my beauty! Two napoleons! How much good they will do you! If you have the courage for it, come this evening to the inn of the Tillac d'Argent, and you will find me there."

Fantine returned home; she was raving, and told the story to her good neighbor Marguerite. "Do you understand that? Pull out my two front teeth! Why, I should be horrible! The hair is bad enough, but the teeth! I would rather throw myself from the fifth story, headfirst, to the pavement!"

"And what was it he offered you?" asked Marguerite.

"Two napoleons."

"That is forty francs."

"Yes," said Fantine.

garrison : a body of troops stationed in a fortress or town to defend it

miliary fever : a medical term used historically for infectious diseases that caused fever and skin rashes similar in appearance to a cereal grain called "proso millet"

declaim : to utter or deliver words or a speech in a rhetorical or impassioned way, as if to an audience

napoleon : gold coins in denominations of 5, 10, 20, 40, 50, and 100 francs

*

She read again the Thénardiers' letter. She said to Marguerite, "What does this mean, a miliary fever? Do you know?"

"Yes," answered the old woman. "It is a disease."

"Then it needs a good many drugs?"

"Yes; terrible drugs."

"How does it come upon you?"

"It is a disease that comes in a moment."

"Does it attack children?"

"Children especially."

"Do people die of it?"

"Very often," said Marguerite.

In the evening Fantine went out and took the direction of the RUE DE PARIS where the inns are.

The next morning, when Marguerite went into Fantine's chamber before daybreak—for they always worked together and so made one candle do for two—she found Fantine seated upon her bed, pale and icy. Her cap had fallen upon her knees. The candle had burned all night and was almost consumed. Marguerite stopped upon the threshold, petrified by this wild disorder, and exclaimed, "Good Lord! The candle is all burned out. Something has happened." Then she looked at Fantine, who sadly turned her shorn head. Fantine had grown ten years older since evening. "Bless us!" said Marguerite. "What is the matter with you, Fantine?"

"Nothing," said Fantine. "Quite the contrary. My child will not die of that frightful sickness for lack of aid. I am satisfied."

She showed the old woman two napoleons that glistened on the table. At the same time, she smiled. The candle lit up her face. It was a sickening smile, for the corners of her mouth were stained with blood, and a dark cavity revealed itself there. The two teeth were gone.

She sent the forty francs to Montfermeil.

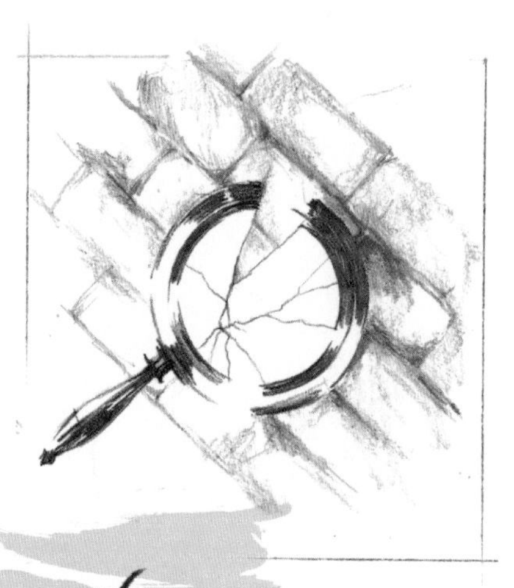

Fantine threw her looking glass out the window. She left her little room on the second story for an attic room with no other fastening than a latch, one of those garret rooms the ceiling of which makes an angle with the floor and hits your head at every moment. She no longer had a bed; she retained a rag that she called her coverlid*, a mattress on the floor, and a worn-out straw chair. Her creditors gave her no rest. She met them in the street, she met them again on her stairs. She passed whole nights in weeping and thinking. She had a strange brilliancy in her eyes and a constant pain in her shoulder. She coughed a great deal. She hated Father Madeleine thoroughly, yet never complained. She sewed seventeen hours a day, but a prison contractor suddenly cut down the price, and this reduced the day's wages to nine sous. Seventeen hours of work, and nine sous a day! Her creditors were more pitiless than ever. O good God! What did they want her to do? She felt herself hunted down, and something of the wild beast began to develop within her.

About the same time, Thénardier wrote to her that he had waited with too much generosity, and that he must have a hundred francs immediately, or else little Cosette, just convalescing after her severe sickness, would be turned out of doors into the cold and upon the highway, and that she would become what she could, and would perish if she must.

"A hundred francs," thought Fantine. "But where is there a place where one can earn even a hundred sous a day?"

"Come!" said she. "I will sell what is left." The unfortunate creature became a woman of the town*.

coverlid : a bed quilt that does not cover the pillow, used chiefly for warmth; bedspread

woman of the town : a prostitute

*

ROUTE DE VERSAILLES À SAINT-GERMAIN, LOUVECIENNES • CAMILLE PISSARRO • 1872

Chapter 13

In January 1823, one evening when it had been snowing, a provincial dandy*, very warmly wrapped in a large, fashionable winter cloak, was amusing himself with tormenting a creature who was walking back and forth before the window of the officers' café, in a ball dress, with her neck and shoulders bare and flowers upon her head.

Every time the woman passed before him, he threw out at her, with a puff of smoke from his cigar, some remark which he thought was witty and pleasant, such as "How ugly you are!" "Are you trying to hide?" "You have lost your teeth!"

The woman, a rueful, bedizened* specter, did not answer him, did not even look at him, but continued in silence and with a dismal regularity. The dandy came up behind her with a stealthy step and, stifling his laughter, stooped down, seized a handful of snow from the sidewalk, and threw it hastily into her back between her naked shoulders.

The girl roared with rage, turned, bounded like a panther, and rushed upon the man, burying her nails in his face and using the most frightful words that ever fell from the offscouring* of a guardhouse. These insults were thrown out from a hideous mouth which lacked the two front teeth. It was Fantine.

At the noise this made, the officers came out of the café, a crowd gathered, and a large circle was formed, laughing, jeering, and applauding. Suddenly a tall man advanced quickly from the crowd, seized the woman by her muddy satin waist, and said, "Follow me!"

The woman raised her head; her furious voice died out at once. Her eyes were glassy; from livid she had become pale, and she shuddered in terror. She recognized Javert.

When they reached the bureau of police, Javert entered with Fantine and closed the door behind him. Javert's grave face betrayed no emotion. The more he examined the conduct of this girl, the more he revolted at it. It was clear that he had seen a crime committed.

He had seen, there in the street, an upright man insulted and attacked by a creature who was an outlaw and an outcast. A prostitute had assaulted a citizen. He, Javert, had seen that himself. He wrote in silence.

When he had finished, he signed his name, folded the paper, and handed it to the sergeant of the guard, saying, "Take three men, and carry this girl to jail." Then, turning to Fantine, "You are in for six months."

The hapless woman shuddered.

"Six months! Six months in prison!" cried she. "Six months to earn seven sous a day! But what will become of Cosette! My daughter! My daughter! Why, I still owe more than a hundred francs to the Thénardiers, Monsieur Inspector. Do you know that?"

She dragged herself along the floor, dirtied by the muddy boots of all these men, without rising, clasping her hands and moving rapidly on her knees.

"Monsieur Javert," said she, "I beg your pity. If you had seen the beginning, you would know. I swear to you by the good God that I was not in the wrong. That gentleman, whom I do not know, threw snow down my back. Don't send me to prison. I must earn money to send to my little daughter. I am not a bad woman at heart. It is not laziness and appetite that have brought me to this. Have pity on me, Monsieur Javert."

"Come," said Javert, "haven't you understood? March off at once! You have your six months! The eternal Father in person could do nothing for you."

At those solemn words, she understood that her sentence was fixed.

She sank down, murmuring, "Mercy!"

Javert turned his back. The soldiers seized her by the arms.

A few minutes before, a man had entered without being noticed. He heard the despairing supplication of Fantine. When the soldiers put their hands upon the wretched being, he stepped forward out of the shadow and said, "One moment, if you please!"

Javert raised his eyes and recognized Monsieur Madeleine. He took off his hat and, bowing with a sort of angry awkwardness, said, "Pardon, Monsieur Mayor—"

At these words—"Monsieur Mayor"—Fantine sprang to her feet at once like a specter rising from the ground, pushed back the soldiers with her arms, walked straight to Monsieur Madeleine before they could stop her, and, gazing at him fixedly with a wild look, she exclaimed, "Ah! It is you then who are Monsieur Mayor!" Then she spit in his face.

Monsieur Madeleine wiped his face and said, "Inspector Javert, set this woman at liberty."

Javert felt as though he were at the point of losing his senses. To see a woman of the town spit in the face of a mayor was a thing so monstrous that he thought it sacrilege to believe it possible.

The mayor's words were no less strange a blow to Fantine. She staggered. Meanwhile she looked all around and began to talk in a low voice, as if speaking to herself. "At liberty! They let me go! I am not to go to prison for six months! Who was it said that? I misunderstood. That cannot be this monster of a mayor! Was it you, my good Monsieur Javert, who told them to set me at liberty? This monstrous mayor, he is the cause of all this. Think of it, Monsieur Javert, he turned me away! On account of a parcel of beggars who told stories in the workshop."

Monsieur Madeleine listened with profound attention. He said to Fantine, "How much did you say that you owed?"

Fantine, who had only looked at Javert, turned toward him. "Who said anything to you?"

Suddenly she hastily adjusted the disorder of her garments, smoothed down the folds of her dress, and walked toward the door. She put her hand upon the latch. One more step and she would be in the street.

Javert until that moment had remained standing, motionless. The sound of the latch roused him. He raised his head with an expression of sovereign authority. "Sergeant," exclaimed he, "don't you see that this vagabond is going off? Who told you to let her go?"

"I," said Madeleine.

At the words of Javert, Fantine had trembled and dropped the latch, as a thief who is caught drops what he has stolen. When Madeleine spoke, she turned, and from that moment, without saying a word, without even daring to breathe freely, she looked by turns from Madeleine to Javert and from Javert to Madeleine, as the one or the other was speaking.

"Monsieur Mayor, that cannot be done."

"Why?" said Monsieur Madeleine.

"This wretched woman has insulted a citizen."

"Inspector Javert," replied Monsieur Madeleine in a calm tone. "Listen. You are an honest man, and I have no objection to explaining myself to you. The truth is this. I was passing through the square when you arrested this woman. There was a crowd still there. I learned the circumstances. I know all about it. It is the citizen who was in the wrong, and who, by a faithful police officer, would have been arrested."

Javert went on, "This wretch has just insulted Monsieur Mayor."

"That concerns me," said Monsieur Madeleine. "The insult to me rests with myself. I can do what I please about it."

"I beg Monsieur Mayor's pardon. The insult rests not with you; it rests with justice."

"Inspector Javert," replied Monsieur Madeleine, "the

dandy : a man unduly devoted to style, neatness, and fashion in dress and appearance

bedizened : dressed up gaudily

offscouring : someone rejected by society; outcast *

highest justice is conscience. I have heard this woman. I know what I am doing."

"I obey my duty. My duty requires that this woman spend six months in prison."

Monsieur Madeleine answered, "She shall not spend a day."

At these decisive words, Javert had the boldness to look the mayor in the eye, and said, but still in a tone of profound respect, "I am very sorry to resist Monsieur Mayor. It is the first time in my life, but he will deign to permit me to observe that I am within the limits of my own authority. This matter belongs to the police of the street. That concerns me, and I detain the woman Fantine."

At this Monsieur Madeleine folded his arms and said in a severe tone, "The matter of which you speak belongs to the municipal police. By the terms of articles 9, 11, 15, and 66 of the code of criminal law, I am the judge of it. I order that this woman be set at liberty."

Javert endeavored to make a last attempt.

"But, Monsieur Mayor—"

"I refer you to article 81 of the law of 13 December 1799, upon illegal imprisonment."

"Monsieur Mayor, permit me—"

"Not another word."

"However—"

"Retire," said Monsieur Madeleine.

Javert received the blow. He bowed before the mayor and went out. Fantine stood by the door and looked at him through her stupor as he passed before her.

She had seen herself somehow disputed about by two opposing powers. She had seen struggling before her very eyes two men who held in their hands her liberty, her life, her soul, her child. One of these men was drawing her to the side of darkness; the other was leading her toward the light. In this contest, seen with distortion through the magnifying power of fright, these two men had appeared to her like two giants: one spoke as her demon, the other as her good angel. The angel had vanquished the demon, and the thought of it made her shudder from head to foot; this angel, this deliverer, was precisely the man whom she abhorred, this mayor whom she had so long considered the author of all her woes, this Madeleine! At the very moment when she had insulted him in a hideous fashion, he had saved her! Had she then been deceived? Ought she then to change her whole heart?

She felt the fearful darkness of her hatred melt within and flow away, while there was born in her heart an indescribable and unspeakable warmth of joy, of confidence, and of love.

When Javert was gone, Monsieur Madeleine turned toward her and said to her, like a man who is struggling that he may not weep, "I have heard you. I knew nothing of what you have said. I believe that it is true. I did not even know that you had left my workshop. Why did you not apply to me? But now I will pay your debts, and I will have your child come to you, or you shall go to her. You shall live here, in Paris, or where you will. I take charge of your child and you. You shall do no more work, if you do not wish to. I will give you all the money that you need. You shall again become honest in again becoming happy. More than that, listen. I declare to you from this moment—if all is as you say, and I do not doubt it—that you have never ceased to be virtuous and holy before God. You poor woman."

This was more than poor Fantine could bear. To have Cosette! To leave this ignominious life! To live free, rich, happy, honest with Cosette! To see suddenly spring up in the midst of her misery all these realities of paradise! She could only pour out two or three sobs. "Oh! Oh! Oh!" Her limbs gave way, she threw herself on her knees before Monsieur Madeleine, and before he could prevent it, he felt that she had seized his hand and carried it to her lips. Then she fainted.

Chapter 14

Monsieur Madeleine had Fantine taken to the infirmary. A violent fever came on, and she passed a part of the night in delirious ravings. Finally she fell asleep.

Toward noon the following day, Fantine awoke. She heard a breathing near her bed, drew aside the curtain, and saw Monsieur Madeleine standing, gazing at something above his head. His look was full of compassionate and supplicating agony. She followed its direction and saw that it was fixed upon a crucifix nailed against the wall.

From that moment Monsieur Madeleine was transfigured in the eyes of Fantine; he seemed to her clothed with light. He was absorbed in a kind of prayer. She gazed at him for a long while without daring to interrupt him; at last she said timidly, "What are you doing?"

Monsieur Madeleine had been in that place for an hour waiting for Fantine to awake. He took her hand, felt her pulse, and said, "How do you feel?"

"Very well. I have slept," she said. "I think I am getting better—this will be nothing."

"I was praying to the martyr who is on high." And in his thought he added, *For the martyr who is here below.*

Monsieur Madeleine had passed the night and morning in informing himself about Fantine. He had learned, in all its poignant details, her history. He went on, "You have suffered greatly, poor mother. Oh! Do not lament. It is in this way that mortals become angels. This hell from which you have come out is the first step toward heaven."

He sighed deeply, but she smiled with a sublime smile from which two teeth were gone.

That same night, Javert wrote a letter. Next morning he carried this letter himself to the post office of Montreuil-sur-Mer. It was directed to Paris, to Monsieur Chabouillet, secretary of the prefect of police.

Monsieur Madeleine wrote immediately to the Thénardiers. Fantine owed them a hundred and twenty francs. He sent them three hundred francs, telling them to pay themselves out of it and to bring the child at once to Montreuil-sur-Mer, where her mother, who was sick, wanted her.

Monsieur Madeleine came to see her twice a day, and at each visit she asked him, "Shall I see my Cosette soon?"

He answered, "Perhaps tomorrow. I expect her every moment."

And the mother's pale face would brighten.

She did not recover; on the contrary, her condition seemed to worsen from week to week. The doctor sounded her lungs and shook his head.

Monsieur Madeleine said to him, "Well?"

"Has she not a child she is anxious to see?" said the doctor.

"Yes."

"Well then, make haste to bring her."

The Thénardiers, however, did not let go of the child; they gave a hundred bad reasons. Cosette was too delicate to travel in the wintertime, and then there were a number of little petty debts.

"I will send somebody for Cosette," said Monsieur Madeleine. "If necessary, I will go myself."

He wrote at Fantine's dictation this letter, which she signed:

Monsieur Thénardier: You will deliver Cosette to the bearer. He will settle all small debts.
—FANTINE

Chapter 15

One morning Monsieur Madeleine was in his office, wondering if he should go to Montfermeil himself, when he was informed that Javert, the inspector of police, wished to speak with him. Monsieur Madeleine could not repress a disagreeable impression. Since the affair of the bureau of police, Javert had avoided him more than ever.

"Let him come in," said he.

Javert entered. The mayor laid down his pen and turned partly round. "Well, what is it? What is the matter, Javert?"

Javert remained silent a moment as if collecting himself, then raised his voice with a sad solemnity. "There has been a criminal act committed, Monsieur Mayor. An inferior agent of the government has been found wanting in respect to a magistrate; in the gravest manner I come, as is my duty, to bring the fact to your knowledge."

"Who is the agent?" asked Monsieur Madeleine.

"I," said Javert.

"And who is the magistrate who has to complain of this agent?"

"You, Monsieur Mayor."

Monsieur Madeleine straightened himself in his chair.

Javert continued, with serious looks and eyes still cast down. "Monsieur Mayor, I come to ask you to be so kind as to make charges and procure my dismissal. Six weeks ago, after that scene about that girl, I was enraged and I denounced you."

"Denounced me?"

"To the prefecture of police in Paris."

Monsieur Madeleine, who did not laugh much oftener than Javert, began to laugh. "As a mayor having encroached upon the police?"

"As a former convict."

The mayor became livid. Javert, who had not raised his eyes, continued, "For a long while I had had suspicions. A resemblance, your immense strength; the affair of old Fauchelevent; your skill as a marksman; your leg, which drags a little—at last I took you for a man named Jean Valjean. He was a convict I saw twenty years ago, when I was adjutant of the galley guard at Toulon. After leaving the galleys, this Valjean, it appears, robbed a bishop's place, then committed another robbery with weapons in his hands, in a highway, on a little Savoyard. For eight years his whereabouts have been unknown, and search has been made for him. Anger determined me, and I denounced you to the prefect."

Monsieur Madeleine, who had taken up the file of papers again, said with a tone of perfect indifference, "And what answer did you get?"

"That I was crazy."

"Well?"

"Well, they were right."

"It is fortunate that you think so!"

"It must be so, for the real Jean Valjean has been found."

The paper that Monsieur Madeleine held fell from his hand; he raised his head, looked steadily at Javert, and said in an inexpressible tone, "Ah!"

Javert continued, "I will tell you how it is, Monsieur Mayor. There was a simple sort of fellow, poor man, who was called Father Champmathieu. There was a theft of cider apples, a wall scaled, branches of trees broken. Champmathieu was arrested; he had even then a branch of an apple tree in his hand. The rogue was caged. So far, it was nothing more than a penitentiary matter. But here comes in the hand of Providence. The jail being in a bad condition, the police justice thought it best to take him to the prison at Arras, where there was a former convict named Brevet, who is there for some trifle. No sooner was Champmathieu set down than Brevet cried out, 'Ha, ha! I know that man. He is a former convict.' Besides Brevet there are two convicts who have seen Jean Valjean. These men were brought from the galleys and confronted with the pretended Champmathieu. They did not hesitate. To them as well as to Brevet it was Jean Valjean. Same age, fifty-four years old; same height; same appearance; in fact the same man. It is he. At this time it was that I sent my denunciation to the prefecture in Paris. They replied that I was out of my mind and that Jean Valjean was at Arras in the hands of justice. I wrote to the justice; he sent for me and brought Champmathieu before me."

"Well?" interrupted Monsieur Madeleine.

Javert replied, with an incorruptible and sad face, "Monsieur Mayor, truth is truth. I am sorry for it, but that man is Jean Valjean. I recognized him also."

Monsieur Madeleine said in a very low voice, "Are you sure?"

"I am sure! And now that I see the real Jean Valjean, I do not understand how I ever could have believed anything else. I beg your pardon, Monsieur Mayor."

Monsieur Madeleine answered, "And what did the man say?"

"He pretends not to understand; he says, 'I am Champmathieu. I have no more to say.' He puts on an appearance of astonishment. The rascal is cunning! But there is the evidence. Four persons have recognized him, and the old villain will be condemned. I am going to testify. I have been summoned."

Monsieur Madeleine had turned again to his desk and was quietly looking over his papers, reading and writing alternately, like a man pressed with business. He turned again toward Javert. "What day then?"

"The case will be tried tomorrow, and I shall leave tonight."

"And how long will the matter last?"

"One day at longest. Sentence will be pronounced at latest tomorrow evening; as soon as my testimony is given, I shall return here."

"Very well," said Monsieur Madeleine. And he dismissed him with a wave of his hand.

Javert did not go.

"Monsieur Mayor, there is one thing more to which I desire to call your attention."

"What is it?"

"It is that I ought to be dismissed."

Monsieur Madeleine arose.

"Javert, you are a man of honor and I esteem you. You exaggerate your fault. Besides, this is an offense which concerns me. You are worthy of promotion rather than disgrace. I desire you to keep your place."

Javert looked at Monsieur Madeleine with his calm eyes, in whose depths it seemed that one beheld his conscience, unenlightened, but stern and pure, and said in a tranquil voice, "Monsieur Mayor, I cannot agree to that. The good of the service demands an example. I simply ask the dismissal of Inspector Javert."

"We will see," said Monsieur Madeleine. And he held out his hand to him.

Javert started back and said fiercely, "Pardon, Monsieur Mayor, but a mayor does not give his hand to a spy. From the moment I abused the power of my position, I have been nothing better than a spy!"

Then he bowed profoundly.

"Monsieur Mayor, I will continue in the service until I am relieved."

He went out. Monsieur Madeleine sat musing, listening to Javert's firm and resolute step as it died away along the corridor. From the mayor's office he went to the outskirts of the city to a man who kept horses and chaises to let, and there bargained for his fleetest horse and lightest tilbury*. These he hired with orders that they be delivered to his house at half past four in the morning.

CHAPTER 16

It was Monsieur Madeleine's intention to go to Arras to the trial of this Champmathieu and there expose himself. But when he reached his home, he hesitated. He was safe; why should he stir up the deeds, the memories of his past life? He had kept in a secret cupboard all he possessed when he first came to Montreuil-sur-Mer. He burned them one by one in his hearth. As the old coat fell apart in charred pieces, a little silver coin fell on the bricks with a ringing sound. It was the forty-sous piece stolen from the little Savoyard. Suddenly his eyes fell upon the two silver candlesticks on the mantel, which were glistening dimly in the firelight.

"Stop!" thought he. "Jean Valjean is contained in them too. They also must be destroyed."

He took the two candlesticks. There was fire enough to melt them quickly into an unrecognizable ingot*. He stirred the embers with one of the candlesticks. A minute more, and they would have been in the fire.

At that moment, it seemed to him that he heard a voice crying within him, "Jean Valjean! Jean Valjean!"

He felt that the bishop was there, that the bishop was present all the more now that he was dead, and was looking fixedly at him, that henceforth Mayor Madeleine with all his virtues would be abominable to him, and the galley slave, Jean Valjean, would be admirable and pure in his sight. That men saw his mask, but the bishop saw his face. That men saw his life, but the bishop saw his conscience. He must then go to Arras, deliver the wrong Jean Valjean, denounce the right one. Alas! That was the greatest of sacrifices, the most poignant of victories, the final step to be taken, but he must do it. He could only enter into sanctity in the eyes of God by returning into infamy in the eyes of men!

He put his books in order. He threw into the fire a package of promissory notes which he held against needy small traders. He wrote a letter, which he sealed, and upon the envelope wrote, *Monsieur Laffitte, banker, Rue d'Artois, Paris.* He drew from a secretary a pocketbook containing some banknotes and his passport.

He put the letter to Monsieur Laffitte in his pocket as well as the pocketbook, and began to walk about the room. He still saw his duty clearly written in luminous letters which flared out before his eyes, and moved with his gaze: "Go! Avow thy name! Denounce thyself!"

The clock struck three. For five hours he had been walking thus, almost without interruption, when he dropped into his chair. He fell asleep and dreamed. But suddenly he awoke. He was chilly. A cold morning wind made the sashes of the still-open window swing on their hinges. The fire had gone out. The candle was low in the socket. The night was yet dark.

He arose and went to the window. There were still no stars in the sky. From his window he could look into the courtyard and into the street. A harsh, rattling noise that suddenly resounded from the ground made him look down. He saw below him two red stars, whose rays danced back and forth grotesquely in the shadow. His mind was still half-buried in the mist of his reverie.

This confusion, however, faded away; a second noise like the first awakened him completely; he looked, and he saw that these two stars were the lamps of a carriage. It was a tilbury drawn by a small white horse. The noise which he had heard was the sound of the horse's hooves upon the pavement.

At that moment there was a loud rap at the door of his room. "Who is there?"

Someone answered, "I, Monsieur Mayor."

He recognized the voice of the old woman, his portress*.

"Monsieur Mayor, what shall I say to the driver?"

"Say that I am coming down."

Chapter 17

All that day Madeleine drove till he finally reached Arras, and there, through the courtesy of the judge of the court of assizes*, he was admitted to the bench where those who were to rule on the case of Champmathieu were sitting. The time had come for closing the case. The judge commanded the accused to rise, and put the usual question: "Have you anything to add to your defense?"

He could not persuade anyone that he was innocent. Finally, to bring added weight against him, the prosecuting attorney brought in the three convicts: Brevet, Chenildieu, and Cochepaille. All three swore that they recognized in him their former fellow prisoner Jean Valjean.

It was evident that the man was lost.

"Officers," said the judge, "enforce order. I am about to sum up the case."

At this moment there was a movement near the judge. A voice was heard exclaiming, "Brevet, Chenildieu, Cochepaille, look this way!"

All eyes turned toward the spot whence it came. A man, who had been sitting among the privileged spectators behind the court, had risen and was standing in the center of the hall. The judge, the prosecuting attorney, and twenty other persons recognized him and exclaimed at once, "Monsieur Madeleine!"

tilbury : a light open two-wheel carriage with or without a top

ingot : a block of gold, silver, or other metal

portress : a woman doorkeeper of a convent or apartment building

court of assizes : a criminal trial court with limited jurisdiction to hear cases involving defendants accused of felonies

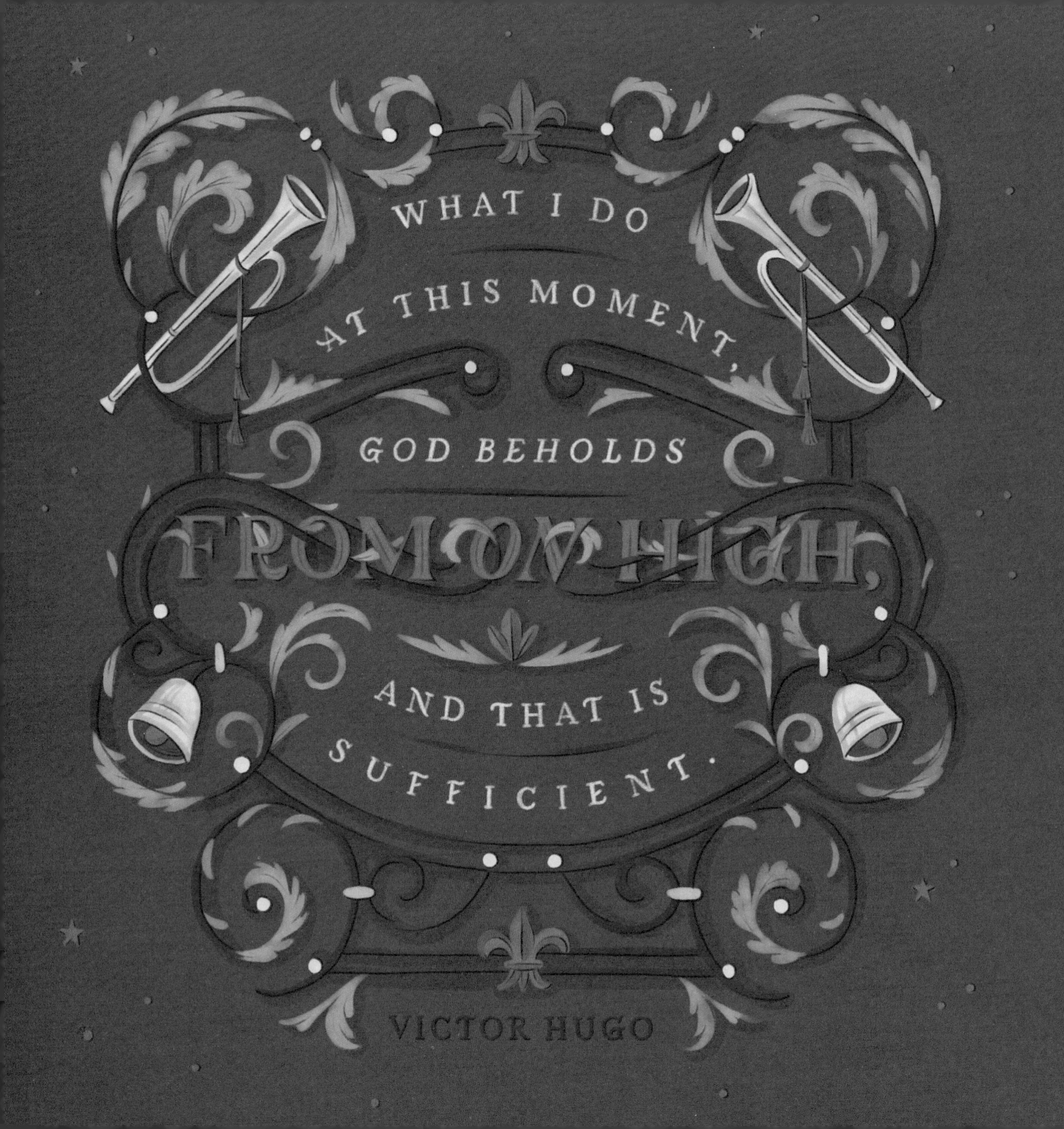
WHAT I DO
AT THIS MOMENT,
GOD BEHOLDS
FROM ON HIGH,
AND THAT IS
SUFFICIENT.
VICTOR HUGO

It was he, indeed. The clerk's lamp lighted up his face. He held his hat in his hand; there was no disorder in his dress; his overcoat was carefully buttoned. He was very pale and trembled slightly. His hair was now perfectly white. All eyes were strained toward him. Before even the judge and prosecuting attorney could say a word, the man, whom all up to this moment called Monsieur Madeleine, had advanced toward the witnesses.

"Do you not recognize me?" said he.

All three stood confounded and indicated by a shake of the head that they did not know him. Monsieur Madeleine turned toward the jurors and court and said in a mild voice, "Gentlemen of the jury, release the accused. Your Honor, order my arrest. He is not the man whom you seek; it is I. I am Jean Valjean."

Not a breath stirred.

Monsieur Madeleine then said, "You were on the point of committing a great mistake. Release that man. I am accomplishing a duty; I am the unhappy convict. I am the only one who sees clearly here, and I tell you the truth. What I do at this moment, God beholds from on high, and that is sufficient. You can take me, since I am here. I have disguised myself under another name; I have become rich; I have become a mayor; I have desired to enter again among honest men. It seems that this cannot be. I did rob monseigneur the bishop; I did rob Petit Gervais. It is true that Jean Valjean was a wicked wretch. Before the galleys, I was a poor peasant, unintelligent; the galleys changed me. I was stupid, and I became wicked. I was a log, and I became a firebrand. Later, I was saved by indulgence and kindness, as I had been lost by severity. But, pardon, you cannot comprehend what I say. You will find in my house, among the ashes of the fireplace, the forty-sous piece of which, seven years ago, I robbed Petit Gervais. I have nothing more to add. Take me. Great God!"

He turned to the three convicts:

"I recognize you, Brevet. Do you remember those checkered knit suspenders that you had in the galleys?"

Brevet started, struck with surprise.

He continued, "Chenildieu, your left shoulder has been burned deeply from lying on a chafing dish full of embers. Three letters, T. F. D., are still to be seen there. Is this true?"

"It is true!" said Chenildieu.

"Cochepaille, you have on your left arm, near where you have been bled, a date in blue letters. It is the date of the landing of the emperor at Cannes, 1 March, 1815. Lift up your sleeve."

Cochepaille lifted up his sleeve; all eyes around him turned to his naked arm. The date was there.

Monsieur Madeleine turned toward the audience and the court with a smile, the thought of which still rends the hearts of those who witnessed it. It was the smile of triumph; it was also the smile of despair.

"You see clearly," said he, "that I am Jean Valjean."

It was evident that Jean Valjean was before their eyes. Without need of any further explanation, the multitude, as by a sort of electric revelation, comprehended instantly, at a single glance, this simple and magnificent story of a man giving himself up that another might not be condemned in his place.

"I will not disturb the proceeding further," continued Jean Valjean. "I am going, since I am not arrested. I have many things to do. The prosecuting attorney knows where I am going and will have me arrested when he chooses."

He walked toward the outer door. All stood aside. There was at this moment an indescribable divinity within him which makes the multitudes fall back and make way before a man. He passed through the throng with slow steps. On reaching the door, he turned and said, "Monsieur Prosecuting Attorney, I remain at your disposal."

Less than an hour afterward, the verdict of the jury discharged from all accusation the said Champmathieu; and Champmathieu, set at liberty forthwith, went his way, thinking all men mad, and understanding nothing of this vision.

Chapter 18

The first thing Monsieur Madeleine did when he returned to Montreuil-sur-Mer was to visit the hospital and see Fantine. She talked constantly of Cosette, but he listened to the words as one listens to the wind that blows, his eyes on the ground.

She did not speak; she did not breathe; she half raised herself in the bed, and the covering fell from her emaciated shoulders; her countenance, radiant a moment before, became livid, and her eyes, dilated with terror, seemed to fasten on something before her at the other end of the room.

"What is the matter, Fantine?"

She did not answer; she did not take her eyes from the object which she seemed to see, but touched his arm with one hand, and with the other made a sign to him to look behind him. He turned, and saw Javert.

Fantine had not seen Javert since the day the mayor had wrested her from him. She was sure that he had come for her. She felt as if she were dying; she hid her face with both hands and shrieked in anguish, "Monsieur Madeleine, save me!"

Jean Valjean—we shall call him by no other name henceforth—had risen. He said to Fantine in his gentlest and calmest tone, "Be composed; it is not for you that he comes."

He then turned to Javert and said, "I know what you want."

Javert answered, "Hurry along."

At the exclamation of Javert, Fantine had opened her eyes again. But the mayor was there—what could she fear? Javert advanced to the middle of the chamber, exclaiming, "Are you coming?"

The unhappy woman looked around her. There was no one but a nun and the mayor. To whom could this contemptuous familiarity be addressed? To herself alone. She shuddered. Then she saw a mysterious thing, so mysterious that its like had never appeared to her in the darkest delirium of fever. She saw Javert seize the arm of Jean Valjean and try to push him out of the room.

"Monsieur Mayor!" she exclaimed.

"Silence," said Javert. "There is no mayor here. Shall I tell you what there is? There is a brigand, a convict called Jean Valjean, and I have got him! That is what there is!"

Fantine started upright, supporting herself by her rigid arms and hands; she looked at Jean Valjean, then at Javert, and then at the nun; she opened her mouth as if to speak; a rattle came from her throat, her teeth struck together, she stretched out her arms in anguish, convulsively opening her hands and groping about her like one who is drowning, then sank suddenly back upon the pillow. Her head struck the head of the bed and fell forward on her breast, the mouth gaping, the eyes open and glazed. She was dead.

Jean Valjean put his hand on that of Javert which held him; then he said, “You have killed this woman.”

“Have done with this!” cried Javert, furious. “I am not here to listen to sermons; save all that. The guard is below; come right along, or the handcuffs!”

There stood in a corner of the room an old iron bedstead in a dilapidated condition, which the sisters used as a camp bed when they watched over patients. Jean Valjean went to the bed, wrenched out the rickety head bar—a thing easy for muscles like his—and, with the bar in his clenched fist, looked at Javert. Javert recoiled toward the door. Jean Valjean, his iron bar in hand, walked slowly toward the bed of Fantine. On reaching it, he turned and said to Javert in a voice that could scarcely be heard, “I advise you not to disturb me now.”

Javert trembled. He had an idea of calling the guard, but Jean Valjean might escape in his absence. He remained therefore, grasped the bottom of his cane, and leaned against the framework of the door without taking his eyes from Jean Valjean.

Jean Valjean rested his elbow upon the bedpost and his head upon his hand, and gazed at Fantine stretched motionless before him. He remained thus, mute and absorbed, evidently lost to everything of this life. His countenance bespoke nothing but inexpressible pity. After a few moments’ reverie, he bent down to Fantine and addressed her in a whisper. The words were heard by none on earth. Did the dead woman hear them? When Jean Valjean whispered in the ear of Fantine, there was an ineffable smile on those pale lips and in those dim eyes, full of the wonder of the tomb.

Jean Valjean took Fantine’s head in his hands and arranged it on the pillow, as a mother would have done for her child, then

fastened the string of her nightdress and replaced her hair beneath her cap. This done, he closed her eyes.

The face of Fantine, at this instant, seemed strangely illumined. Death is the entrance into the great light.

Fantine’s hand hung over the side of the bed. Jean Valjean knelt before this hand, raised it gently, and kissed it. Then he rose and, turning to Javert, said, “Now I am at your disposal.”

Javert put Jean Valjean in the city prison.

Chapter 19

On the evening of this same day, the old portress who had been Monsieur Madeleine’s servant was sitting in her lodge, still quite bewildered and sunk in sad reflections. The factory had been closed all day; the carriage doors were bolted; the street was deserted.

Toward the time when Monsieur Madeleine had been accustomed to return, the honest portress rose mechanically, took the key of his room from a drawer with the taper stand that he used at night to light himself up the stairs, then hung the key on a nail from which he had been in the habit of taking it and placed the taper stand by its side as if she were expecting him. She then seated herself again in her chair and resumed her reflections. The poor old woman had done all this without being conscious of it.

More than two hours had elapsed when the window of her box opened and a hand passed through the opening, took the key and stand, and lighted the taper at the candle which was burning.

The portress raised her eyes; she was transfixed with astonishment; a cry rose to her lips, but she could not give it utterance. She knew the hand, the arm, the coat sleeve. It was Monsieur Madeleine.

"Good heavens! Monsieur Mayor!" she exclaimed. "I thought you were—"

She stopped; the end of her sentence would not have been respectful to the beginning. To her, Jean Valjean was still Monsieur Mayor.

He completed her thought. "In prison," said he. "I was there; I broke a bar from a window, I let myself fall from the top of a roof, and here I am. I am going to my room."

He gave his servant no caution, very sure she would guard him better than he would guard himself.

He ascended the staircase and opened his door with little noise, felt his way to the window and closed the shutter, then came back, took his taper, and went into the chamber. The precaution was not useless; his window could be seen from the street.

He cast a glance about him, over his table, his chair, his bed, which had not been slept in for three days. There remained no trace of the disorder of the night bef ore the last. The portress had put the room to rights. Only, she had picked up from the ashes and laid on the table the forty-sous piece, blackened by the fire.

He took a sheet of paper and wrote, *This is the forty-sous piece stolen from Petit Gervais*, then placed the piece of silver on the sheet in such a way that it would be the first thing perceived on entering the room. He took from a wardrobe an old shirt, which he tore into several pieces and in which he packed the two silver candlesticks. In all this there was neither haste nor agitation.

Very soon two gentle taps were heard at the door. It was Sister Simplice. She had wept, and she was trembling.

Jean Valjean had written a few lines on a piece of paper, which he handed to the nun, saying, "Sister, you will give this to the curé."

The paper was not folded. She cast her eyes on it.

"You may read it," said he.

She read, "'I beg Monsieur Curé to take charge of all that I leave here. He will please defray therefrom the expenses of my trial and of the burial of the woman who died this morning. The remainder is for the poor.'"

There was a loud noise on the staircase. They heard a tumult of steps ascending and the old portress exclaiming in her loudest and most piercing tones.

"My good sir, I swear to you in the name of God that nobody has come in here the whole day and the whole evening, that I have not even once left my door!"

A man replied, "But yet, there is a light in this room."

They recognized the voice of Javert.

The chamber was so arranged that the door in opening covered the corner of the wall to the right. Jean Valjean blew out the taper and placed himself in this corner. Sister Simplice fell on her knees near the table.

The door opened. Javert entered.

The nun did not raise her eyes. She was praying. The candle was on the mantel and gave but a dim light. Javert perceived the sister and stopped.

His first impulse was to retire. But there was also another duty which held him, and which urged him imperiously in the opposite direction. His second impulse was to remain, and to venture at least one question. This was Sister Simplice, who had never lied in her life. Javert knew this and venerated her especially on account of it.

"Sister," said he, "are you alone in this room?"

There was a fearful instant during which the poor portress felt her limbs falter beneath her.

The sister raised her eyes and replied, "Yes."

Then continued Javert, "Excuse me if I persist; it is my duty—you have not seen this evening a person, a man? He has escaped, and we are in search of him—Jean Valjean—you have not seen him?"

The sister answered, "No."

She lied. Two lies in succession, one upon another, without hesitation, quickly, as if she were adept in it.

“Your pardon!” said Javert, and he withdrew, bowing reverently.

The affirmation of the sister was to Javert something so decisive that he did not even notice the singularity of the taper just blown out and smoking on the table.

An hour afterward, a man was walking rapidly in the darkness beneath the trees, from Montreuil-sur-Mer in the direction of Paris. This man was Jean Valjean.

Chapter 20

Javert never allowed a convict to wander long in liberty, and so, when Jean Valjean had escaped him at Montreuil-sur-Mer, he went posthaste to Paris, where he was sure the former mayor would try to conceal himself. One day as he was walking down a side street, he saw a carter struggling with a heavy weight he wanted to place in his wagon. For some time he wrestled with it, but though a man of powerful frame, he was unable to move it. When he was about to give up, an old man dressed in the coarse clothes of a laborer came by. He saw the fruitless efforts of the teamster, so he stepped up to lend his aid. He looked at the weight for a moment and then, stooping down, lifted it with ease into the wagon.

Javert had been watching the proceedings and immediately stepped up. An almost-imperceptible shudder passed over the frame of the old man, and he made to walk away. But before he had taken two steps, Javert's hand was on his shoulder.

Together they went to the department of police, and some days later, Jean Valjean was again in the galleys at Toulon.

Toward the end of October, the inhabitants of Toulon saw coming back into their port, in order to repair some damages from heavy weather, the ship *Orion*, which then formed a part of the Mediterranean squadron. This ship, crippled as she was, produced some sensation on entering the roadstead*. She flew a pennant which entitled her to a salute of eleven guns.

One morning, the throng witnessed an accident. The crew were furling the sail. The topman*, whose duty it was to take in the starboard upper corner of the main topsail, lost his balance. He was seen tottering; the dense throng assembled on the wharf uttered a cry, the man's head overbalanced his body, and he whirled over the yard, his arms outstretched toward the deep. As he went over, he grasped a rope and hung suspended. The sea lay far below him at a giddy depth. The poor fellow hung dangling to and fro at the end of this line like a stone in a sling.

To go to his aid was to run a frightful risk. None of the crew dared attempt it. In the meantime, the poor topman was becoming exhausted. He did not cry out, for fear of losing his strength. The crowd that watched all turned their heads away that they might not see him fall.

Suddenly, a man was discovered clambering up the rigging with the agility of a wildcat. This man was clad in red—it was a convict; he wore a green cap—it was a convict for life. As he reached the round-top*, a gust of wind blew off his cap and revealed a head entirely white. It was not a young man.

In fact, it was one of the convicts employed on board in some prison task, who had, at the first alarm, run to the officer of the watch, and, amid the confusion and hesitation of the crew, asked permission to save the topman's life at the risk of his own. A sign of assent being given, with one blow of a hammer he broke the chain riveted to the iron ring at

roadstead : a sheltered stretch of water near the shore in which ships can ride at anchor

topman : the man stationed in the top on a sailing vessel, responsible for the setting of the sails

round-top : a platform at the top of a ship's mast

his ankle, then took a rope in his hand and flung himself into the shrouds*.

In a twinkling this volunteer was upon the top of the mast. He paused a few seconds and seemed to measure it with his glance. At length, the convict raised his eyes to heaven and took a step forward. The crowd drew a long breath. He ran along the yard. On reaching its extreme tip, he fastened one end of the rope he had with him and let the other hang at full length. He began to let himself down by his hands along this rope; instead of one man, two were seen dangling at that giddy height.

You would have said it was a spider seizing a fly; only, in this case, the spider was bringing life and not death. Ten thousand eyes were fixed upon the pair. Every man held his breath. However, the convict, at length, managed to make his way down to the seaman. One minute more, and the man, exhausted and despairing, would have fallen into the deep. The convict firmly secured him to the rope to which he clung with one hand while he worked with the other. Finally, he was seen reascending to the yard and hauling the sailor after him. He supported him there, for an instant, to let him recover his strength, and then, lifting him in his arms, carried him as he walked along the yard to the round-top, where he left him in the hands of his messmates.

Then the throng applauded and shouted, "This man must be pardoned!"

He, however, had made it a point of duty to descend again immediately and go back to his work. In order to arrive more quickly, he slid down the rigging and started to run along a lower yard. There was a certain moment when everyone felt alarmed; whether it was that he felt fatigued, or because his head swam, people thought they saw him hesitate and stagger. Suddenly, the convict fell into the sea.

The fall was perilous. The poor convict had plunged between two ships. It was feared that he would be drawn under one or the other. Four men sprang, at once, into a boat. The people cheered them on, and anxiety again took possession of all minds. The man had not again risen to the surface. He had disappeared into the sea, without making even a ripple. The search was continued until night, but not even the body was found.

The next morning, the *Toulon Journal* published the following lines:

> November 17, 1823. Yesterday, a convict at work on board the *Orion*, on his return from rescuing a sailor, fell into the sea and was drowned. His body was not recovered. It is presumed that it has been caught under the piles at the pier head of the arsenal. This man was registered by the number 9430, and his name was Jean Valjean.

CHAPTER 21

On Christmas evening in the year 1823, several men, wagoners and peddlers, were seated at the table and drinking around four or five candles in the low hall of the Thénardier tavern. Cosette was at her usual place, under the kitchen table near the fireplace; she was clad in rags; her bare feet were in wooden shoes, and by the light of the fire she was knitting woolen stockings for the little Thénardiers. In a neighboring room two children were heard prattling—the Thénardiers' daughters, Éponine and Azelma.

At intervals, the cry of a very young child was heard above the noise of the barroom. This was a little boy named Gavroche which the woman had had some winters before. The mother

shroud : one of the ropes, usually in pairs, leading from a ship's mastheads to give lateral support to the masts *

had nursed him but did not love him. When the hungry clamor of the brat became too much to bear, Thénardier said, "Your boy is squalling. Why don't you go and see what he wants?"

"Bah!" answered the mother. "I am sick of him." And the poor little fellow continued to cry in the darkness.

This man and this woman were a hideous and terrible pair. Cosette was between them, like a creature who is at the same time being bruised by a millstone and lacerated with pincers.

Cosette was beaten unmercifully; that came from the woman. She went barefoot in winter; that came from the man.

Cosette ran up and down stairs; she washed, brushed, scrubbed, swept, ran, tired herself, got out of breath, lifted heavy things, and, puny as she was, did the rough work. No pity; a ferocious mistress, a malignant master. The Thénardier chophouse was like a snare in which Cosette had been caught, and was trembling.

Four new guests had just come in. Cosette was only eight years old, and she had already suffered so much that she mused with the mournful air of an old woman. She realized that there was no water in the cistern. One thing comforted her a little: they did not drink much water in the Thénardier tavern.

From time to time, one of the drinkers would look out into the street and exclaim, "It would take a cat to go along the street without a lantern tonight!"

All at once, one of the peddlers who lodged in the tavern came in, and said in a harsh voice, "You have not watered my horse."

"Oh, yes, monsieur!" said Cosette. "The horse did drink a full bucket, and 'twas me that carried it to him, and I talked to him."

This was not true. Cosette lied.

"Here is a girl as big as my fist, who can tell a lie as big as a house," exclaimed the peddler. "I tell you that he has not had any water, little wench! He has a way of blowing when he has not had any water, that I know well enough."

"Well, of course that is right," said the Thénardiess. "If the beast has not had any water, he must have some."

"But, ma'am," said Cosette feebly, "there is no water."

The Thénardiess threw the street door wide open. "Well, go after some!"

Cosette hung her head and went for an empty bucket that was by the chimney corner. The bucket was larger than she, and the child could have sat down in it comfortably. The Thénardiess went back to her range and tasted what was in the kettle with a wooden spoon, grumbling the while, "There is some at the spring."

Then she fumbled in a drawer. "Here, Ma'm'selle Toad," added she. "Get a big loaf at the baker's as you come back. Here is fifteen sous."

Cosette had a little pocket in the side of her apron; she took the piece without saying a word, and put it in that pocket. Then she remained motionless, bucket in hand, the open door before her. She seemed to be waiting for somebody to come to her aid.

"Get along!" cried the Thénardiess.

The door closed. She thought no more; she saw nothing more. The immensity of night engulfed this little creature.

It was a short walk to the spring. Cosette knew the road, from traveling it several times a day, and did not lose her way. A remnant of instinct guided her blindly. But she turned her eyes neither to the right nor to the left, for fear of seeing things in the trees and in the bushes.

It was a small natural basin, about two feet deep, surrounded with moss and with long, reedy grass, and paved with a few large stones. A brook escaped from it with a gentle, tranquil murmur.

Cosette did not take time to breathe. She felt with her left hand in the darkness for a young oak which bent over the spring and usually served her as a support, found a branch, swung herself from it, bent down, and plunged the bucket in the water. She was for a moment so excited that her strength was tripled. When bent over, she did not notice that the pocket of her apron emptied itself into the spring. The fifteen-sous piece fell into the water.

Cosette neither saw it nor heard it fall. She drew out the bucket almost full and set it on the grass. She breathed an instant, then grasped the handle and started on. She walked bending forward, her head down, like an old woman; the weight of the bucket strained and stiffened her thin arms. The iron handle was numbing and freezing her little wet hands; from time to time she had to stop, and every time she stopped, the cold water that splashed from the bucket fell upon her naked knees. This took place in the depth of a wood, at night, in the winter, far from all human sight; it was a child of eight years; there was none but God at that moment who saw this sad thing.

She was worn out with fatigue and was not yet out of the forest. Arriving near an old chestnut tree which she knew, she made a last halt, longer than the others, to get well rested; then she gathered all her strength, took up the bucket again, and began to walk on courageously. Meanwhile the poor little despairing thing could not help crying, "Oh! My God, help me!"

At that moment she felt all at once that the weight of the bucket was gone. A hand, which seemed enormous to her, had just caught the handle and was carrying it easily. She raised her head. A large, dark form, straight and erect, was walking beside her in the gloom. It was a man who had come up behind her, and whom she had not heard. Without saying a word, he had grasped the handle of the bucket.

The child was not afraid.

Chapter 22

In the afternoon of that same Christmas Day, 1823, after walking a long time, a man came to the most deserted portion of the BOULEVARD DE L'HÔPITAL IN PARIS. He had the appearance of someone who was looking for lodgings and seemed to stop by preference before the most modest houses. This man combined extreme misery with extreme neatness. From his hair, which was entirely white, from his wrinkled brow, from his face, evincing exhaustion and weariness of life, one would have supposed him considerably over sixty. From his firm though slow step and the vigor of his motions, one would hardly have thought him fifty. There was in the depths of his eye an indescribably mournful serenity. He carried in his left hand a small package tied in a handkerchief; he leaned upon a sort of staff cut from a hedge.

This was the man who had fallen in step with Cosette. As he made his way through the copse in the direction of Montfermeil, he had perceived that little shadow struggling along with a groan, setting her burden on the ground, then taking it up and going on again. He had approached her and seen that it was a very young child carrying an enormous bucket of water. Then he had gone to the child and silently taken hold of the handle of the bucket.

Cosette, we have said, was not afraid. The man spoke to her. His voice was serious and was almost a whisper.

"My child, that is very heavy for you."

Cosette raised her head and answered, "Yes, monsieur."

"Give it to me," the man continued. "I will carry it for you."

Cosette let go of the bucket. The man walked along with her.

"It is very heavy, indeed," said he to himself. Then he added, "Little girl, how old are you?"

"Eight years, monsieur."

"And have you come far in this way?"

"From the spring in the woods."

"And are you going far?"

"A good quarter of an hour from here."

The man remained a moment without speaking; then he said abruptly, "You have no mother then?"

"I don't know. I don't believe I have. All the rest have one. For my part, I have none. I believe I never had any." The man stopped, put the bucket on the ground, stooped down, and placed his hands upon the child's shoulders, making an effort to look at her and see her face in the darkness.

"What is your name?" said the man.

"Cosette."

It seemed as if the man had an electric shock. He looked at her again; then, letting go of her shoulders, he took up the bucket and walked on. A moment after, he asked, "Little girl, where do you live?"

"In Montfermeil, if you know it."

"It is there that we are going?"

"Yes, monsieur."

"Who is it that has sent you out into the woods after water at this time of night?"

"Madame Thénardier."

"What does she do, your Madame Thénardier?"

"She is my mistress," said the child. "She keeps the tavern."

"The tavern," said the man. "Well, I am going there to lodge tonight. Show me the way."

The man walked very fast. Cosette followed him without difficulty. She felt fatigue no more. From time to time, she raised her eyes toward this man with a sort of tranquility and inexpressible confidence. She had never been taught to turn toward Providence and to pray. However, she felt in her bosom something that resembled hope and joy, and which rose toward heaven.

As they drew near the tavern, Cosette timidly touched his arm. "Monsieur?"

"What, my child?"

"Here we are close by the house. Will you let me take the bucket now? Because if madame sees that anybody brought it for me, she will beat me."

The man gave her the bucket. A moment later, they were at the door of the chophouse. The door opened. The Thénardiess appeared with a candle in her hand.

"Madame," said Cosette, trembling, "there is a gentleman who is coming to lodge."

The Thénardiess very quickly replaced her fierce air with an amiable grimace and looked for the newcomer with eager eyes.

"Is it monsieur?" said she.

"Yes, madame," answered the man, touching his hat.

Rich travelers are not so polite. This gesture and the sight of the stranger's costume—and his baggage, which the Thénardiess reviewed at a glance—made the amiable grimace disappear and the fierce air reappear. She added dryly, "Ah, my brave man, I am very sorry, but I have no room."

"Put me where you will," said the man, "in the garret, in the stable. I will pay as if I had a room."

"Forty sous. In advance."

Meanwhile the man, after leaving his stick and bundle on a bench, had seated himself at a table on which Cosette had been quick to place a bottle of wine and a glass. The peddler, who had asked for the bucket of water, had gone himself to carry it to his horse. Cosette had resumed her place under the kitchen table and her knitting. The man, who hardly touched his lips to the wine, was contemplating the child with a strange attention.

Cosette might, perhaps, have been pretty. Thin and pale, she was eight years old, but one would hardly have thought her six. Her large eyes, sunk in a sort of shadow, were almost put out by continual weeping. The corners of her mouth had that curve of habitual anguish, which is seen in the condemned and in the hopelessly sick. The light of the fire, which was shining upon her, made her bones stand out and rendered her thinness fearfully visible. As she was always shivering, she had acquired the habit of drawing her knees together. Her whole dress was nothing but a rag. Her skin showed here and there, and black-and-blue spots could be distinguished, which indicated the places where the Thénardiess had touched her. Her naked legs were red and rough. The hollows under her collarbones would make one weep.

The man did not take his eyes from Cosette. Suddenly, the Thénardiess exclaimed out, "Oh! I forgot! That bread!"

Cosette had entirely forgotten the bread. Like children who are always terrified, she had no recourse but to lie.

"Madame, the baker was shut."

"You ought to have knocked."

"I did knock, madame, but he didn't open."

"I'll find out tomorrow if that is true," said the Thénardiess, "and if you are lying, you will lead a pretty dance. Meantime, give me back the fifteen-sous piece."

Cosette plunged her hand into her apron pocket and turned white. The fifteen-sous piece was not there.

"Come," said the Thénardiess, "didn't you hear me?"

Cosette turned her pocket inside out; there was nothing there. What could have become of that money? The little unfortunate could not utter a word. She was petrified.

"Have you lost it, the fifteen-sous piece?" screamed the Thénardiess. "Or do you want to steal it from me?"

At the same time she reached her arm toward the cowhide hanging in the chimney corner.

Meanwhile the man in the yellow coat had been fumbling in his waistcoat pocket without being noticed. Cosette was writhing with anguish in the chimney corner, trying to gather up and hide her poor half-naked limbs. The Thénardiess raised her arm.

"I beg your pardon, madame," said the man, "but I just now saw something fall out of the pocket of that little girl's apron and roll away. That may be it."

At the same time he stooped down and appeared to search on the floor for an instant.

"Just so, here it is," said he, rising. And he handed a silver piece to the Thénardiess.

"Yes, that is it," said she.

That was not it, for it was a twenty-sous piece, but the Thénardiess found her profit in it. She put the piece in her pocket, casting a ferocious look at the child. Cosette went back to what the Thénardiess called "her hole," and her large eye, fixed upon the unknown traveler, began to assume an expression that it had never known before, artless astonishment with a blind confidence associated with it.

Several hours passed away. The drinkers had gone, the revel* was done, the house was closed, the room was deserted, the fire had gone out. The stranger still remained in the same place and in the same posture. But he had not spoken a word since Cosette had gone. Finally, Thénardier took off his cap, approached softly, and ventured to say, "Is monsieur not going to repose?"

"Yes," said the stranger, "you are right. Where is your stable?"

"Monsieur," said Thénardier, with a smile, "I will conduct monsieur." Thénardier took the candle and led him into a room on the first floor, which was very showy, furnished all in mahogany, with a high-post bedstead and red calico curtains.

revel : lively and noisy enjoyment, especially with drinking and dancing *

Something in the manner of this strange wayfarer had caused both the innkeeper and his wife to suspect that this man whom they took for a pauper was none other than the banker who sent them their remittances, in disguise. It was this suspicion that made Thénardier conduct his guest into his best chamber.

"What is this?" said the traveler.

"It is properly our bridal chamber; this is not open more than three or four times in a year."

"I should have liked the stable as well," said the man bluntly.

Thénardier ignored the uncivil answer. He lighted two entirely new wax candles on the mantel; a good fire was blazing in the fireplace.

When the traveler turned again, the host had disappeared. Thénardier had discreetly taken himself out of the way without daring to say good night, not desiring to treat with a disrespectful cordiality a man whom he proposed to skin royally in the morning.

The stranger sat down in an armchair and remained some time thinking. Then he drew off his shoes, took one of the two candles, blew out the other, pushed open the door, and went out of the room, looking about him as if he were searching for something. He passed through a hall and came to the stairway. There he heard a very soft little sound, which resembled the breathing of a child. Guided by this sound, he came to a sort of triangular nook built under the stairs. There, among all sorts of old baskets and rubbish, in the dust and among the cobwebs, he spied a bed. It was placed on the floor immediately on the tiles, and in it Cosette was sleeping.

An open door near Cosette's nook disclosed a large, dark room. The stranger entered. At the further end, through a glass window, he perceived two little beds with very white spreads. They were those of the two little daughters of the house. His eye fell upon the fireplace; there was no fire; there were not even any ashes, but there were two little children's shoes, of coquettish shape and different sizes. He remembered the custom of children putting their shoes by the fireplace on Christmas night, in expectation of some shining gift from their good fairy. Éponine and Azelma had not forgotten to each put one of their shoes there.

The traveler bent over them and saw that the fairy—the mother—had already made her visit, placing a beautiful new ten-sous piece in each shoe. He also noticed in the darkest corner of the fireplace a wooden shoe of the clumsiest sort, half-broken and covered with ashes and dried mud. Cosette, with that touching confidence of childhood which can always be deceived without ever being discouraged, had also placed her shoe in the fireplace. There was nothing in this wooden shoe.

Chapter 23

Early the next morning, after the stranger had paid his bill, Thénardier complained of the hardness of the times, of the difficulty he had in earning sufficient money to keep his family and little Cosette from starving or freezing to death. It was this that the guest had been leading to.

All of a sudden he turned to Thénardier and asked, "How much would you take in return for the little Lark?"

Thénardier was staggered, but quick as a flash he recovered himself and answered, "Monsieur, I must have fifteen hundred francs."

The stranger took from his side pocket an old black leather pocketbook, opened it, and drew forth three bank bills, which he placed upon the table. He then rested his large thumb on these bills and said to the tavern keeper, "Bring Cosette."

The Thénardiess at her husband's command went to get her, and an instant later the little girl entered the barroom.

The stranger took the bundle he had brought and untied it. This bundle contained a little woolen frock, woolen stockings, and shoes—a complete dress for a little girl. It was all in black.

"My child," said the man, "take this and go and dress yourself quickly."

The day was breaking when the inhabitants of Montfermeil, who were beginning to open their doors, saw pass on the road to Paris a poorly clad goodman leading a little girl dressed in mourning. It was the stranger and Cosette. No one recognized the man; as Cosette was not now in tatters, few recognized her.

Cosette was going away. All she understood was that she was leaving behind the Thénardier chophouse. Nobody had thought of bidding her good-bye, nor had she of bidding good-bye to anybody. She went out from that house, hated and hating. Cosette walked seriously along, opening her large eyes and looking at the sky. From time to time she bent over and cast a glance at her new frock and then looked at the goodman. She felt somewhat as if she were near God.

The two had hardly been gone a quarter of an hour when the innkeeper and his wife began to think they had let Cosette go too cheaply. At the wife's suggestion, Thénardier started in pursuit of them. They had the start of him, but a child walks slowly, and Thénardier went rapidly. And then the country was well known to him.

The man had sat down to give Cosette a little rest. The chophouse keeper pushed aside the bushes and suddenly appeared before the eyes of those whom he sought.

"Pardon me, monsieur," said he, all out of breath, "but here are your fifteen hundred francs."

So saying, he held out the three bank bills to the stranger.

The man raised his eyes. "What does that mean?"

Thénardier answered respectfully, "Monsieur, that means that I take back Cosette."

Cosette shuddered and hugged close to the goodman.

He answered, looking Thénardier straight in the eye and spacing his syllables. "You—take—back—Cosette?"

"Yes, monsieur, I take her back. I have reflected. Indeed, I haven't the right to give her to you. This little girl is not mine. She belongs to her mother, who has confided her to me; I can only give her up to her mother. You will tell me her mother is dead. Well. In that case, I can only give up the child to a person who shall bring me a written order, signed by the mother, stating I should deliver the child to him. That is clear."

The man, without answering, felt in his pocket, and Thénardier saw the pocketbook containing the bank bills reappear. The tavern keeper felt a thrill of joy.

Before opening the pocketbook, the traveler cast a look

about him. The place was entirely deserted. There was not a soul either in the wood or in the valley. The man opened the pocketbook and drew from it not the handful of bank bills which Thénardier expected but a little piece of paper, which he unfolded and presented open to the innkeeper, saying, "You are right. Read that!"

Thénardier took the paper and read.

Monsieur Thénardier: You will deliver Cosette to the bearer. He will settle all small debts.
—FANTINE

"You know that signature?" asked the man.

It was indeed the signature of Fantine. Thénardier recognized it. There was nothing to say. He felt doubly enraged—enraged at being compelled to give up the bribe which he'd hoped for, and enraged at being beaten.

The man added, "You can keep this paper as your receipt."

"This signature is very well imitated," Thénardier grumbled between his teeth. "Well, so be it!"

Then he made a desperate effort. "Monsieur," said he, "it is all right. But you must settle 'all small debts.' There is a large amount due to me."

The man rose to his feet and said, "Monsieur Thénardier, in January the mother reckoned that she owed you 120 francs; you sent her in February a memorandum of five hundred francs; you received three hundred francs at the end of February and three hundred at the beginning of March. There have since elapsed nine months, which, at fifteen francs per month, the price agreed upon, amounts to 135 francs. You had received a hundred francs in advance. There remain thirty-five francs due you. I have just given you fifteen hundred francs."

"Monsieur, I—don't know your name," said he resolutely, putting aside this time all show of respect. "I shall take back Cosette or you must give me a thousand crowns."

The stranger said quietly, "Come, Cosette."

He took Cosette with his left hand, and with the right picked up his staff, which was on the ground. Thénardier noted the enormous size of the cudgel* and the solitude of the place. The man disappeared in the wood with the child, leaving the chophouse keeper motionless.

As they walked away, Thénardier observed his broad shoulders, a little rounded, and his big fists. Then his eyes fell back upon his own puny arms and thin hands. "I must have been a fool indeed," thought he, "not to have brought my gun, as I was going on a hunt."

However, the innkeeper did not abandon the pursuit. "I must know where he goes," said he, and he began to follow them at a distance. There remained two things in his possession: one a bitter mockery—the piece of paper signed *Fantine*—and the other a consolation—the fifteen hundred francs.

The man was leading Cosette and was walking slowly, his head bent down, in an attitude of reflection and sadness. The winter had left the wood bereft of foliage, so that Thénardier did not lose sight of them, though remaining at a considerable distance behind. From time to time the man turned and looked to see if he were followed.

He perceived the innkeeper. He looked at him so forbiddingly that Thénardier judged it unprofitable to go farther. Thénardier went home.

Jean Valjean was this mysterious stranger and was not dead. When he fell into the sea—or rather when he threw himself into it—he was already free from his irons. He swam underwater to a ship at anchor to which a boat was fastened. He found means to conceal himself in this boat until evening. At night he betook himself again to the water and reached land. There he could procure clothes. Then Jean Valjean, endeavoring to throw the law off the track, followed a wandering path to Paris.

His first care, on reaching Paris, had been to purchase a mourning dress for a little girl of eight years, then to procure lodgings. That done, he had gone to Montfermeil. He was believed to be dead, and that thickened the obscurity which surrounded him. At Paris there had fallen into his hands a paper which chronicled that a prisoner had drowned saving another. He felt reassured, and almost as much at peace as if he really had been dead.

The evening of the same day that Jean Valjean had rescued Cosette from the clutches of the Thénardiess was when he entered Paris again, at nightfall, with the child. There they took a cabriolet* to the observatory; then both walked through the deserted streets toward the BOULEVARD DE L'HÔPITAL.

The day had been strange and full of emotion for Cosette; they had eaten behind hedges bread and cheese bought at isolated chophouses; they had often changed carriages and had traveled short distances on foot. She did not complain, but she was tired, and Jean Valjean perceived it by her pulling more heavily at his hand while walking. He took her in his arms, and Cosette laid her head on Jean Valjean's shoulder and went to sleep.

Chapter 24

Jean Valjean's lodgings were in a rickety old dwelling on the BOULEVARD DE L'HÔPITAL, known as the Gorbeau house. There were three rooms upstairs, one of which he planned for Cosette, a second he reserved for himself, the third remained tenantless. The old woman who acted as caretaker slept in the entry downstairs.

He took the still-sleeping child, laid her on the cot in her room, and sat down by the side. The dawn of the next day found Jean Valjean again near the bed of Cosette. He waited there, motionless, to see her wake. Something new was entering his soul.

Jean Valjean had never loved anything. For twenty-five years he had been alone in the world. He had never been a father, lover, husband, or friend. At the galleys, he was cross, sullen, abstinent, ignorant, and intractable. His sister and her children had left in his memory only a vague and distant impression, which had finally almost entirely vanished. He had made every exertion to find them again, and, not succeeding, yet had not forgotten. The other tender emotions of his youth, if any such he had, were lost in an abyss.

When he saw Cosette, when he had taken her, carried her away, and rescued her, he felt his heart moved. Every feeling and affection he possessed was awakened and drawn toward this child. He would approach the bed where she slept and feel inward yearnings, like a mother, and know not what they were; for it is something very incomprehensible and very sweet, this grand and strange emotion of a heart in its first love. But, as he was fifty-five, and Cosette was but eight years old, all that he might have felt of love in his entire life melted into a sort of radiance. This was the second white vision he had seen. The bishop had caused the dawn of virtue on his horizon; Cosette evoked the dawn of love.

Jean Valjean was prudent enough never to go out in the daytime. Every evening, however, about twilight, he would walk for an hour or two, sometimes alone, often with Cosette, selecting the most unfrequented side alleys of the boulevards and going into the churches at nightfall. They lived frugally, always with a little fire in the stove, but like people in embarrassed circumstances.

He still wore his yellow coat, his black pantaloons, and his old hat. On the street he was taken for a beggar. It sometimes happened that kindhearted dames, in pas sing, would

cudgel : a short, thick stick used as a weapon

cabriolet : a light two-wheeled carriage with a hood, drawn by one horse

*

turn and hand him a penny. Jean Valjean accepted the penny and bowed humbly. It chanced sometimes also that he would meet some wretched creature begging alms, and then, glancing about him to be sure that no one was looking, he would stealthily approach the beggar, slip a piece of money, often silver, into his hand, and walk rapidly away. He began to be known in the quarter as the beggar who gives alms.

The old landlady, a crabbed creature, fully possessed with that keen observation as to all that concerned her neighbors, watched Jean Valjean closely without exciting his suspicion. One morning she saw Jean Valjean go, with an appearance which seemed peculiar to the old busybody, into one of the uninhabited apartments of the building. She followed him with the steps of an old cat, and could see him without herself being seen, through the chink of the door directly opposite. Jean Valjean had, doubtless for greater caution, turned his back toward the door in question. The old woman saw him fumble in his pocket and take from it a needle case, scissors, and thread, and then proceed to rip open the lining of one lapel of his coat and take from under it a piece of yellowish paper, which he unfolded. The beldame* remarked with surprise that it was a bank bill for a thousand francs.

A moment afterward, Jean Valjean accosted her and asked her to get this thousand-franc bill changed for him, adding that it was the half-yearly interest on his property which he had received on the previous day. The old woman got the note changed, all the while forming her conjectures.

There was, in the neighborhood, a mendicant* who sat crouching over the edge of a condemned public well nearby, and whom Jean Valjean never passed without giving him a few pennies. Sometimes he spoke to him. Some said this poor creature was in the pay of the police. He was an old man of seventy-five who was always mumbling prayers.

One evening, as Jean Valjean was passing that way, unaccompanied by Cosette, he noticed the beggar sitting in his usual place, under the streetlamp which had just been lighted. The man, according to custom, seemed to be praying and was bent over. Jean Valjean walked up to him and put a piece of money in his hand, as usual. The beggar suddenly raised his eyes, gazed intently at Jean Valjean, and then quickly dropped his head. This movement was like a flash; Jean Valjean shuddered; it seemed to him that he had just seen, by the light of the streetlamp, not the calm, sanctimonious face of the aged beggar, but a terrible and well-known countenance. He experienced the sensation one would feel on finding himself suddenly face-to-face, in the gloom, with a tiger.

Some days after, he was in his room, giving Cosette her spelling lesson, which the child was repeating in a loud voice, when he heard the door of the building open and close again. He sent Cosette to bed, telling her in a suppressed voice to lie down very quietly. As he kissed her forehead, the footsteps stopped. Jean Valjean remained silent and motionless, his back turned toward the door, still seated on his chair, from which he had not moved, and holding his breath in the darkness. After a considerable interval, not hearing anything more, he threw himself on his bed without undressing but could not shut his eyes that night.

At daybreak, as he was sinking into slumber from fatigue, he was aroused again by the same footstep which had ascended the stairs on the preceding night. He started from his bed and placed his eye to the keyhole, hoping to get a glimpse of the person, whoever it might be, who had made his way into the building in the nighttime. A man passed by Jean Valjean's room without stopping. He was tall, wore a long frock coat, and had a cudgel under his arm. It was the redoubtable form of Javert.

All that day Jean Valjean remained in the house. When evening came, he made a roll of a hundred francs he had in a drawer and put it into his pocket. At dusk, he went to the street door and looked carefully up and down. The boulevard seemed to be utterly deserted.

He went upstairs again. "Come," said he to Cosette. He took her by the hand, and they both went out.

Chapter 25

Jean Valjean had begun to thread the streets, making as many turns as he could, returning sometimes upon his track to make sure that he was not followed. The moon was full. Jean Valjean was not sorry for that, for he could glide along the houses and the walls on the dark side and observe the light side.

Cosette walked without asking any questions. The sufferings of the last six years of her life had introduced something of the passive into her nature. She felt safe, being with him.

Jean Valjean knew no more than Cosette where he was going, but he was determined not to enter the Gorbeau house again. Like the animal hunted from his den, he was looking for a hole to hide in until he could find one to remain in.

As eleven o'clock struck, he crossed the RUE DE PONTOISE in front of the bureau of police. Some moments afterward, the instinct of which we have already spoken made him turn his head. At this moment he saw distinctly, thanks to a lamp which revealed them, three men following him quite near, passing one after another under this lamp on the dark side of the street. They stopped in the center of the square and formed a group like people consulting. The man who seemed to be the leader turned and energetically pointed in the direction of Jean Valjean. At the instant when the leader turned, the moon shone full in his face. Jean Valjean recognized Javert perfectly.

Uncertainty was at an end; he took Cosette in his arms and ran. The three men were at his heels in a moment, and for about a quarter of an hour the pursued and the pursuers tore through the deserted streets. But the strength of Jean Valjean, burdened though he was with Cosette, began to tell; he gained on Javert and his assistants, and at a dark corner, he ran up a narrow alley unobserved. For a moment he thought he was safe, but quickly he discovered that there was no opening at the other end, and he turned back.

Javert, meanwhile, having lost the scent, stationed one of his men at the entrance of the alley. Javert knew that the alley was closed at the other end and hoped Jean Valjean had run in there, but he was too old a hand to take chances and did not want to run the risk of losing his prey by stopping to make a search.

Jean Valjean became desperate. He tried the doors along the alley, but found them locked and barred; he looked up at the walls, but they were too high to be scaled. At the further end, however, he came to a sharp corner above which he saw a lime tree.

Among other resources, thanks to his numerous escapes from the galleys at Toulon, he had, it will be remembered, become master of that incredible art of raising himself in the right angle of a wall—if need be to the height of a sixth story—without ladders or props, by mere muscular strength, supporting himself by the back of his neck, his shoulders, his hips, and his knees, hardly making use of the few projections of the stone.

Jean Valjean measured with his eyes the wall above which he saw the lime tree. It was about eighteen feet high. The wall was capped by a flat stone without any projection.

The difficulty was Cosette. Cosette did not know how to scale a wall. Abandon her? Jean Valjean did not think of it. To carry her was impossible. The whole strength of a man is necessary to accomplish these strange ascents. He needed a cord. Jean Valjean had none. Truly, at that instant, if Jean Valjean had had a kingdom, he would have given it for a rope.

beldame : a malicious and ugly woman, especially an old one; a witch

mendicant : a beggar

All extreme situations have their flashes which sometimes make us blind, sometimes illuminate us. The despairing gaze of Jean Valjean encountered the lamppost in the cul-de-sac. At nightfall they lighted the streetlamps, which were placed at intervals and were raised and lowered by means of a rope traversing the street from end to end, running through the grooves of posts. The reel on which this rope was wound was enclosed below the lantern in a little iron box, the key of which was kept by the lamplighter, and the rope itself was protected by a casing of metal.

There was such a post in the alley, put there for the convenience of the people who lived along it. But this night, thanks to the ample light afforded by the moon, it was not lit. Jean Valjean crossed at a bound, sprang the bolt of the little box with the point of his knife, and an instant after was back at the side of Cosette. He had a rope!

Meanwhile the hour, the place, the darkness, the preoccupation of Jean Valjean, his actions, his going to and fro, all this began to disturb Cosette. Any other child would have uttered loud cries long before. She contented herself with pulling Jean Valjean by the skirt of his coat. The sound of an approaching patrol was constantly becoming more and more distinct.

"Father," said she, in a whisper, "I am afraid. Who is it that is coming?"

"Hush!" answered the unhappy man. "It is the Thénardiess."

Cosette shuddered. He added, "Don't say a word; I'll take care of her. If you cry, if you make any noise, the Thénardiess will hear you. She is coming to catch you."

Then, without any haste, with a firm and rapid decision, so much the more remarkable at such a moment when the patrol and Javert might come upon him at any instant, he took off his cravat, passed it around Cosette's body under the arms, taking care that it should not hurt the child, attached this cravat to an end of the rope, took the other end of the rope in his teeth, took off his shoes and stockings and threw them over the wall, climbed upon a pile of masonry, and began to raise himself in the angle of the wall and the gable with as much solidity and certainty as if he had the rungs of a ladder under his heels and his elbows. Half a minute had not passed before he was on his knees on the top of the wall.

Cosette watched him, stupefied, without saying a word. Jean Valjean's charge and the name of Thénardiess had made her dumb. All at once, she heard Jean Valjean's voice calling to her in a low whisper, "Put your back against the wall."

She obeyed.

"Don't speak, and don't be afraid," added Jean Valjean. And she felt herself lifted from the ground.

Before she had time to think where she was, she was at the top of the wall. Jean Valjean seized her, put her on his back, took her two little hands in his left hand, lay down flat and crawled along the top of the wall until he reached the lime tree, and made his way to the ground. Whether from terror or from courage, Cosette had not uttered a whisper.

Jean Valjean found himself in a sort of garden, very large, oblong, with a row of large poplars at the further end, some tall forest trees in the corners, and a clear space in the center. There were here and there stone benches which seemed black with moss. The walks were bordered with sorry little shrubs perfectly straight.

On one side there was a small building in ruins, but with some dismantled rooms, one of which was well filled and appeared to serve as a shed. A larger building ran back on the alley and presented upon this garden two square facades.

No other house could be seen. The further end of the garden was lost in mist and in darkness. Still, he could make out walls intersecting it, as if there were other cultivated grounds beyond. Nothing can be imagined more wild and more solitary than this garden. There was no one there, which was very natural on account of the hour, but it did not seem as if the place were made for anybody to walk in, even in broad noon.

Jean Valjean put on his shoes; then he entered the shed with Cosette. Cosette trembled and pressed close to his side. They heard the tumultuous clamor of the patrol ransacking the cul-de-sac and the street, the clatter of their muskets against the stones, the calls and imprecations of Javert to the watchmen he had stationed, some indistinguishable. At the end of a quarter of an hour it seemed as though this stormy rumbling began to recede. Suddenly, in the midst of this deep calm, a new sound arose; a celestial, divine, ineffable sound, as ravishing as the other was horrible. It was a hymn which came forth from the darkness, a bewildering mingling of prayer and harmony in the obscure and fearful silence of the night; voices of women, but voices with the pure accents of virgins and the artless accents of children; those voices which are not of earth, and which resemble those that the newborn still hear and the dying hear already. This song came from the gloomy building which overlooked the garden. At the moment when the uproar of the demons receded, one would have said, it was a choir of angels approaching in the darkness.

Cosette and Jean Valjean fell on their knees.

They knew not what it was; they knew not where they were; but they both felt, the man and the child, the penitent and the innocent, that they ought to be on their knees.

The chant ceased. Perhaps it had lasted a long time. Jean Valjean could not have told. Hours of ecstasy are never more than a moment. All had again relapsed into silence. There was nothing more in the street, nothing more in the garden. That which threatened, that which reassured, all had vanished. The wind rattled the dry grass on the top of the wall, which made a low, soft, and mournful noise.

The night wind indicated that it must be between one and two o'clock in the morning. Poor Cosette did not speak. She was still trembling.

"Are you sleepy?" said Jean Valjean.

"I am very cold," she answered.

A moment after she added, "Is she there yet?"

"Who?" said Jean Valjean.

"Madame Thénardier."

"Oh!" said he. "She has gone." The child sighed as if a weight were lifted from her breast.

The ground was damp, the shed open on all sides; the wind freshened every moment. The goodman took off his coat and wrapped Cosette in it.

"Are you warmer, so?"

"Oh yes, Father!"

The child had laid her head upon a stone and went to sleep.

He sat down near her and looked at her. Little by little, as he beheld her, he grew calm and regained possession of his clearness of mind. He plainly perceived this truth, the basis of his life henceforth, that so long as she should be alive, so long as he should have her with him, he should need nothing except for her, and fear nothing save on her account. He did not even realize that he was very cold.

Meanwhile, through the reverie into which he had fallen, he had heard for some time a singular noise. It sounded like a little bell that someone was shaking in the garden. It resembled the dimly heard tinkling of cowbells in the pastures at night.

He turned and looked and saw that there was someone in the garden. This being appeared to limp.

Jean Valjean shuddered with the continual tremor of the outcast. To them everything is hostile and suspicious. He took the sleeping Cosette gently in his arms and carried her into the furthest corner of the shed behind a heap of old furniture that was out of use. Cosette did not stir. From there he watched the strange motions of the man. The sound of the bell followed every movement of the man. It seemed evident that the bell was fastened to this man; but then what could that mean? What was this man?

While he was revolving these questions, he touched Cosette's hands. They were icy. He called to her in a low voice, "Cosette."

She did not open her eyes.

"Could she be dead?" said he, and he sprang up, shuddering from head to foot. He listened for her breathing; she was breathing, but with a respiration that appeared feeble and about to stop. How should he get her warm again? How rouse her? All else was banished from his thoughts. He rushed desperately out of the ruin. It was absolutely necessary that in less than a quarter of an hour Cosette should be in bed and before a fire.

He walked straight to the man whom he saw in the garden.

He had taken in his hand the roll of money which was in his vest pocket. This man had his head down and did not see him coming. With a few strides, Jean Valjean was at his side, exclaiming, "A hundred francs!"

The man started and raised his eyes.

"A hundred francs for you," continued Jean Valjean, "if you will give me refuge tonight."

The moon shone full in Jean Valjean's bewildered face.

"Father Madeleine!" said the man. "How did you come here? How did you get in? And what has happened to you? You have no cravat, you have no hat, you have no coat? But how did you get in?"

"Who are you? And what is this house?" asked Jean Valjean.

"What!" exclaimed the old man. "You don't remember me?"

"No," said Jean Valjean. "And how does it happen that you know me?"

"You saved my life," said the man. He turned, a ray of the moon lighted up his face, and Jean Valjean recognized old Fauchelevent.

"What is this house?"

"Why, you know very well; you got me this place here as a gardener. It is the convent of the Petit Picpus."

Jean Valjean remembered. Chance—that is to say, Providence—had thrown him precisely into this convent, to which old Fauchelevent, crippled by his fall from his cart, had been admitted, upon Jean Valjean's recommendation, two years before.

"But now," resumed Fauchelevent, "how did you manage to get in, Father Madeleine? You are a man, and no men come in here."

"But you are here."

"There is none but me."

He approached the old man and said to him in a grave voice, "Father Fauchelevent, I saved your life, and now you can do for me what I once did for you."

Fauchelevent grasped in his old wrinkled and trembling hands the robust hands of Jean Valjean, and it was some seconds before he could speak. At last he exclaimed, "Oh! That would be a blessing of God if I could do something for you, in return for that! I save your life!"

A wonderful joy had, as it were, transfigured the old gardener. A radiance seemed to shine forth from his face. "What do you want me to do?" he added.

"I will explain. You have a room?"

"I have a solitary shanty, over there, behind the ruins of the old convent, in a corner that nobody ever sees. There are three rooms."

"Good," said Jean Valjean. "Now I ask of you two things. First, that you will not tell anybody what you know about me. Second, that you will not attempt to learn anything more."

"As you please. I know that you can do nothing dishonorable, and that you have always been a man of God."

"Very well. But now come with me. We will go for the child."

"Ah!" said Fauchelevent. "There is a child!"

He said not a word more but followed Jean Valjean as a dog follows his master. In half an hour Cosette, again become rosy before a good fire, was asleep in the old gardener's bed.

Chapter 27

It was through the supplications and testimony of Fauchelevent to the mother prioress of the convent that Jean Valjean was accorded employment as a gardener. Fauchelevent introduced him as his brother, and Valjean was allowed to stay in a small two-room shed on the property, far removed from the sight of the convent. The prioress immediately took Cosette and gave her a place in the school as a charity pupil.

Father Fauchelevent was recompensed for his good deed; in the first place it made him happy, and then he had less work to do, as it was divided. Finally, as he was very fond of tobacco, he found the presence of M. Madeleine advantageous from another point of view. He took three times as much tobacco as before, since M. Madeleine paid for it.

The convent was to Jean Valjean like an island surrounded by wide waters. These four walls were, henceforth, the world to him. Within them he could see enough of the sky to be calm and enough of Cosette to be happy. A very pleasant life began again for him.

Jean Valjean worked every day in the garden and was very useful there. He had formerly been a pruner and now found it quite in his way to be a gardener. Nearly all the orchard trees were wild stock; he grafted them and made them bear excellent fruit.

Cosette was allowed to come every day and pass an hour with him. As the sisters were melancholy, and he was kind, the child compared him with them and worshiped him. Every day, at the hour appointed, she would hurry to the little building. When she entered the old place, she filled it with paradise. Jean Valjean basked in her presence and felt his own happiness increase by reason of the happiness he conferred on Cosette. The delight we inspire in others has this enchanting peculiarity that, far from being diminished like every other reflection, it returns to us more radiant than ever. At the hours of recreation, Jean Valjean from a distance watched her playing and romping, and he could distinguish her laughter from the laughter of the rest. For, now, Cosette laughed.

Even Cosette's countenance had, in a measure, changed. The gloomy cast had disappeared. Laughter is sunshine; it chases winter from the human face.

When the recreation was over and Cosette went in, Jean Valjean watched the windows of her schoolroom and, at night, would rise from his bed to take a look at the windows of the room in which she slept.

God has his own ways. The convent contributed, like Cosette, to confirm and complete in Jean Valjean the work of the bishop.

Often, in the middle of the night, he would rise from his bed to listen to the grateful anthem of these innocent beings thus overwhelmed with austerities, and he felt the blood run cold in his veins as he reflected that they who were justly punished never raised their voices toward heaven except to blaspheme, and that he, wretch that he was, had uplifted his clenched fist against God.

When he thought of these things, all that was in him gave way before this mystery of sublimity. In these meditations, pride vanished. He reverted, again and again, to himself; he felt his own pitiful unworthiness and often wept. All that had occurred in his existence for the last six months led him back toward the holy injunctions of the bishop: Cosette through love, the convent through humility.

Sometimes, in the evening, about dusk, at the hour when the garden was solitary, he was seen kneeling in the middle of the walk that ran along the chapel, before the window through which he had looked on the night of his first arrival, turned toward the spot where he knew that the sister who was performing the reparation* was prostrate in prayer. Thus he prayed kneeling before this sister. It seemed as though he dared not kneel directly before God.

Everything around him—this quiet garden, these children shouting with joy, these meek and simple women, this silent cloister—gradually entered into all his being, and little by little, his soul subsided into silence like this cloister, into peace like this garden, into simplicity like these women, into joy like these children. And then he reflected that two houses of God had received him in succession at the two critical moments of his life—the first when every door was closed and human society repelled him; the second when human society again howled upon his track, and the galleys once more gaped for him—and that, had it not been for the first, he should have fallen back into crime, and had it not been for the second, into punishment. His whole heart melted in gratitude, and he loved more and more.

Several years passed thus. Cosette was growing.

Chapter 28

In the Marais, there lived some years before, in 1817, an old man named Monsieur Gillenormand. He was a peculiar old man and very truly a man of another age—the genuine bourgeois* of the eighteenth century. He had passed his eightieth year but walked erect, spoke in a loud voice, saw clearly, drank hard, ate, and slept well. He had every one of his thirty-two teeth. He wore glasses only when reading. This jovial old man was always in good health. He was hasty, easily angered. He got into a rage on all occasions. When anybody contradicted him, he raised his cane; he beat his servants as in the time of Louis XIV. He had an unmarried daughter over fifty years old whom he belabored severely when he was angry, and whom he would gladly have horsewhipped. She seemed to him about eight years old.

He lived at RUE DES FILLES DU CALVAIRE, number six. The house was his own. He occupied an ancient and ample apartment on the first story, between the street and the gardens, covered to the ceiling with fine tapestry. Long, full curtains hung at the windows and made great, magnificent broken folds. In addition to a library adjoining his room, he had a boudoir hung with magnificent straw-colored tapestry, covered with

reparation : the making of amends for a wrong one has done
bourgeois : middle class

fleurs-de-lis and with figures from the galleries of Louis XIV. He was kind when he wished to be. In his youth, he had been the most disagreeable husband and the most charming lover in the world. This old man had had two wives. The first had presented him with a daughter, who had remained unmarried, and the second, another daughter, who died when about thirty years old and who had married—for love, or luck, or otherwise—a soldier of fortune, who had served in the armies of the republic and the empire, had won the cross at Austerlitz*, and had been made colonel at Waterloo. "This is the disgrace of my family," said the old bourgeois.

There was besides in the house, between this old maid and this old man, a child, a little boy, always trembling and mute before M. Gillenormand. M. Gillenormand never spoke to this child but with stern voice, and sometimes with uplifted cane. But he idolized him. It was his grandson.

Chapter 29

Whoever had read the military memoirs, the biographies, the *Moniteur**, and the bulletins of the Grand Army* would have been struck by a name which appears rather often: the name of Georges Pontmercy. When quite young, this Georges Pontmercy was a soldier, and when the revolution broke out, he fought many battles, and at the battle of Mont Palissel, he had his arm broken by a musket ball. He distinguished himself at Austerlitz in that wonderful march in echelon* under the enemy's fire. When the cavalry of the Russian Imperial Guard crushed a battalion of the Fourth of the Line, Pontmercy was one of those who overthrew the guard.

The emperor, well pleased, cried to him, "You are a colonel, you are a baron, you are an officer of the Legion of Honor*!"

Pontmercy answered, "Sire, I thank you for my widow." An hour afterward, he fell wounded again.

After Waterloo, Pontmercy succeeded in regaining the army and was passed along from ambulance to ambulance to the cantonments* of the Loire.

The Restoration* put him on half pay, then sent him to a residence under surveillance at Vernon. The king, Louis XVIII, ignoring all that had been done in the Hundred Days*, recognized neither his position of officer of the Legion of Honor nor his rank of colonel nor his title of baron.

Under the empire, between two wars, he had found time to marry Mademoiselle Gillenormand. The girl's father, who really felt outraged, consented with a sigh, saying, "The greatest families are forced to it." In 1815, Madame Pontmercy, an admirable woman in every respect, noble and rare, and worthy of her husband, died, leaving a child. This child would have been the colonel's joy in his solitude, but the grandfather had imperiously demanded his grandson, declaring that unless he were given up to him, he would disinherit the boy. The father yielded for the sake of the little boy, and not being able to have his child, he set about tending to his own garden.

M. Gillenormand had no dealings with his son-in-law. The colonel was to him "a bandit." M. Gillenormand never spoke of his son-in-law unless to make mocking allusions to "his barony." It was expressly understood that Pontmercy should never endeavor to see his son or speak to him, under pain of the boy being turned away and disinherited. To the Gillenormands, Pontmercy was pestiferous. They intended to bring up the child to their liking. The colonel did wrong perhaps to accept these conditions, but he submitted to them, thinking that he was doing right and sacrificing himself alone.

While the boy was thus growing up, every two or three months the colonel would escape, come furtively to Paris like a fugitive, and go to Saint-Sulpice* at the hour when Aunt Gillenormand took Marius to Mass. There, trembling lest the aunt should turn round, concealed behind a pillar, motionless, not daring to breathe, he saw his child.

Twice a year Marius wrote filial letters to his father, which his aunt dictated. This was all that M. Gillenormand allowed, and the father answered with very tender letters, which the grandfather thrust into his pocket without reading.

Marius had his years at college; then he entered the law school. He was a royalist*, fanatical, and austere. He had little love for his grandfather, whose cynicism wounded him, and the place of his father was a dark void. For the rest, he was an ardent but cool lad, noble, generous, proud, religious, lofty; honorable even to harshness, pure even to unsociableness.

Chapter 30

In 1827, Marius was eighteen. One evening, he saw his grandfather with a letter in his hand.

"Marius," said M. Gillenormand, "you will set out tomorrow for Vernon."

"What for?" said Marius.

"To see your father."

Marius shuddered. He had thought of everything but this, that a day might come when he would have to see his father. Marius, besides his feelings of political antipathy, was convinced that his father did not love him. That was clear, since he had abandoned him. Feeling that he was not loved at all, Marius had no love.

He was so astounded that he did not question M. Gillenormand. The grandfather continued, "It appears that he is sick. He asks for you. Start tomorrow morning. I think there is a conveyance which starts at six o'clock and arrives at night. Take it. He says the case is urgent."

The next day at dusk, Marius arrived at Vernon. Candles were just beginning to be lighted. He asked the first person he met for the house of Monsieur Pontmercy. He agreed with the Restoration, and he, too, recognized his father neither as baron nor as colonel. At the house, a woman opened the door with a small lamp in her hand.

"Is this the home of Monsieur Pontmercy?" asked Marius.

The woman gave an affirmative nod of the head.

"Can I speak with him?"

The woman gave a negative sign.

"But I am his son!" resumed Marius. "He expects me."

"He expects you no longer," said the woman. Then he perceived that she was in tears.

Austerlitz : a battle that occurred in 1805 near the town of Austerlitz in the Austrian Empire, also known as the Battle of the Three Emperors; one of the most significant battles of the Napoleonic Wars; viewed by many as the greatest victory of Napoleon's army, who defeated the larger Russian and Austrian army

Moniteur (*Le Moniteur universel*) : a French newspaper in print between 1789 and 1901, at times the official journal of the French government

bulletins of the Grand Army : Napoleon's war bulletins; accounts of his battles sent to his home government

echelon : a formation of troops in parallel rows with the end of each row projecting farther than the one in front

Legion of Honor : the highest French order of merit for military and civil merits, established in 1802 by Napoleon Bonaparte

cantonment : military garrison or camp

The Restoration : the period following the first fall of Napoleon in 1814, when the brother of Louis XVI came to power and reigned in a highly conservative fashion

Hundred Days : the period between Napoleon's return from exile on the island of Elba to Paris on 20 March 1815 and the second restoration of King Louis XVIII on 8 July 1815

Saint-Sulpice : a Roman Catholic church in Paris; the second-largest church in the city, only slightly smaller than Notre-Dame

royalist : one who supports a monarchy *

She pointed to the door of a low room; he entered. In this room, which was lighted by a tallow candle on the mantel, there were three men: a physician, standing; a priest, praying on his knees; and one stripped to his shirt and lying at full length upon the floor, who was the colonel.

The colonel had been three days before attacked with a fever. At the beginning of the sickness, he had written to Monsieur Gillenormand to ask for his son. His illness had grown worse. On the very evening of Marius's arrival at Vernon, the colonel had had a fit of delirium; he sprang out of his bed crying, "My son has not come! I am going to meet him!" Then he had fallen upon the floor, and had but just died. The doctor had come too late; the curé had come too late. The son also had come too late.

By the dim light of the candle, they could distinguish upon the cheek of the pale and prostrate colonel a big tear which had fallen from his death-stricken eye. The eye was glazed, but the tear was not dry. This tear was for his son's delay.

Marius looked upon this man, whom he saw for the first time and for the last—this venerable and manly face, these open eyes which saw not, this white hair, these robust limbs upon which he distinguished here and there brown lines which were saber cuts and red stars which were bullet holes. He looked upon that gigantic scar which imprinted heroism upon this face on which God had impressed goodness. He thought that this man was his father and that this man was dead, and he remained unmoved. The sorrow which he experienced was the sorrow which he would have felt before any other man whom he might have seen stretched out in death.

Mourning, bitter mourning was in that room. The servant was lamenting by herself in a corner; the curé was praying, and his sobs were heard; the doctor was wiping his eyes; the corpse itself wept. This doctor, this priest, and this woman looked at Marius through their affliction without saying a word; it was he who was the stranger. Marius, too little moved, felt ashamed and embarrassed at his attitude. At the same time he felt something like remorse, and he despised himself for acting thus. But was it his fault? He did not love his father, indeed!

The colonel left nothing. The sale of his furniture hardly paid for his burial. The servant found a scrap of paper which she handed to Marius. It contained this, in the handwriting of the colonel:

For my son—
The emperor made me a baron upon the battlefield of Waterloo. Since the Restoration contests this title which I have bought with my blood, my son will take it and bear it. I need not say that he will be worthy of it.

On the back, the colonel had added,

At this same battle of Waterloo, a sergeant saved my life. This man's name is Thénardier. Not long ago, I believe he was keeping a little tavern in a village in the suburbs of Paris, at Chelles or at Montfermeil. If my son meets him, he will do Thénardier all the service he can.

Not from duty toward his father, but on account of that vague respect for death which is always so imperious in the heart of man, Marius took this paper.

No trace remained of the colonel. Monsieur Gillenormand

had his sword and uniform sold to a secondhand dealer. Marius remained only forty-eight hours at Vernon. After the burial, he returned to Paris and went back to his law studies, thinking no more of his father than if he had never lived. In two days the colonel had been buried, and in three days forgotten. Marius wore crepe on his hat. That was all.

Chapter 31

Marius had preserved the religious habits of his childhood. One Sunday he went to hear Mass at Saint-Sulpice. He took his place behind a pillar and knelt down before a chair without noticing that on the back was written this name: *Monsieur Mabeuf, churchwarden*. The Mass had hardly commenced when an old man presented himself and said to Marius, "Monsieur, this is my place."

Marius moved away readily, and the old man took his chair. After Mass, Marius remained absorbed in thought a few steps distant. The old man approached him again and said, "I beg your pardon, monsieur, for having disturbed you a little while ago, and for disturbing you again now, but you must have thought me impertinent, and I must explain myself."

"Monsieur," said Marius, "it is unnecessary."

"Yes!" resumed the old man. "I do not wish you to have a bad opinion of me. For ten years I have seen, regularly, every two or three months, a poor, brave father come to that place, a man who had no other opportunity and no other way of seeing his child, being prevented through some family arrangements. He came at the hour when he knew his son was brought to Mass. The little one never suspected that his father was here. He did not even know, perhaps, that he had a father, the innocent boy! The father, for his part, kept behind a pillar so that nobody should see him. He looked at his child and wept. This poor man worshiped this little boy. He had a father-in-law, rich relatives—I do not remember exactly—who threatened to disinherit the child if he, the father, should see him. He had sacrificed himself that his son might someday be rich and happy. They were separated by political opinions. Having been at Waterloo does not make a man a monster; a father should not be separated from his child for that. He was one of Bonaparte's colonels. He is dead, I believe. He lived at Vernon, where my brother is curé, and his name is something like Pontmarie, or Montpercy. He had a scar from the blade of a saber."

"Pontmercy," said Marius, turning pale.

"Exactly. Pontmercy. Did you know him?"

"Monsieur," said Marius, "he was my father."

The old churchwarden clasped his hands and exclaimed, "Ah! You are the child! Yes, that is it; he ought to be a man now. Well! Poor child, you can say that you had a father who loved you well."

When Marius left Saint-Sulpice, he went straight to the library of the law school and asked for the file of the *Moniteur*.

He read the *Moniteur*; he read all the histories of the republic and the empire; all the memoirs, journals, bulletins, proclamations; he devoured everything. The first time he met his father's name in the bulletins of the Grand Army, he had a fever for a whole week. He went to see the generals under whom Georges Pontmercy had served. The churchwarden, Mabeuf, whom he had gone to see again, gave him an account of the colonel's life at Vernon, his retreat, his garden, and his solitude. Marius came to understand fully this rare, sublime, and gentle man, this sort of lion-lamb who was his father.

In the meantime, engrossed in this study, which took up all his time as well as all his thoughts, he hardly saw the Gillenormands. At the hours of meals he appeared; then when they looked for him, he was gone. The aunt grumbled. The grandfather smiled. Sometimes the old man added, "The devil! I thought that it was some gallantry. It seems to be a passion." It was a passion, indeed. Marius was on the way to adoration for his father.

At the same time an extraordinary change took place in his ideas. This history on which he had now cast his eyes startled him. The republic, the empire, had been to him till then nothing but monstrous words. The republic, a guillotine at twilight; the empire, a saber in the night. He had looked into them, and there, where he expected to find only a chaos of darkness, he had seen, with a sort of astounded surprise mingled with fear and joy, stars shining. The revolution and the empire set themselves in luminous perspective before his straining eyes. He saw each of these two groups of events and men arrange themselves into two enormous facts: the republic into the sovereignty of the civic right restored to the masses; the empire into the sovereignty of the French idea imposed upon Europe. He saw spring out of the revolution the grand figure of the people, and out of the empire the grand figure of France. He declared to himself that all of this had been good.

Marius perceived then that up to that time he had comprehended his country no more than he had his father. He now saw. And on the one hand he admired; on the other he worshiped.

He was full of regret and remorse. Oh, if his father were living, if he had him still, if God in his mercy and in his goodness had permitted that his father might still be alive, how he would have run, how he would have plunged headlong, how he would have cried, "Father! I am here! It is I! My heart is the same as yours! I am your son!"

On reading his history, the veil which covered Napoleon from Marius's eyes gradually fell away. He perceived something immense and suspected that he had been deceiving himself up to that moment about Bonaparte as well as about everything else; each day he saw more clearly.

One night he was alone in his little room next to the roof. His candle was lighted; he was reading, leaning on his table by the open window. All manner of reveries came over him from the expanse of space and mingled with his thought. He was reading the bulletins of the Grand Army, those heroic lines written on the battlefield; he saw there at intervals his father's name, the emperor's name everywhere; the whole of the grand empire appeared before him; he felt as if a tide were swelling and rising within him; it seemed to him at moments that his father was passing by him like a breath and whispering in his ear; he thought he heard the drums, the cannon, the trumpets, the measured tread of the battalions, the dull and distant gallop of the cavalry; from time to time he lifted his eyes to the sky and saw the colossal constellations shining in the limitless abysses; then they fell back upon the book, and he saw there other colossal things moving about confusedly. His heart was full. He was transported, trembling, breathless—suddenly, without himself knowing what moved him or what he was obeying. He arose, stretched his arms out of the window, gazed fixedly into the gloom, the silence, the darkling infinite, the eternal immensity, and cried, *"Vive l'empereur!"*

All these revolutions were accomplished in him without a suspicion of it in his family. When he had entirely cast off his old Bourbon* skin, when he had shed the aristocrat and the royalist, when he was fully revolutionary, thoroughly democratic, and almost republican, he went to an engraver and ordered a hundred cards bearing this name: *Baron Marius Pontmercy*. However, as he knew nobody and could not leave his cards at anybody's door, he put them in his pocket.

By another natural consequence, in proportion as he drew nearer to his father's memory and the things for which the colonel had fought for twenty-five years, he drew away from his grandfather. For a long time M. Gillenormand's capriciousness had been disagreeable to him. Above all, Marius felt inexpressibly revolted when he thought that M. Gillenormand had pitilessly torn him from the colonel, thus depriving the father of the child and the child of the father. Through affection and veneration for his father, Marius had almost reached aversion for his grandfather.

Marius often took short journeys to Montfermeil in obedience to the injunction which his father had left him, and sought for the former sergeant of Waterloo, the innkeeper Thénardier. Thénardier had failed, the inn was closed, and nobody knew what had become of him.

Chapter 32

When Marius finally summoned the courage to confront his grandfather about the truth that he had learned of his own recently beloved father, his grandfather became apoplectic. He banished his only grandson from his house and demanded that he never darken the doors again.

At that period, apparently indifferent, something of a revolutionary thrill was vaguely felt. Each one took the step forward which was before him. Royalists became liberals; liberals became democrats. Other groups of minds were more serious. They fathomed principle; they attached themselves to right. They longed for the absolute.

There was in Paris, among other affiliations of this kind, a society having as its aim the elevation of men. They declared themselves the Friends of the A B C—the *abaissé* (the abased)—who were the people. They met in Paris at two places: in a wineshop called Corinth, and near the Panthéon in a little coffeehouse on the Place Saint Michel called the Café Musain. The first of these two places of rendezvous was near the workingmen, the second near the students.

The ordinary conventicles* of the Friends of the A B C were held in a back room of the Café Musain. They smoked, drank, played, and laughed there. They talked very loudly about everything, and in whispers about something else. On the wall was nailed an old map of France under the republic, an indication sufficient to awaken the suspicion of a police officer.

Most of the Friends of the A B C were students, in thorough understanding with a few workingmen. The names of the principal ones are as follows; they belong to a certain extent to history: Enjolras, Combeferre, Courfeyrac, and Laigle, also known as Bossuet. These young men constituted a sort of family among themselves, by force of friendship.

Bourbon : The House of Bourbon was a European royal line that ruled for a time in France, as well as in Spain, Naples, and Sicily.

conventicle : a secret or unlawful religious meeting, typically of people with nonconformist views

*

Enjolras was an only son and was rich. He was a charming young man who was capable of being terrible. He was angelically beautiful, officiating and militant; from the immediate point of view, a soldier of democracy; above the movement of the time, a priest of the ideal. He had deep-set eyes, lids a little red, thick lower lip, easily becoming disdainful, and a high forehead. He was severe in his pleasures. Before everything but the republic, he chastely dropped his eyes. He was the marble lover of liberty.

Beside Enjolras, who represented the logic of the revolution, Combeferre represented its philosophy. Combeferre completed and corrected Enjolras. He said, "Revolution, but civilization." Hence, in all Combeferre's views, there was something attainable and practicable. Enjolras was a chief; Combeferre was a guide. You would have preferred to fight with the one and march with the other.

Courfeyrac was a brave fellow, the center.

In this conclave of young heads there was one bald member, Laigle, a cheery fellow who was unlucky. His specialty was to succeed in nothing. On the other hand, he laughed at everything. At twenty-five he was bald. His father had died owning a house and some land, but he, the son, had found nothing more urgent than to lose this house and land in a bad speculation. He had nothing left. He had considerable knowledge and wit, but everything failed him, everything deceived him; whatever he built up fell upon him. Laigle was slowly making his way toward the legal profession.

All these young men, diverse as they were, and of whom, as a whole, we ought only to speak seriously, had the same religion: Progress.

One afternoon, Laigle was thinking, without melancholy, of a little mishap which had befallen him the day before at the law school, and which modified his personal plans for the future—plans which were, moreover, rather indefinite.

Reverie does not hinder a cabriolet from going by, nor the dreamer from noticing the cabriolet. Laigle, whose eyes were wandering in a sort of general stroll, perceived a vehicle turning into the square, moving at a walk, as if undecided. Why was it moving at a walk? Laigle looked at it. There was inside, beside the driver, a young man, and before the young man, a large carpetbag. The bag exhibited to the passers this name, written in big black letters upon a card sewed to the cloth: *MARIUS PONTMERCY*.

This name changed Laigle's attitude. He straightened up and addressed the young man in the cabriolet. "Monsieur Marius Pontmercy?"

The cabriolet, thus called upon, stopped. The young man, who also seemed to be profoundly musing, raised his eyes. "Well?" said he.

"You are Monsieur Marius Pontmercy?"

"Certainly."

"I was looking for you," said Laigle. "I heard your name called by the professor—and in your absence, I answered, 'Present.' By doing so, I saved you from being erased from the class."

"Then I must offer you my thanks."

"That is unnecessary." Laigle thought for a moment. "And do you live near this place?" Laigle asked of Marius.

"Alas, I have no home address at the moment," Marius answered.

Courfeyrac exited the café and also stepped into the cabriolet. "Driver," said he, "Hôtel de la Porte Saint Jacques." And that same evening, Marius was installed in a room at the Hôtel de la Porte Saint Jacques, side by side with Courfeyrac.

Chapter 33

In a few days, Marius was the friend of Courfeyrac. Youth is the season of prompt weldings and rapid cicatrizations*. Marius, in Courfeyrac's presence, breathed freely, a new thing for him. Courfeyrac asked him no questions. One morning, however, Courfeyrac abruptly put this question to him.

"By the way, have you any political opinions?"

"What do you mean?" said Marius, almost offended at the question.

"What are you?"

"Bonapartist democrat."

"Gray shade of quiet mouse color," said Courfeyrac.

The next day, Courfeyrac introduced Marius to the Café Musain. Then he whispered in his ear with a smile, "I must give you your admission into the revolution." And he took him into the room of the Friends of the A B C. He presented him to the other members, saying in an undertone this simple word, which Marius did not understand: "A pupil."

Marius had fallen into a mental wasps' nest. Up to this time solitary and inclined to soliloquy and privacy by habit and by taste, he was a little bewildered at this flock of young men about him. All these different progressives attacked him at once and perplexed him. The tumultuous sweep and sway of all these minds at liberty and at work set his ideas in a whirl. On abandoning his grandfather's opinions for his father's, he had thought himself settled; he now suspected, with anxiety and without daring to confess it to himself, that he was not. The angle from which he saw all things was beginning to change anew.

These new friends of Marius offered much debate over the state—and future—of France. The talk was inflamed with their newly ignited passion for freedom. This freedom could only come, they declared, through the shedding of old skins and the abandoning of old beliefs.

"Citizens," said Enjolras, "our new mother is the Republic. That is our only path to the freedom of the common man."

Chapter 34

That evening left Marius in a profound agitation, with a sorrowful darkness in his soul. He had but just attained a faith; could he so soon reject it? He decided within himself that he could not. He declared to himself that he would not doubt, and he began to doubt in spite of himself. To be between two religions—one which you have not yet abandoned, and another which you have not yet adopted—is insupportable. Whatever might be his desire to stop where he was and to hold fast there, he was irresistibly compelled to continue, to advance, to examine, to think, to go forward. He was on good terms neither with his grandfather nor with his friends; rash toward the former, backward toward the others; he felt doubly isolated, from old age and also from youth.

In this trouble in which his mind was plunged, he scarcely gave a thought to certain serious phases of existence. The realities of life do not allow themselves to be forgotten. They came and jogged his memory sharply.

One morning, the keeper of the house entered Marius's room and said to him, "Monsieur Courfeyrac is responsible for you?"

"Yes."

cicatrization : scar formation at the site of a healing wound *

"But I am in need of money."

"Ask Courfeyrac to come and speak with me," said Marius.

Courfeyrac came; the host left them. Marius related to him what he had not thought of telling him before, that he was, so to speak, alone in the world, without any relatives.

"Have you any money?"

"Fifteen francs."

"Do you wish me to lend you some?"

"Never."

"Have you any clothes? Have you any jewelry?"

"What clothes you see, and a watch, gold; here it is."

"I know a dealer in clothing and a watchmaker who will buy your watch."

The clothes dealer was sent for. He gave twenty francs for the clothes. They went to the watchmaker. He gave forty-five francs for the watch.

"That is not bad," said Marius to Courfeyrac, on returning to the house. "With my fifteen francs, this makes eighty francs."

"The hotel bill?" observed Courfeyrac.

"Ah! I forgot," said Marius.

The host presented his bill. It amounted to seventy francs.

"I have ten francs left," said Marius.

Meanwhile, Aunt Gillenormand, who was really a kind person, had finally unearthed Marius's lodgings. One morning when Marius came home from the school, he found a letter from his aunt and six hundred francs in gold, in a sealed box.

Marius sent the thirty louis back to his aunt with a respectful letter, in which he told her that he had the means of living and that he could provide henceforth for all his necessities. At that time he had three francs left.

The aunt did not inform the grandfather of this refusal, lest she should exasperate him. Marius left the Hôtel de la Porte Saint Jacques, unwilling to contract debt.

When Marius became a lawyer, he informed his grandfather of it in a letter which was frigid but full of submission and respect. M. Gillenormand took the letter with trembling hands, read it, and tore it in pieces.

Misery, as with everything else, gradually becomes endurable. By dint of hard work, courage, perseverance, and will, Marius had succeeded in earning by his labor about seven hundred francs a year. He had learned German and English. He made out prospectuses, translated from the journals, compiled biographies; net result, year in and year out, seven hundred francs. He lived on this.

In Paris, of course, there were areas that only the poor and wretched lived. Among those who lived in the Gorbeau building were the most wretched of all: a family of four persons, father, mother, and two daughters nearly grown, all four lodging in the garret room. This family at first sight presented nothing very peculiar but its extreme destitution; the father, in renting the room, had given his name as Jondrette.

Now, this family was the family of a sprightly little barefoot urchin. When he came there, he found distress and what is sadder still, no smile; a cold hearthstone and cold hearts.

When he came in, they would ask, "Where have you come from?"

He would answer, "From the street."

When he was going away, they would ask him, "Where are you going to?"

He would answer, "Into the street."

The child felt no suffering from this mode of existence and bore no ill will toward anybody. He did not know how a father and mother ought to be. But yet his mother loved his sisters.

On the BOULEVARD DU TEMPLE this boy went by the name of little Gavroche.

The room occupied by the Jondrettes in the Gorbeau tenement was the last at the end of the hall. Marius occupied, at an annual rent of thirty francs, the adjacent cell in the tenement, with no fireplace, in which there was no more furniture than was indispensable. He ate frugally and spent nothing for pleasures and luxuries, and so succeeded even in saving a little each year.

For Marius to arrive at this flourishing condition had required years, hard and difficult. Marius had never given up for a single day. He had undergone everything; he had done everything except get into debt. He gave himself this credit, that he had never owed a sou to anybody. Rather than borrow, he did not eat. He had many days of fasting. Feeling that all extremes meet, and that if we do not take care, abasement of fortune may lead to baseness of soul, he watched jealously over his pride. In all his trials he felt encouraged and sometimes even borne up by a secret force within. The soul helps the body, and at certain moments uplifts it.

By the side of his father's name, another name was engraved upon Marius's heart: the name of Thénardier. Marius, in his enthusiastic yet serious nature, surrounded with a sort of halo the man to whom, as he thought, he owed his father's life, that brave sergeant who had saved the colonel in the midst of the balls and bullets of Waterloo. He never separated the memory of this man from the memory of his father, and he associated them in his veneration. The idea of the misfortune into which he knew that Thénardier had fallen intensified his feeling of gratitude. Marius had learned at Montfermeil of the ruin and bankruptcy of the unlucky innkeeper. Since then, he had made untold effort to find him in that dark abyss of misery into which Thénardier had disappeared. For three years he had been devoted to spending in these explorations what little money he could spare. Thénardier's creditors had sought for him also, with less love than Marius, but with as much zeal, and had not been able to put their hands on him. This was the only debt which the colonel had left him, and Marius made it a point of honor to pay it. Indeed, to find Thénardier, Marius would have given one of his arms, and to save him from his wretchedness, all his blood. To see Thénardier, to render some service to Thénardier—this was the sweetest and most magnificent dream of Marius.

Marius was now twenty years old. It was three years since he had left his grandfather. They remained on the same terms on both sides, without attempting a reconciliation and without seeking to meet.

To tell the truth, Marius was mistaken as to his grandfather's heart. He imagined that M. Gillenormand had never loved him, and that this crusty and harsh old man, who swore, screamed, stormed, and lifted his cane, felt for him at most only the affection of an old man. Marius was deceived. There are fathers who do not love their children; rarely does a grandfather not adore his grandson. In reality, as we have said, M. Gillenormand worshiped Marius in his own way, with an accompaniment of cuffs and even of blows, but when the child was gone, he felt a dark void in his heart.

While the old man was regretting, Marius was rejoicing. As with all good hearts, suffering had taken away his bitterness. He thought of M. Gillenormand only with kindness, but he had determined to receive nothing more from the man who had been cruel to his father. Marius had two friends: one young, Courfeyrac; and one old, M. Mabeuf. He inclined toward the old one. First he was indebted to him for the revolution through which he had gone; he was also indebted to him for having known and loved his father.

It was Marius's delight to take long walks alone in the less-frequented paths of the Luxembourg Gardens. It was in one of these walks that he had discovered the Gorbeau tenement, and its isolation and cheapness being an attraction to him, he had taken a room in it. He was only known in it by the name of Monsieur Marius.

Toward the middle of the year 1831, the old woman who waited upon Marius told him that his neighbors, the wretched Jondrette family, were to be turned into the street. Marius, who passed almost all his days out of doors, hardly knew that he had any neighbors.

"Why are they turned out?" said he.

"Because they do not pay their rent; they owe for two terms."

"How much is that?"

"Twenty francs," said the old woman.

Marius had thirty francs in reserve in a drawer.

"Here," said he, to the old woman, "there are twenty-five francs. Pay for these poor people, give them five francs, and do not tell them that it is from me."

Chapter 35

Marius was now a fine-looking young man, of medium height, with heavy jet-black hair, a high intelligent brow, a frank and calm expression, the reddest lips, and the whitest teeth. At the time of his most wretched poverty, he noticed that girls turned when he passed, and with a deathly feeling in his heart he fled or hid himself. He thought they looked at him on account of his old clothes and that they were laughing at him; the truth is, they looked at him because of his graceful appearance. This wordless misunderstanding between him and the pretty girls he met had rendered him hostile to society. He attached himself to none; he fled before all.

There were, however, in all the immensity of creation, two women whom Marius never fled from nor avoided. One was the old woman with the beard who swept his room; the other was a little girl whom he saw very often and whom he never looked at.

For more than a year Marius had noticed in a retired walk of the Luxembourg Gardens a man and a girl quite young, nearly always sitting side by side on the same seat, near the RUE DE L'OUEST. Whenever chance led Marius to this walk, and it was almost every day, he found this couple there. The man might be sixty years old; he seemed sad and serious; his whole person presented the robust but wearied appearance of a soldier retired from active service. Had he worn a decoration, Marius would have said he was an old officer. His expression was kind, but it did not invite approach, and he never returned a look. He wore a blue coat and a broad-brimmed hat, a black cravat, and Quaker linen. His hair was perfectly white.

The young girl who accompanied him looked about thirteen or fourteen. She wore the dress peculiar to the convent schoolgirl, an ill-fitting garment of coarse black. They appeared to be father and daughter. For two or three days Marius scrutinized this old man, who was not yet an aged man, and this little girl, not yet a woman; then he paid no more attention to them. For their part they did not even seem to see him.

Marius had acquired a sort of mechanical habit of promenading on this walk. He would generally reach the walk at the end opposite their seat, promenade the whole length of it, passing before them, then return to the end by which he entered, and so on. He performed this turn five or six times in his promenade, and this promenade five or six times a week, but they and he had never come to exchange bows. Courfeyrac had noticed them at some time or other and had named the daughter Mademoiselle Lanoire (Black) and the father Monsieur Leblanc (White). Marius, too, found it convenient to call this unknown gentleman M. Leblanc.

The second year it so happened that Marius broke off this habit of going to the Luxembourg, without really knowing why, for nearly six months. At last he went back there again one day; it was a serene summer morning, and Marius was as happy as one always is when the weather is fine.

He went straight to his walk, and as soon as he reached it, he saw, still on the same seat, this pair. When he came near them, however, he saw that it was indeed the same man, but it seemed to him that it was no longer the same girl. The woman whom he now saw was a noble, beautiful creature, with all the most bewitching outlines of woman, at the precise moment

LUXEMBOURG GARDENS AT TWILIGHT • JOHN SINGER SARGENT • 1879

at which they are yet combined with all the most charming graces of childhood.

When Marius passed near her, he could not see her eyes, which were always cast down. He saw only her long chestnut lashes, eloquent of mystery and modesty. But that did not prevent the beautiful girl from smiling as she listened to the white-haired man, who was speaking to her, and nothing was so transporting as this maidenly smile with these downcast eyes.

At the first instant Marius thought it was another daughter of the same man, a sister doubtless of her whom he had seen before. But when the invariable habit of his promenade led him for the second time near the seat, and he had looked at her attentively, he recognized that she was the same. In six months the little girl had become a young woman.

One day the air was mild, the Luxembourg was flooded with sunshine and shadow, the sky was as clear as if the angels had washed it in the morning, and Marius had opened his whole soul to nature. He passed near this seat, the young girl raised her eyes, their glances met, but what was there now in the glance of the young girl? Marius could not have told. It was a strange flash.

She cast down her eyes, and he continued on his way. What he had seen was not the simple, artless eye of a child; it was a mysterious abyss, half-opened, then suddenly closed.

Chapter 36

The next day, at the usual hour, Marius took from his closet his new coat, his new pantaloons, his new hat, and his new boots; he put on his gloves and went to the Luxembourg. When he entered the walk, he saw M. Leblanc and the young girl at the other end on their seat.

He approached them, but then he stood silent and motionless. For the first time in fifteen months, he said to himself that this gentleman, who sat there every day with his daughter, had undoubtedly noticed him and probably thought his assiduity* very strange. He remained thus for some minutes with his head down; then he turned abruptly away from the seat, away from Monsieur Leblanc and his daughter, and went home.

The next day Marius was there again. He approached as near as he could, seeming to be reading a book.

Thus a fortnight* rolled away. Marius went to the Luxembourg, no longer to promenade but to sit down, always in the same place, near the Gladiator*. Once there he did not stir.

Marius's love grew for this young woman, whom he had never once even spoken to. He dreamed of her every night. And then there came to him a good fortune for which he had not even hoped. One night, at dusk, he found on the seat which M. Leblanc and his daughter had just left, a handkerchief marked with the letters *U. F.* Marius knew nothing of this beautiful girl, neither her family, nor her name, nor her dwelling; these two letters were the first thing he had caught of her. The *U* was evidently her first name. Ursula, thought he. He kissed the handkerchief, put it over his heart in the daytime, and at night went to sleep with it on his lips.

This handkerchief belonged to the old gentleman, who had simply let it fall from his pocket.

Marius had committed one blunder in falling into the snare of the seat by the Gladiator. He had committed a second by not remaining at the Luxembourg when Monsieur Leblanc came there alone. He committed a third, a monstrous one. He followed "Ursula." She lived in the RUE DE L'OUEST, in the least frequented part of it, in a new three-story house of modest appearance. From that moment Marius added to his happiness in seeing her at the Luxembourg the happiness of following her home.

His hunger increased. He knew her name—her first name, at least, the charming name, the real name of a woman; he knew where she lived. He desired to know who she was. One night after he had followed them home and seen them disappear, he entered after them and said boldly to the porter, "Is it the gentleman on the first floor who has just come in?"

"No," answered the porter. "It is the gentleman on the third."

Another fact. This success made Marius still bolder.

"And what is this gentleman?"

"He lives on his income, monsieur. A very kind man, who does a great deal of good among the poor, though not rich."

"What is his name?" continued Marius.

The porter raised his head and said, "Is monsieur a detective?"

Marius retired, much abashed.

Next day Monsieur Leblanc and his daughter made but a short visit to the Luxembourg; they went away while it was yet broad daylight. Marius followed them into the RUE DE L'OUEST, as was his custom. On reaching the door, Monsieur Leblanc let his daughter in and then stopped, and before entering himself, turned and looked steadily at Marius. The day after that they did not come to the Luxembourg.

At nightfall Marius went to the RUE DE L'OUEST and saw a light in the windows of the third story. He walked beneath these windows until the light was put out. He passed a week in this way. Monsieur Leblanc and his daughter appeared at the Luxembourg no more. Marius made melancholy conjectures; he dared not watch the house during the day. He limited himself to going at night to gaze upon the reddish light of the windows. At times he saw shadows moving, and his heart beat high.

On the eighth day, when he reached the house, there was no light in the windows. "What!" said he. "The lamp is not yet lighted. But it is dark. Or they have gone out?" He remained till one o'clock in the morning. No light appeared in the third-story windows, and nobody entered the house. He went away very gloomy.

On the morrow he found nobody at the Luxembourg, though he waited; at dusk he went to the house. No light in the windows; the blinds were closed; the third story was entirely dark. Marius knocked at the door, went in, and said to the porter, "The gentleman of the third floor?"

"Moved," answered the porter.

Marius tottered. "Where does he live now?"

"I don't know." And the porter, looking up, recognized Marius.

assiduity : constant attention to someone

fortnight : a period of two weeks

Gladiator : a copy of a life-size marble sculpture of a swordsman in the Luxembourg Gardens. The original, created in Ephesus about 100 BC, was known as the Borghese Gladiator, since the original sculpture was in the Borghese Collection in Rome.

*

Chapter 37

Marius still lived in the Gorbeau tenement. There were no occupants remaining in the house but himself and those Jondrettes; however, Marius had never spoken either to the father, or to the mother, or to the daughters. The other tenants had moved away or died, or had been turned out for not paying their rent.

One day in the course of the winter, Marius went slowly up the boulevard. He was walking thoughtfully, with his head down.

Suddenly he felt that he was elbowed in the dusk; he turned and saw two young girls in rags, one tall and slender, the other a little shorter, passing rapidly by, breathless, frightened, and apparently in flight; they had met him, had not seen him, and had jostled him in passing. Marius could see in the twilight their livid faces, their tattered skirts, and their naked feet. As they ran they were talking to each other in low slang. The girls had just escaped from the clutches of the police.

Marius stopped for a moment. He perceived a little grayish packet on the ground at his feet. It was a sort of envelope which appeared to contain papers. He retraced his steps, he called, but he did not find the girls; he concluded they were already beyond hearing, put the packet in his pocket, and went to dinner.

Later that evening, he opened the envelope. It was unsealed and contained four letters, also unsealed. All four exhaled an odor of wretched tobacco. Marius read them through; they were addressed to different individuals—one, for instance, to the beneficent gentleman of the Church Saint Jacques du Haut Pas. All begged for money; but, strangely enough, these letters were all four written in the same hand.

After reading these four letters, Marius did not find himself much wiser than before. Nothing, however, indicated that these letters belonged to the girls whom Marius had met on the boulevard. After all, they were but wastepaper evidently without value. Marius put them back into the envelope and went to bed.

The following morning, he breakfasted and was setting about his work when there was a gentle rap at his door. "Come in," said Marius.

"I beg your pardon, Monsieur—"

It was a hollow rasping voice, the voice of an old man, roughened by brandy and by liquors. Marius turned quickly and saw a girl of perhaps fifteen.

The face was not unknown to Marius. He remembered having seen it somewhere. "What do you wish, mademoiselle?" asked he.

The young girl answered, "Here is a letter for you, Monsieur Marius."

She called Marius by his name; he could not doubt that her business was with him; but what was this girl? How did she know his name? Without waiting for an invitation, she entered resolutely, looking at the whole room and the unmade bed. She was barefooted. Great holes in her skirt revealed her long limbs and her sharp knees. She was shivering. She had in her hand a letter which she presented to Marius.

Marius, in opening this letter, noticed that the enormously large wafer* was still wet. The message could not have come far. He read,

My amiable neighbor, young man!
I have learned your kindness toward me, that you paid my rent six months ago. I bless you, young man. My eldest daughter will tell you that we four have been without a morsel of bread for two days, and my spouse sick. I think I may hope that your generous heart will soften at this exposure by deigning to lavish upon me some light gift.
—JONDRETTE, PS—My daughter will await your orders, dear Monsieur Marius.

This letter, in the midst of the obscure accident which had occupied Marius's thoughts since the previous evening, was a candle in a cave. Everything was suddenly cleared up. This letter came from the same source as the other four. It was the same writing, the same paper, the same odor of tobacco.

During the time that Marius had lived in the tenement, he must have met the Jondrettes in the passage and on the stairs more than once, but to him they were only shadows. He had taken so little notice that on the previous evening he had brushed against the Jondrette girls upon the boulevard without recognizing them; and it was with great difficulty that this girl, who had just come into his room, had awakened in him a vague remembrance of having met with her elsewhere.

Now he saw everything clearly. He understood that the occupation of his neighbor Jondrette in his distress was to work upon the sympathies of benevolent persons; that he procured their addresses and that he wrote under assumed names letters to people whom he deemed rich and compassionate, which his daughters carried, at their risk and peril; for this father was one who risked his daughters.

The Jondrette girl went to the table. "Ah!" said she. "Books!" A light of happiness flashed through her glassy eye. "I can read, I can."

She hastily caught up the book which lay open on the table and read fluently, "'The general received the order to take five battalions of his brigade and carry the chateau of Hougoumont, which is in the middle of the plain of Waterloo—'"

She stopped. "Ah, Waterloo! I know that. It is a battle in old times. My father was there; my father served in the armies."

She put down the book, took up a pen, and exclaimed, "And I can write, too!"

She dipped the pen in the ink and wrote upon a sheet of blank paper which was in the middle of the table, *The cognes* are here.*

Then she looked at Marius and said to him, "Do you know, Monsieur Marius, that you are a very pretty boy?"

She went to him and laid her hand on his shoulder. "You pay no attention to me, but I know you, Monsieur Marius. I meet you here on the stairs."

Her voice tried to be very soft but succeeded only in being very low. Marius drew back quietly.

"Mademoiselle," said he with cold gravity, "I have here a packet, which is yours, I think. Permit me to return it to you." And he handed her the envelope that contained the four letters.

She clapped her hands and exclaimed, "We have looked everywhere!" Then she snatched the packet.

Meanwhile, after a thorough exploration of his pockets, Marius had at last got together five francs and sixteen sous. This was at the time all that he had in the world. *That is enough for my dinner today*, thought he. *Tomorrow we will see.* He took the sixteen sous and gave the five francs to the young girl. She took the piece eagerly.

"Good," said she, "there is some sunshine!"

She made a low bow to Marius, then a friendly wave of the hand, and moved toward the door, saying, "Good morning, monsieur. I am going to find my old man."

wafer : a small disk of dried paste used for fastening letters or holding papers together

cognes : a vernacular reference to the police *

CHAPTER 38

For five years Marius had lived in poverty, in privation, in distress even, but he perceived that he had never known real misery. Real misery he had just seen. This young girl was to Marius a sort of messenger from the night. She revealed to him an entire and hideous aspect of the darkness.

Marius almost reproached himself with the fact that he had been so absorbed in his reveries and passion that he had not, until now, cast a glance upon his neighbors. Paying their rent was a mechanical impulse—everybody would have had that impulse—but he, Marius, should have done better. What! A mere wall separated him from these abandoned beings, who lived by groping in the night without the pale of the living; he came in contact with them, he was in some way the last link of the human race which they touched, he heard them live or rather breathe beside him, and he took no notice of them! Every day at every moment, he heard them through the wall, walking, going, coming, talking, and he did not lend his ear! And in these words there were groans, and he did not even listen; his thoughts were elsewhere, upon dreams, upon impossible glimmerings, upon loves in the sky, upon infatuations; and all the while human beings, his brothers in Jesus Christ, his brothers in the people, were suffering death agonies beside him! He even caused a portion of their suffering and aggravated it. For had they had another neighbor, a more observant neighbor, an ordinary and charitable man, it was clear that their poverty would have been noticed, their signals of distress would have been seen, and long ago perhaps they would have been gathered up and saved! Undoubtedly they seemed very depraved, very corrupt, very vile, very hateful, even, but those are rare who fall without becoming degraded. There is a point, moreover, at which the unfortunate and the infamous are associated and conflated in a single word, a fatal word: *les misérables*; whose fault is it? And then, is it not when the fall is lowest that charity ought to be greatest?

While he thus preached to himself, he looked at the wall which separated him from the Jondrettes, as if he could send his pitying glance through that partition. The wall was a thin layer of plaster upheld by laths and joists, through which voices and words could be distinguished perfectly. Marius examined this partition. Suddenly he arose; he noticed toward the top, near the ceiling, a triangular hole, where three laths left a space between them. Pity has and should have its curiosity. This hole was a kind of Judas. *Let us see what these people are,* thought Marius, *and to what they are reduced.* He climbed upon the bureau, put his eye to the crevice, and looked.

Marius was poor and his room was poorly furnished, but even as his poverty was noble, his garret was clean. The den into which his eyes were at that moment directed was abject,

gloomy, filthy. All the furniture was a straw chair, a rickety table, a few old broken dishes, and in two of the corners two indescribable pallets; all the light came from a dormer window of four panes, curtained with spiders' webs. Just enough light came through that loophole to make a man's face appear like the face of a phantom.

Marius's room had a broken brick pavement; this one was neither paved nor floored; the inmates walked immediately upon the old plastering of the ruinous tenement, which had grown black under their feet. However, this room had a fireplace, so it rented for forty francs a year. In the fireplace there was a little of everything: a kettle, some broken boards, rags hanging on nails, a birdcage, some ashes, and even a little fire. Two embers were smoking sullenly.

The size of this garret added still more to its horror. It had projections, angles, black holes, recesses under the roof, bays, and promontories. Beyond, unfathomable corners, which seemed as if they must be full of spiders as big as one's fist.

One of the pallets was near the door, the other near the window. Each had one end next to the chimney, and both were opposite Marius. In a corner near the opening through which Marius was looking, hanging upon the wall in a black wooden frame, was a colored engraving at the bottom of which was written in large letters *THE DREAM*.

By the table, upon which Marius saw a pen, ink, and paper, was seated a man of about sixty, small, thin, haggard, with a keen, cruel, and restless air. He had a long gray beard. He was dressed in a woman's chemise*, which showed his shaggy breast and his naked arms bristling with gray hairs. Below this chemise were a pair of muddy pantaloons and boots from which the toes stuck out. He was smoking a pipe. There was no more bread in the den, but there was tobacco. He was writing, probably some such letter as those which Marius had read.

A big woman, who might have been forty years old or a hundred, was squatting near the fireplace upon her bare feet. She also was dressed only in a chemise and a knit skirt patched with pieces of old cloth. A coarse apron covered half the skirt. Although bent and drawn up into herself, it could be seen that she was very tall. She had light-red hair sprinkled with gray, which she pushed back from time to time with her huge shining hands.

Upon one of the pallets Marius could discern a sort of slender, wan little girl seated, with her feet hanging down, having the appearance neither of listening, nor of seeing, nor of living.

The younger sister, doubtless, of the one who had come to his room.

Nothing indicated the performance of any labor in this room; not a loom, not a wheel, not a tool. It was that gloomy idleness which follows despair, and which precedes the death agony.

Chapter 39

Marius was about to get down from the observatory when a sound attracted his attention and induced him to remain in his place. The door of the garret was hastily opened. The eldest daughter appeared upon the threshold. She came in, pushed the door shut behind her, stopped to take breath, then cried with an expression of joy and triumph, "He is coming! The philanthropist. I went into the church, he was at his usual place, I made a curtsy to him, and I gave him the letter; he read it and said to me, 'Where do you live, my child?' I said, 'Monsieur,

chemise : a garment worn by women under their dresses *

I will show you.' He said to me, 'No, give me your address. My daughter has some purchases to make; I am going to take a carriage, and I will get to your house as soon as you do.' I gave him the address. When I told him the house, he appeared surprised and hesitated an instant. Then he said, 'It is all the same; I will go.' When Mass was over, I saw him leave the church with his daughter. I saw them get into a fiacre*. And I told him plainly, the last door at the end of the hall on the right."

"And how do you know that he will come?"

"I just saw the fiacre coming. That is what made me run."

The man sprang up. There was a sort of illumination on his face. "Wife!" cried he. "Here is the philanthropist. Put out the fire."

The astounded woman did not stir. The father, with the agility of a mountebank, caught a broken pot which stood on the mantel and threw some water upon the embers. He seized the chair, and with a kick he ruined the seat. He turned toward the younger girl, who was on the pallet near the window, and cried in a thundering voice, "Quick! Off the bed! Break a pane of glass!"

The child, with a sort of terrified obedience, rose upon tiptoe and struck her fist into a pane. The glass broke and fell with a crash.

"Good," said the father.

The mother asked, "Dear, what is it you want me to do?"

"Get into bed," answered the man.

The mother obeyed and threw herself heavily upon one of the pallets.

Meanwhile a sob was heard in a corner. "What is that?" cried the father.

The younger daughter, without coming out of the darkness into which she had shrunk, showed her bleeding fist. In breaking the glass she had cut herself; she had gone to her mother's bed, and she was weeping in silence.

"So much the better!" said the man. "I knew she would."

Then, tearing the chemise which he had on, he made a bandage with which he hastily wrapped up the little girl's bleeding hand.

An icy wind whistled at the window and came into the room. The mist from without entered and spread about like a whitish wadding picked apart by invisible fingers. Through the broken pane the falling snow was seen.

The father cast a glance about him as if to assure himself that he had forgotten nothing. Then, rising and standing with his back to the chimney, "Now," said he, "we can receive the philanthropist."

Just then there was a light rap at the door. The man rushed forward and opened it, exclaiming with many low bows and smiles of adoration, "Come in, monsieur! Deign to come in, my noble benefactor, as well as your charming young lady."

A man of mature age and a young girl appeared at the door of the garret. Marius had not left his place. What he felt at that moment escapes human language. It was she.

Marius could hardly discern her through the luminous vapor which suddenly spread over his eyes. It was that sweet being, that star which had been his light for six months, it was that eye, that brow, that mouth, that beautiful vanished face which had produced night when it went away. The vision was reappearing. She stepped into the room and laid a large package on the table. It contained two coverlids and an overcoat.

For some moments, Jondrette had been looking at the philanthropist in a strange manner. Even while speaking, he seemed to scrutinize him closely as if he were trying to recall some reminiscence. Suddenly, taking advantage of a moment when the newcomers were anxiously questioning the smaller girl about her mutilated hand, he passed over to his wife and said to her quickly and in a very low tone, "Notice that man!"

Then, turning toward M. Leblanc, he said, "Tomorrow is the fourth of February, the fatal day, the last delay that my landlord will give me; if I do not pay him this evening, tomorrow my eldest daughter, myself, my spouse with her fever, my child with her wound—we shall all four be turned out of doors and driven off into the street. You see, monsieur, I owe four quarters a year! That is sixty francs."

Jondrette lied. Four quarters would have made but forty francs, and he could not have owed for four, since it was not six months since Marius had paid for two.

M. Leblanc took five francs from his pocket and threw them on the table. "Monsieur," said he, "I have only these five francs with me, but I am going to take my daughter home, and I will return this evening; is it not this evening that you have to pay?"

Jondrette's face lighted up with a strange expression. He answered quickly, "Yes, my noble monsieur. At eight o'clock I must be at my landlord's."

"I will be here at six o'clock, and I will bring you the sixty francs."

"My benefactor!" cried Jondrette distractedly. And he added in an undertone, "Take a good look at him, Wife!"

M. Leblanc took the arm of the beautiful young girl and turned toward the door. "Till this evening, my friends," said he.

And they went out all three, Jondrette preceding the two strangers.

Marius had lost nothing of all this scene, and yet in reality he had seen nothing of it. His eyes had remained fixed upon the young girl; his heart had, so to speak, seized upon her and enveloped her entirely, from her first step into the garret.

When they went out, he had but one thought: to follow her, not to give up her track, not to leave her without knowing where she lived, not to lose her again, at least, after having so miraculously found her! He leaped down from the bureau and took his hat. As he was putting his hand on the bolt and was just going out, he reflected and stopped. The hall was long, the stairs steep, Jondrette a great talker. M. Leblanc doubtless had not yet got into his carriage; if he should turn round in the passage, or on the stairs, or on the doorstep, and perceive him, Marius, in that house, he would certainly be alarmed and would find means to escape him anew, and it would be all over at once. Marius was perplexed. At last he took the risk and went out of his room.

Marius would have offered chase in a public cab, but alas, he only had sixteen sous in his pocket. That was not enough to travel a single block.

As Marius returned to his room, he noticed Jondrette on the other side of the boulevard, talking to a man of dangerous appearance. These two men quietly talked while the snow whirled about them.

Chapter 40

Marius mounted the stairs of the old tenement with slow steps. Just as he was going into his cell, he perceived in the hall behind him the elder Jondrette girl, who was following him. It was she who had his five francs, but it was too late to ask her for them. The cab was there no longer, and the fiacre was far away. Moreover, she would not give them back to him. As to questioning her about the address of the people who had just come, that was useless; it was plain that she did not know, since the letter had been addressed to the beneficent gentleman of the Church Saint Jacques du Haut Pas. Marius went into his room and shut his door behind him.

It did not close; he turned and saw a hand holding the door partly open. "What is it?" he asked. "Who is there?"

It was the Jondrette girl.

fiacre : a small four-wheeled carriage for public fare *

"Is it you again?" said Marius almost harshly. "What do you want of me?"

She raised her mournful eyes, in which a sort of confused light seemed to shine dimly, and said to him, "Monsieur Marius, you look sad. Can I serve you in anything? I do not ask your secrets—you need not tell them to me—but yet I may be useful. When it is necessary to carry letters, go into houses, inquire from door to door, find out an address, follow somebody, I do it. Make use of me."

An idea came into Marius's mind. He approached the girl.

"You brought this old gentleman here with his daughter. Do you know their address?"

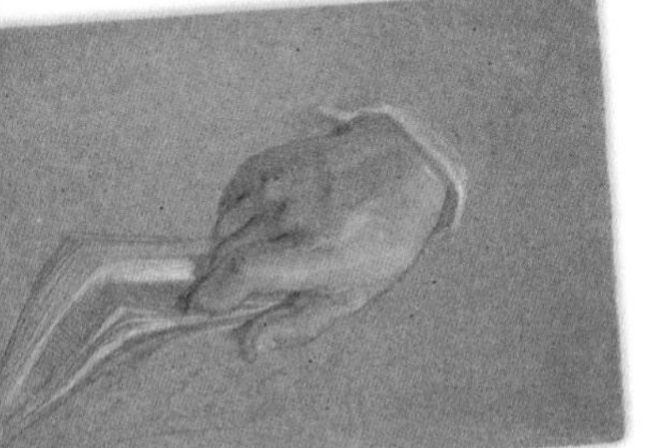

"No."

"Find it for me."

The girl's eyes, which had been gloomy, had become joyful; they now became dark.

"Do you know them?"

"No."

"That is to say," said she hastily, "you do not know her, but you want to know her."

"Can you do it?" said Marius.

"You shall have the beautiful young lady's address."

There was again, in these words *the beautiful young lady*, an expression which made Marius uneasy.

She looked steadily at him. "What will you give me?"

"Anything you wish!"

"You shall have the address."

She looked down and then closed the door.

Marius was alone. Suddenly he was violently awakened from his reverie. He heard the loud, harsh voice of Jondrette pronounce these words for him, full of the strangest interest: "I tell you that I am sure of it, and I recognized him!"

Of whom was Jondrette talking? He had recognized whom? M. Leblanc? The father of his Ursula? Was Marius just about to get in this sudden and unexpected way all the information the lack of which made his life obscure to himself?

He sprang upon the bureau and resumed his place near the little aperture in the partition. He again saw the interior of the Jondrette den.

Nothing had changed in the appearance of the room except that the two new coverlids were thrown over the two beds. Jondrette had evidently just come in. He had not yet recovered his regular breathing. His eyes had an extraordinary look.

"It was eight years ago! But I recognize him! I recognize him! Immediately. It is the same height, the same face, hardly any older; there are some men who do not grow old; it is the same tone of voice. He is better dressed; that is all!"

Just as his daughters approached the door to the hall, the father caught the elder daughter by the arm and said with a peculiar tone, "You will be here at five o'clock precisely. Both of you. I shall need you."

Marius redoubled his attention.

Alone with his wife, Jondrette began to walk the room again and took two or three turns in silence. Suddenly he turned toward the woman, folded his arms, and exclaimed, "And the young lady . . . !"

"Well, what?" said the woman. "The young lady?"

Marius could doubt no longer—it was indeed of her that they were talking. He listened with an intense anxiety. His whole life was concentrated in his ears. Jondrette stooped down and whispered to his wife. Then he straightened up and finished aloud, "It is she!"

"That girl?" said the wife.

"That girl!" said the husband.

She sprang up and remained a moment standing, her hair flying, her nostrils distended, her mouth half-open, her fists clenched and drawn back. Then she fell back upon the pallet. The man still walked back and forth, paying no attention to his wife.

"My fortune is made."

"What do you mean?" asked the woman.

"Listen attentively. He is caught; it is all right. It is already done. Everything is arranged. I have seen the men. He will come this evening at six o'clock to bring his sixty francs, the rascal! He will come at six o'clock; our neighbor is gone to dinner then. There is nobody in the house. Our neighbor never comes back before eleven o'clock. The girls will stand watch. He will be his own executor."

"And if he should not be his own executor?" asked the wife.

"We will execute him."

Just then the clock of Saint Médard struck one.

Chapter 41

Marius now was into a viper's hole, a nest of monsters. Across the dark words which had been uttered, he saw a few things distinctly: that an ambuscade* was preparing, obscure but terrible; that they were both running a great risk, she probably, her father certainly; that Marius must foil the hideous machinations of the Jondrettes and break the web of these spiders.

But what was he to do? Warn the persons threatened? Where should he find them? He did not know their address. They had reappeared to his eyes for an instant; then they had again plunged into the boundless depths of Paris. Wait at the door for M. Leblanc at six o'clock in the evening, and warn him of the plot? But Jondrette and his men would see him watching, the place was solitary, they would be stronger than he, they would find means to seize him, and he whom Marius wished to save would be lost. The clock of Saint Médard had just struck one, and the ambuscade was to be carried out at six. Marius had five hours before him. There was but one thing to be done.

He put on his presentable coat, tied a cravat about his neck, took his hat, and went out without making any noise.

On reaching number fourteen RUE DE PONTOISE, he asked for the commissary of police.

"He is not in," said one of the office boys. "But there is an inspector who answers for him."

The office boy introduced him into the commissary's private room. A man of tall stature was standing there behind a railing, in front of a stove, and holding up with both hands the flaps of a huge overcoat. He had a square face, a thin and firm mouth, very fierce, bushy, grayish whiskers, and an eye that would turn your pockets inside out.

"What do you wish?" said he to Marius.

Marius related his adventure: that a person whom he only knew by sight was to be drawn into an ambuscade that very evening; that occupying the room next to the place, he, Marius Pontmercy, attorney, had heard the whole plot through the partition; that the scoundrel who had contrived the plot was named Jondrette; that he had accomplices; that Jondrette's daughters would stand watch; that there was no means of warning the threatened man, as not even his name was known; and finally, that all this was to be done at six o'clock that evening, at the most desolate spot on the BOULEVARD DE L'HÔPITAL, in the house numbered 50-52.

At that number the inspector raised his head and said coolly, "It is then in the room at the end of the hall?"

"Exactly," said Marius.

The inspector remained silent a moment, then resumed, "Number 50-52. I know the shanty. Impossible to hide ourselves in the interior without the actors perceiving us; then they would leave and break up the play."

The inspector looked at Marius still more steadily and continued with a sententious solemnity, "Give me your latchkey."

ambuscade : an ambush *

RUE DE ROUEN • SANTIAGO RUSIÑOL • 1861–1931

Marius took his key from his waistcoat, handed it to the inspector, and added, "If you trust me, you will come in force."

The inspector, with a single movement, plunged both his enormous hands into the immense pockets of his overcoat and took out two small steel pistols. He presented them to Marius, saying, "Take these. Go back home. Hide yourself in your room; let them think you have gone out. They are loaded. Each with two balls. You will watch at the hole in the wall. The men will come. Let them go on a little. When you deem the affair at a point to stop it, you will fire off a pistol. Not too soon. The rest is my affair. Above all, not too soon."

Marius took the pistols and put them in the side pocket of his coat.

"Now," pursued the inspector, "there is not a minute to be lost. Forget nothing of what I have told you."

And as Marius placed his hand on the latch of the door to go out, the inspector called to him, "By the way, if you need me, ask for Inspector Javert."

Chapter 42

That afternoon, Marius saw Jondrette passing along and watched him. Jondrette went straight on without suspecting that there was now an eye fixed upon him. He stopped at a hardware store, and, a few minutes afterward, Marius saw him come out of the shop holding in his hand a large chisel with a white wooden handle which he concealed under his coat. The light was waning; it was snowing.

Marius thought it best to take advantage of Jondrette's absence to get home. He succeeded in getting into his room without being perceived and without any noise.

Marius took his boots off softly and pushed them under his bed. Many minutes passed. Marius heard the lower door turn on its hinges; a heavy and rapid step ascended the stairs and passed along the corridor; the latch of the garret was noisily lifted; Jondrette came in. Several voices were heard immediately. The whole family was in the garret.

Jondrette said, "All goes to a charm. You will forget nothing of what I told you! You will do the whole of it."

Marius heard him put something heavy on the table, probably the chisel which he had bought. Then he added, lowering his voice, "Put that into the fire. Have you greased the hinges of the door, so that they shall not make any noise?"

"Yes," answered the mother.

"What time is it?"

"Six o'clock, almost. The girls must go and stand watch."

Jondrette's voice rose. "Are you sure there is nobody at home in our neighbor's room?"

"He has not been back today, and you know that it is his dinnertime."

"Pay attention, now!" said Jondrette. "One toward the barrière*, the other at the corner. Don't lose sight of the house door a minute."

They went down the stairs and out. There were now in the house only Marius, Jondrette, and his wife.

Marius judged that the time had come to resume his place at his observatory. In a twinkling, and with the agility of his age, he was at the hole in the partition.

The entire den was illuminated by lighted charcoal; a blue flame danced, showing the form of the chisel bought by Jondrette, which was growing ruddy* among the coals. The Jondrette lair was admirably chosen for the theatre of a deed of darkness and violence and for the concealment of a crime.

barrière : fence; barrier; gate
ruddy : having a reddish color

It was the most retired room of the most isolated house of the most solitary boulevard in Paris.

Jondrette had sat down on the dismantled chair and was smoking. Suddenly he raised his voice. "We must have two chairs here."

Marius felt a shiver run down his back on hearing the woman make this quiet reply: "I will get our neighbor's."

With rapid movements she opened the door of the den and went out into the hall. Marius physically had not the time to get down from the bureau and hide himself under the bed.

"Take the candle," cried Jondrette.

"No," said she, "that would bother me; I have two chairs to bring. There is moonlight."

Marius heard the heavy hand of the mother Jondrette groping after his key in the dark. The door opened. The mother Jondrette raised her eyes, did not see Marius, took the two chairs—the only chairs which Marius had—and went back into the den. Then she went downstairs to await the coming of the benefactor.

Jondrette arranged the two chairs on two sides of the table. Marius then perceived that what he had taken for a shapeless heap was a rope ladder, very well made, with wooden rounds and two large hooks to hang it by. This ladder had evidently been brought there in the afternoon during Marius's absence.

There was in the room a calm which was inexpressibly threatening. The approach of some appalling thing could be felt. Marius grasped the pistol which was in his right pocket, took it out, and cocked it.

CHAPTER 43

Just then the distant and melancholy vibration of a bell shook the windows. Six o'clock struck on Saint Médard. Jondrette marked each stroke with a nod of his head. At the sixth stroke, he snuffed the candle with his fingers. Then he began to walk about the room, listened in the hall; then he returned to his chair. He had hardly sat down when the mother Jondrette opened the door and stood in the hall making a horrible grimace. "Walk in," said she.

"Walk in, my benefactor," repeated Jondrette, rising precipitously.

Monsieur Leblanc appeared. He had an air of serenity which made him singularly venerable. He laid four louis upon the table.

"Monsieur," said he, "that is for your rent and your pressing wants. We will see about the rest."

"God reward you, my generous benefactor!" said Jondrette, and rapidly approaching his wife, he said, "Send away the fiacre."

She slipped away, while her husband was lavishing bows and offering a chair to Monsieur Leblanc. A moment afterward she came back. The snow, which had been falling ever since morning, was so deep that they had not heard the fiacre arrive, and did not hear it go away. Meanwhile Monsieur Leblanc had taken a seat. Jondrette sat opposite Monsieur Leblanc.

The night was chilly, the solitudes of La Salpêtrière* covered with snow and white in the moonlight like immense shrouds, the flickering light of the streetlamps here and there, not a passer perhaps within a mile around, the Gorbeau tenement at its deepest degree of silence in the midst of these solitudes, this darkness. The vast Jondrette garret was lighted by a single candle, and in this den were two men seated at a table, Monsieur Leblanc tranquil, Jondrette smiling and terrible, his wife, in a corner; and, behind the partition, Marius, invisible, alert, losing no word, losing no movement, his eye on them, waiting next door, the pistol in his grasp.

Marius, moreover, was experiencing nothing but an emotion of horror. He clasped the butt of the pistol and felt reassured. "I shall stop this wretch when I please," thought he.

He felt that the police were somewhere near, awaiting the signal agreed upon. He hoped, moreover, that from this terrible meeting between Jondrette and Monsieur Leblanc, some light would be thrown upon all that he was interested to know.

No sooner was Monsieur Leblanc seated than he turned his eyes toward the empty pallets. "How does the poor little injured girl do?" he inquired.

"Badly," answered Jondrette with a doleful yet grateful smile. "Very badly, my worthy monsieur. Her elder sister has taken her to have her arm dressed."

While Jondrette was talking, Marius raised his eyes and perceived at the back of the room somebody whom he had not before seen. A man had come in so noiselessly that nobody had heard the door turn on its hinges. He sat down in silence and with folded arms.

"Who is that man?" said M. Leblanc.

"That man?" said Jondrette. "That is a neighbor. Pay no attention to him."

M. Leblanc breathed with confidence. He resumed, "Pardon me; what were you saying to me, monsieur?"

"I was telling you, monsieur and dear patron," replied Jondrette, leaning his elbows on the table and gazing at M. Leblanc with fixed and tender eyes, "that I had a picture to sell."

A slight noise was made at the door. A second man entered, and although this man had literally slipped into the room, he could not prevent M. Leblanc from perceiving him.

"Do not mind them," said Jondrette. "They are people of the house. I was telling you, then, that I have a valuable painting left. Here, monsieur, look."

He got up, went to the wall, and turned the thing round, still leaving it resting against the wall. It was something that resembled a picture, and which the candle scarcely revealed. Marius could make nothing out of it, Jondrette being between him and the picture.

"What is that?" asked M. Leblanc.

Jondrette exclaimed, "A painting by a master; a picture of great price, my benefactor! I cling to it as to my two daughters; it calls up memories to me! I am so unfortunate that I would part with it."

Whether by chance or whether there was some beginning of distrust, while examining the picture, M. Leblanc glanced toward the back of the room. There were now four men there, three seated on the bed, one standing near the door casing; all four bare-armed, motionless, and with blackened faces. None of them had shoes on. Jondrette noticed that M. Leblanc's eye was fixed upon these men.

"They are friends. They live nearby," said he. "They are dark because they work in charcoal. Do not occupy your mind with them, my benefactor, but buy my picture. Take pity on my misery. I shall not sell it to you at a high price. How much do you estimate it worth?"

"But," said M. Leblanc, looking Jondrette full in the face and like a man who puts himself on his guard, "this is some tavern sign. It is worth about three francs."

Jondrette answered calmly, "Have you your pocketbook here? I will be satisfied with a thousand crowns."

La Salpêtrière : a mental hospital in Paris that was known for its abhorrent conditions *

M. Leblanc rose to his feet, placed his back to the wall, and ran his eyes over the room. Jondrette kept his eyes on the door.

Jondrette took a step toward M. Leblanc and cried in a voice of thunder, "Do you know me?"

The door of the garret had been suddenly flung open, disclosing three men in blue blouses with black paper masks. The first was spare and had a long iron-bound cudgel; the second, who was a sort of colossus, held by the middle of the handle a butcher's ax. The third, a broad-shouldered man, held in his clenched fist an enormous key stolen from some prison door. It appeared that it was the arrival of these men for which Jondrette was waiting. A rapid dialogue commenced between him and the man with the cudgel.

"Is everything ready?" said Jondrette.

"Yes," answered the spare man.

"Is there a fiacre below?"

"Yes."

"With two good horses?"

"It is waiting where I said it should wait."

"Good," said Jondrette.

M. Leblanc was very pale. He looked over everything in the room like a man who understands into what he has fallen, and his head, directed in turn toward all the heads which surrounded him, moved on his neck with an attentive and astonished slowness, but there was nothing in his manner which resembled fear; he, who the moment before had the appearance only of an old man, had suddenly become a sort of athlete, and placed his powerful fist upon the back of his chair with a surprising and formidable gesture.

Three of the men had between them a large pair of shears, a steel bar, and a hammer. Marius thought that in a few seconds more the time would come to interfere, and he raised his right hand toward the ceiling, in the direction of the hall, ready to let off his pistol shot.

Jondrette turned again toward M. Leblanc and repeated his question, accompanying it with that low, smothered, and terrible laugh of his: "You do not recognize me, then?"

M. Leblanc looked him in the face and answered, "No."

Then Jondrette came up to the table. He leaned forward over the candle, folding his arms and pushing his angular and ferocious jaws up toward the calm face of M. Leblanc, and in that posture, like a wild beast just about to bite, he cried, "My name is not Jondrette; my name is Thénardier! I am the innkeeper of Montfermeil! Do you understand me? Thénardier! Now do you know me?"

A slight flush passed over M. Leblanc's forehead, and he answered without tremor or elevation of voice, and with his usual placidness, "No more than before."

Marius did not hear this answer: he was thunderstruck. Upon hearing Jondrette's words, Marius trembled in every limb and supported himself against the wall as if he had felt the chill of a sword blade through his heart. Then his right arm, which was just ready to fire the signal shot, dropped slowly down, and at the moment that Jondrette had repeated, "Do you understand me? Thénardier!" Marius's nerveless fingers had almost dropped the pistol. Jondrette, in unveiling who he was, had not moved M. Leblanc, but he had completely unnerved Marius. That name of Thénardier, which M. Leblanc did not seem to know, Marius knew. That name he had worn on his heart, written in his father's will! He carried it in the innermost place of his thoughts, in the holiest spot of his memory, in that sacred command: "A sergeant saved my life. This man's name is Thénardier. . . . If my son meets him, he will do Thénardier all the service he can." Here was Thénardier! He had found him at last, and how? This savior of his father was a bandit! A monster! This deliverer of Colonel Pontmercy was in the actual commission of a crime, which looked like a murder! And upon whom? What a fatality! What a bitter mockery of fate!

If he fired the pistol, M. Leblanc was saved and Thénardier was lost; if he did not, M. Leblanc was sacrificed. He seemed on the one hand to hear Ursula entreating him for her father, and on the other the colonel commending Thénardier to him. His knees gave way beneath him; he was on the point of fainting.

Chapter 44

Meanwhile Thénardier was walking to and fro before the table in a sort of bewilderment and frenzied triumph. He turned toward M. Leblanc with a frightful look.

"You do not know me? Well, I know you! I knew you immediately as soon as you stuck your nose in here. Ah! You are going to find out at last that it is not all roses to go into people's houses like that, under pretext of their being inns, with worn-out clothes, with the appearance of a pauper, to deceive persons, take their help away, and threaten them in the woods, and that you do not get quit of it by bringing back afterward, when people are ruined, an overcoat that is too large and two paltry hospital coverlids, old beggar, child-stealer. I will gnaw your heart tonight!"

For some moments, Monsieur Leblanc had seemed to follow and to watch all the movements of Thénardier, who, blinded and bewildered by his own rage, turned his back to Monsieur Leblanc.

Monsieur Leblanc seized this opportunity, pushed the chair away with his foot, the table with his hand, and at one bound, with a marvelous agility, before Thénardier had had time to turn around, he was at the window. To open it, get up, and step through it was the work of a second. He was half outside when six strong hands seized him and drew him forcibly back into the room. At the same time the Thénardiess had clutched him by the hair.

At the disturbance which this made, the other bandits ran in from the hall. One of them raised a club over Monsieur Leblanc's head. Marius could not endure this sight. *Father,* thought he, *pardon me!* And his finger sought the trigger of the pistol.

The shot was just about to be fired when Thénardier's voice cried, "Do him no harm!"

The first result of this was to stop the pistol which was just ready to go off and to paralyze Marius, to whom the urgency seemed to disappear, and who now saw no impropriety in waiting longer. He thought some chance might arise which would save him from the fearful alternative of letting the father of Ursula perish, or destroying the savior of the colonel.

A Herculean struggle had commenced. With one blow full in the chest M. Leblanc had sent one man sprawling into the middle of the room, then with two back strokes had knocked down two other assailants, whom he held one under each knee. The wretches screamed under the pressure as if they were under a granite millstone, but the four others had seized the formidable old man by the arms and the back and held him down. They succeeded in throwing him over upon the bed nearest to the window and held him there.

M. Leblanc seemed to have given up all resistance. They searched him. There was nothing upon him but a leather purse which contained six francs and his handkerchief. Thénardier went to the corner by the door and took a bundle of ropes, which he threw to them.

"Tie him to the foot of the bed," said he.

The pallet upon which M. Leblanc had been thrown was a sort of hospital bed supported by four big roughly squared wooden posts. M. Leblanc made no resistance. The brigands bound him firmly. Thénardier took a chair and came and sat down nearly in front of M. Leblanc. Thénardier looked no longer like himself; in a few seconds the expression of his face had passed from unbridled violence to tranquil and crafty mildness.

"Monsieur, you were wrong in trying to jump out of the window. You might have broken your leg. Now, if you please, we will talk quietly. In the first place I must inform you of a circumstance I have noticed, which is that you have not yet made the least outcry."

Thénardier was right, although it had escaped Marius in his anxiety. M. Leblanc had only uttered a few words without raising his voice, and, even in his struggle by the window with the six bandits, he had preserved the most remarkable silence.

Thénardier continued, "You did not cry out. I make you my compliments for it, and I will tell you what I conclude from it. My dear monsieur, when a man cries out, who is it that comes? The police. And after the police? Justice. Well! You did not cry out because you were no more anxious than we to see justice and the police come. It is because—I suspected as much long ago—you have some interest in concealing something. For our part we have the same interest. Now we can come to an understanding."

The observation of Thénardier, well founded as it was, added in Marius's eyes still more to the mysterious cloud that enveloped the strange and serious face of Monsieur Leblanc. But whatever he might be, bound with ropes, surrounded by cutthroats, half-buried, so to speak, in a grave which was deepening beneath him every moment, before the fury as well as before the mildness of Thénardier this man remained impassible; and Marius could not repress at such a moment his admiration for that superbly melancholy face.

Thénardier quietly got up, went to the fireplace, took away

the screen, and thus revealed the glowing coals in which the prisoner could plainly see the chisel at a white heat. Then Thénardier came back and sat down by Monsieur Leblanc.

"I continue, now we can come to an understanding. Let us arrange this amicably. I am willing to go halfway and make some sacrifice on my part. I need only two hundred thousand francs."

Monsieur Leblanc did not breathe a word.

Thénardier went on, "I do not know the state of your fortune, but I know that you do not care much for money, and a benevolent man like you can certainly give two hundred thousand francs to a father of a family who is unfortunate. You will say, 'I have not two hundred thousand francs with me.' I am not exacting. I only ask one thing. Have the goodness to write what I shall dictate."

Here Thénardier paused, casting a smile toward the fireplace. He pushed the table close up to Monsieur Leblanc and took the inkstand, a pen, and a sheet of paper from the drawer, which he left partly open and from which gleamed the long blade of a knife.

He laid the sheet of paper before Monsieur Leblanc. "Write," said he.

The prisoner spoke at last. "How do you expect me to write? I am tied."

"That is true; pardon me!" said Thénardier. "You are quite right."

When the prisoner's right hand was free, Thénardier dipped the pen into the ink and presented it to him.

"Remember, monsieur, that you are in our power, at our discretion, that no human power can take you away from here, and that we should be really grieved to be obliged to proceed to unpleasant extremities. I know neither your name nor your address, but I give you notice that you will remain tied until the person whose duty it will be to carry the letter which you are about to write has returned. Have the kindness now to write."

Thénardier began to dictate.

"'My daughter—'"

The prisoner shuddered.

"Put 'My dear daughter,'" said Thénardier.

M. Leblanc obeyed.

Thénardier continued: "'Come immediately—'" He stopped. "You call her daughter, do you not?"

"Who?" asked M. Leblanc.

"The little girl!" said Thénardier. "The Lark."

M. Leblanc answered without the least apparent emotion. "I do not know what you mean."

"Well, go on," said Thénardier, and he began to dictate again. "'Come immediately. I have imperative need of you. The person who will give you this note is directed to bring you to me. I am waiting for you. Come secretly.'

"Now," continued Thénardier, "sign it. What is your name?"

The prisoner laid down the pen and asked, "For whom is this letter?"

"You know very well," answered Thénardier. "For the little girl—I have just told you."

It was evident that Thénardier avoided naming the young girl in question. He said "the Lark" and he said "the little girl," but he did not pronounce the name. The precaution of a shrewd man preserving his own secret before his accomplices. To speak the name would have been to tell them more than they needed to know.

He resumed, "Sign it. What is your name?"

"Urbain Fabre," said the prisoner.

Thénardier, with the movement of a cat, thrust his hand into his pocket and pulled out the handkerchief taken from M. Leblanc. He looked for the mark upon it and held it up to the candle.

"*U. F.* That is it. Urbain Fabre. Well, sign *U. F.*"

The prisoner signed.

"As it takes two hands to fold the letter, give it to me; I will fold it."

This done, Thénardier resumed, "Put on the address—Mademoiselle Fabre, at your house. I know that you live not very far from here, but I do not know in what street. I see that you understand your situation. As you have not lied about your name, you will not lie about your address. Put it on yourself."

The prisoner remained thoughtful for a moment; then he took the pen and wrote,

Mademoiselle Fabre, at Monsieur Urbain Fabre's, Rue d'Enfer, no. 17.

Thénardier seized the letter with a sort of feverish convulsive movement.

"Wife!" cried he.

The Thénardiess sprang forward.

"Here is the letter. You know what you have to do. There is a fiacre below. Go!"

And addressing the man with the ax, "Go with the woman. You will get up behind the fiacre."

A minute had not passed when the snapping of a whip was heard.

"Good!" muttered Thénardier. "They are going at good speed. The bourgeoise will be back in three-quarters of an hour."

He drew a chair near the fireplace and sat down, folding his arms and holding his muddy boots up to the fire. There were now but five bandits left in the den with Thénardier and the prisoner. They were heaped together in a corner like brutes and were silent. Thénardier was warming his feet. The prisoner had relapsed into his taciturnity. A gloomy stillness had succeeded the savage tumult which filled the garret a few moments before.

Marius was waiting in an anxiety which everything increased. The riddle was more impenetrable than ever. Who was this "little girl" whom Thénardier had also called "the Lark"? Was it his Ursula? The prisoner had not seemed to be moved by this name, "the Lark," and had answered in the most natural way in the world, *"I do not know what you mean."* On the other hand, the two letters *U. F.* were explained; it was Urbain Fabre, and Ursula's name was no longer Ursula. This Marius saw most clearly. He was waiting, hoping for some movement, no matter what, unable to collect his ideas and not knowing what course to take.

At all events, thought he, *if the Lark is she, I shall certainly see her, for the Thénardiess is going to bring her here. Then all will be plain. I will give my blood and my life if need be, but I will deliver her. Nothing shall stop me.*

Nearly half an hour passed thus. Thénardier appeared absorbed in a dark meditation; the prisoner did not stir. Nevertheless Marius thought he had heard at intervals and for some moments a little dull noise from the direction of the prisoner.

Suddenly Thénardier addressed the prisoner. "My spouse is coming back; do not be impatient. I think the Lark is really your daughter, and I find it quite natural that you should keep her. But listen a moment; with your letter, my wife is going to find her. I told my wife to dress up, as you saw, so that your young lady would follow her without hesitation. They will both get into the fiacre with my comrade behind. There is somewhere outside one of the barrières a carriage with two very good horses. They will take your young lady there. My comrade will get into the carriage with her, and my wife will come back here to tell us it is done. As to your young lady, no harm will be done her. He will take her to a place where she will be quiet, and as soon as you have given me the little two hundred thousand francs, she will be sent back to you. If you have me arrested, my comrade will give the Lark a pinch; that is all."

The prisoner did not utter a word. After a pause, Thénardier continued, "As soon as my spouse has got back and said, 'The Lark is on her way,' we will release you, and you will be free to go home to bed. You see that we have no bad intentions."

Appalling images passed before Marius's mind. Marius felt his heart cease to beat. What was he to do? Fire off the pistol? Put all these wretches into the hands of justice? But the hideous man of the ax would nonetheless be out of all reach with the young girl, and Marius remembered these words of Thénardier, the bloody signification of which he divined: *"If you have me arrested, my comrade will give the Lark a pinch."* Now it was not by the colonel's will alone; it was by his love itself, by the peril of her whom he loved, that he felt himself held back.

This fearful situation, which had lasted now for more than an hour, changed its aspect at every moment. The tumult of his thoughts strangely contrasted with the deathly silence of the den. In the midst of this silence they heard the sound of the door of the stairway, which opened, then closed. The prisoner made a movement in his bonds.

The Thénardiess burst into the room, red, breathless, panting, with glaring eyes, and cried, "False address!"

Marius breathed. She, Ursula or the Lark, she whom he no longer knew what to call, was safe.

Chapter 45

"A false address! What did you hope for by that?"

"To gain time!" cried the prisoner with a ringing voice. And at the same time he shook off his bonds; they were cut. The prisoner was no longer fastened to the bed save by one leg.

Before the seven men had had time to recover themselves and to spring upon him, he had bent over to the fireplace, reached his hand toward the furnace, then risen up, and now Thénardier, the Thénardiess, and the bandits, thrown by the shock into the back part of the room, beheld him with stupefaction, holding above his head the glowing chisel, from which fell an ominous light.

The prisoner now raised his voice.

"You are pitiable, but my life is not worth the trouble of so long a defense. As to your thought that you could make me speak, that you could make me write what I do not wish to write, that you could make me say what I do not wish to say—"

He pulled up the sleeve of his left arm, and added, "Here."

At the same time he extended his arm and laid upon the naked flesh the glowing chisel, which he held in his right hand by the wooden handle. They heard the hissing of the burning flesh; the odor peculiar to chambers of torture spread through the den. Marius staggered, lost in horror; the brigands themselves felt a shudder; the face of the astonishing old man hardly contracted, and while the red iron was sinking into the smoking wound, he turned upon Thénardier his fine face, in which there was no hatred, and in which suffering was swallowed up in a serene majesty.

"Wretches," said he, "have no more fear of me than I have of you."

And drawing the chisel out of the wound, he threw it through the window, which was still open. The horrible glowing tool disappeared, whirling into the night, and fell in the distance, and was quenched in the snow.

The prisoner resumed, "Do with me what you will."

"Lay hold of him," said Thénardier.

Two of the brigands laid their hands upon his shoulders, and the masked man placed himself in front of him, ready to knock out his brains with a blow of the key.

At the same time Marius heard beneath him—at the foot of the partition, but so near that he could not see those who were talking—this colloquy exchanged in a low voice:

"There is only one thing more to do."

"To kill him?"

"That is it."

It was the husband and wife who were holding counsel.

Thénardier walked with slow steps toward the table, opened the drawer, and took out the knife. Marius was tormenting the trigger of his pistol. Unparalleled perplexity! For an hour there had been two voices in his conscience, one telling him to respect the will of his father, the other crying to him to succor the prisoner, which threw him into agony. He had vaguely hoped up to that moment to find some means of reconciling these two duties, but no possible way had arisen. The peril was now urgent, the last limit of hope was passed; at a few steps from the prisoner, Thénardier was reflecting, with the knife in his hand.

Marius cast his eyes wildly about him, the last mechanical resource of despair. Suddenly he started. At his feet, on the table, a clear ray of the full moon illuminated a sheet of paper. Upon that sheet he read this line, written in large letters that very morning by the elder of the Thénardier girls: *The cognes are here*.

An idea, a flash crossed Marius's mind; that was the means he sought, the solution of this dreadful problem which was torturing him, to spare the killer and to save the victim. He

LEARN TO DO
GOOD,
SEEK JUSTICE.
HELP THE
OPPRESSED.
DEFEND THE CAUSE OF ORPHANS.
FIGHT
FOR THE
RIGHTS OF WIDOWS.
ISAIAH 1:17

knelt down upon his bureau, reached out his arm, caught up the sheet of paper, quietly detached a bit of plaster from the partition, wrapped it in the paper, and threw it into the middle of the den. It was time. Thénardier had conquered his last fears, or his last scruples, and was moving toward the prisoner.

"Something fell!" cried the Thénardiess.

"What is it?" said the husband.

The woman had sprung forward and picked up the piece of plaster wrapped in the paper. She handed it to her husband.

"How did this come in?" asked Thénardier.

"Egad!" said the woman. "It came through the window."

Thénardier hurriedly unfolded the paper and held it up to the candle.

"It is Éponine's writing. The devil!"

He made a sign to his wife, who approached quickly, and he showed her the line written on the sheet of paper; then he added in a hollow voice, "Quick! The ladder! Leave the meat in the trap, and clear the camp!"

"Without cutting the man's throat?" asked the Thénardiess.

"We have not the time."

"Which way?"

"Through the window," answered Thénardier. "Éponine threw the stone through the window; that shows the house is not watched on that side."

The brigands who were holding the prisoner let go of him; in the twinkling of an eye, the rope ladder was unrolled out the window and firmly fixed to the casing by the two iron hooks. The prisoner paid no attention to what was passing around him. He seemed to be dreaming or praying.

As soon as the ladder was fixed, Thénardier cried, "Come, bourgeois!" And he rushed toward the window.

But as he was stepping out, a bandit seized him roughly by the collar.

"No, old joker! After us."

"You are children," said Thénardier. "We are losing time."

"Well," said one of the bandits, "let us draw lots who shall go out first."

"Would you like my hat?" cried a voice from the door.

They all turned around. It was Javert. He had his hat in his hand and was holding it out, smiling.

Javert, at nightfall, had posted his men and hid himself behind the trees on the RUE DES GOBELINS, which fronts the Gorbeau tenement on the other side of the boulevard. Two young girls had been charged with watching the approaches to the den. But he only bagged Azelma. Éponine was not at her post; she had disappeared, and he could not take her. Then he listened for the signal agreed upon. The going and coming of the fiacre fretted him greatly. At last, he became impatient, and, sure that there was a nest there, sure of being in good luck, having recognized several of the bandits who had gone in, he finally decided to go up without waiting for the pistol shot. After all, he had Marius's passkey.

He had come at the right time. In less than a second, these seven frightened men, terrible to look upon, were grouped in a posture of defense.

Javert put on his hat again and stepped into the room, his arms folded, his cane under his arm, his sword in its sheath.

"Halt there," said he. "You will not pass out through the window; you will pass out through the door. It is less unwholesome. There are seven of you, fifteen of us." And turning round, he called behind him, "Come in now!"

A squad of *sergents de ville* with drawn swords and officers armed with axes and clubs rushed in at Javert's call. They bound the bandits.

"Handcuffs on all!" cried Javert.

The Thénardiess, completely crushed, looked at her manacled hands and those of her husband, dropped to the floor, and exclaimed, with tears in her eyes, "My daughters!"

"They are provided for," said Javert.

Just then he perceived the prisoner of the bandits, who, since the entrance of the police, had not uttered a word and had held his head down.

"Untie monsieur!" said Javert.

He sat down with authority before the table on which the candle and the writing materials still were, drew a stamped sheet from his pocket, and commenced his procès-verbal*. When he had written the first lines, a part of the formula which is always the same, he raised his eyes.

"Bring forward the gentleman whom these gentlemen bound."

The officers looked about them. The prisoner of the bandits, M. Leblanc, M. Urbain Fabre, the father of Ursula or the Lark, had disappeared.

The door was guarded, but the window was not. As soon as he saw that he was unbound, and while Javert was writing, M. Leblanc had taken advantage of the disturbance, the tumult, the confusion, the obscurity, and a moment when their attention was not fixed upon him, to leap out of the window.

An officer ran to the window and looked out; nobody could be seen outside. The rope ladder was still trembling.

"The devil!" said Javert, between his teeth. "That must have been the best one."

Marius had seen the unexpected denouement of the ambuscade, but hardly had Javert left the old ruin, carrying away his prisoners, when Marius also slipped out of the house and went to Courfeyrac's.

Chapter 46

The day following these events, a child went toward the Gorbeau house, and finding the door locked, began to batter it with kicks. Ma'am Burgon opened the door, then suddenly stopped. She recognized the gamin*.

"Hullo," said the child. "I have come to see my ancestors."

The old woman responded, "There is nobody here."

"Pshaw!" said the child. "Where are my father, my mother, and my sisters?"

"In prison."

The child scratched the back of his ear and said, "Ah!" then turned on his heel. A moment afterward, the old woman heard him sing with his clear, fresh voice as he disappeared under the black elms shivering in the wintry winds.

That same day, by seven o'clock in the morning, Marius went back to the tenement, paid his rent to Ma'am Burgon, had his possessions loaded upon a handcart, and went off without leaving his address, so that when Javert came back in the forenoon to question Marius about the events of the evening, he found only Ma'am Burgon, who answered him, "Moved!"

Marius had two reasons for this prompt removal. The first was that he now had a horror of that house where he had seen, so near at hand and in all its most repulsive and most ferocious development, a social deformity perhaps still more hideous than the evil rich man—the evil poor. The second was that he did not wish to figure in the trial which would probably follow, and be brought forward to testify against Thénardier.

Javert thought that the young man, whose name he had not retained, had been frightened and had escaped, or, perhaps, had not even been home at the time of the ambuscade.

A month rolled away, then another. Marius was still with Courfeyrac. He knew from a young attorney, a habitual attendant in the anterooms of the court, that Thénardier was in solitary confinement. Every Monday, Marius sent to the clerk of La Force* five francs for Thénardier. Marius, having now no money, borrowed the five francs of Courfeyrac, for the first time in his life. This periodical five francs was a double enigma, to Courfeyrac who furnished them, and to Thénardier who received them.

Marius, moreover, was in sore affliction. Everything had relapsed into darkness. He had for a moment seen close at hand in that obscurity the young girl whom he loved, the old man who seemed to be her father, these unknown beings who were his only interest and his only hope in this world; and at the moment he had thought to hold them fast, a breath had swept all those shadows away. What should he think of the old man? Was he really hiding from the police? Why had he not called for help? Why had he escaped? Was he the father of the young girl? Finally, was he really the man whom Thénardier thought he recognized? All this detracted nothing from the angelic charms of the young girl of the Luxembourg. All had vanished, except love.

A certain amount of reverie is good; it soothes the fever of the brain at work and produces in the mind a soft and fresh vapor which fills up the gaps and intervals here and there, binds them together, and blunts the sharp corners of ideas. But woe to the brain-worker who allows himself to fall entirely from thought into reverie! One no longer goes out of the house except to walk and dream.

A single sweet idea remained to Marius, that she had loved him; that her eyes had told him so; that she did not know his name but that she knew his soul; and that, perhaps, wherever she was, whatever that mysterious place might be, she loved him still.

It happened one day that Marius's solitary walks conducted him to an open place in the long and monotonous circuit of the boulevards of Paris, a spot which on inquiry he found was called the Field of the Lark. *The Lark* was the appellation which, in the depths of Marius's melancholy, had replaced *Ursula*. "Yes," said he in the kind of unreasoning stupor peculiar to these mysterious asides, "this is her field. I shall learn here where she lives." And he came every day to this Field of the Lark.

That morning the bright sun was gleaming through the new and glossy leaves. He was thinking of "Her!"

All at once, in the midst of his ecstasy of exhaustion, he heard a voice which was known to him say, "Ah! There he is!"

He raised his eyes and recognized the unfortunate child who had come to his room one morning, the elder of the Thénardier girls, Éponine; he now knew her name. She had become more wretched and more beautiful, two steps which together seemed impossible. She was barefoot and in rags, as on the day when she had so resolutely entered his room, only her rags were two months older; the holes were larger, the tatters dirtier. It was the same rough voice, the same forehead tanned and wrinkled by exposure; the same free, wild, and wandering gaze. She had, in addition to her former expression, that mixture of fear and sorrow which the experience of a prison adds to misery. She had spears of straw and grass in her hair because she had slept in some stable loft.

Meantime, she had stopped before Marius with an expression of pleasure upon her livid face, and something which resembled a smile. She stood for a few seconds as if she could not speak.

"I have found you, then?" said she at last. "How I have looked for you, if you only knew! I have been in prison a fortnight! They have let me out seeing that there was nothing

procès-verbal : trial report

gamin : a street urchin

La Force : a former prison located in central Paris *

against me, and I was not of the age of discernment. Oh! How I have looked for you! You don't live down there any longer?"

"No," said Marius.

"Oh! I understand. On account of the affair. You have moved. But tell me, where do you live now?"

Marius did not answer.

She resumed with an expression which gradually grew darker. "You don't seem to be glad to see me? But if I would, I could easily make you glad!"

"How?" inquired Marius.

She bit her lip; she seemed to hesitate, as if passing through a kind of interior struggle. At last, she said, "You look sad; I want you to be glad. Poor Monsieur Marius! You know, you promised me that you would give me whatever I should ask—"

"Yes! But tell me!"

She looked into Marius's eyes and said, "I have the address."

Marius turned pale. All his blood flowed back to his heart. "What address?"

"The address you asked me for, of the young lady!" Having pronounced this word, she sighed deeply.

Marius sprang up from the bank on which he was sitting and took her wildly by the hand. "Come! Show me the way, tell me! Ask me for whatever you will! Where is it?"

"Come with me," she answered. "I am not sure of the street and the number; it is away on the other side from here, but I know the house very well. I will show you."

She withdrew her hand and added in a tone which would have pierced the heart of an observer, but which did not even touch the intoxicated and transported Marius, "How glad you are!"

A cloud passed over Marius's brow. He seized Éponine by the arm. "Swear to me one thing! Promise me, Éponine! Swear to me that you will not give this address to your father!"

She turned toward him with an astounded appearance. "Éponine! How do you know that my name is Éponine?"

"Promise what I ask you!"

But she did not seem to understand. "That is nice! You called me Éponine!"

Marius caught her by both arms at once. "But answer me now, in heaven's name! Swear to me that you will not give the address you know to your father!"

"My father?" said she. "Do not be concerned on his account. He is in solitary. But I promise you that! I swear to you that! There! Will that do?"

"Nor to anybody?" said Marius.

"Nor to anybody."

"Now," added Marius, "show me the way."

"Come. How glad he is!" said she.

After a few steps, she stopped. "You follow too near me, Monsieur Marius. Let me go forward, and follow me like that, without seeming to. It won't do for a fine young man like you to be seen with a woman like me."

She went on a few steps and stopped again; Marius rejoined her. She spoke to him aside and without turning. "By the way, you know you have promised me something?"

Marius fumbled in his pocket. He had nothing in the world but the five francs intended for Thénardier. He took it and put it into Éponine's hand.

She opened her fingers, let the piece fall on the ground, and looked at him with a gloomy look. "I don't want your money," said she.

In the month of October 1829, a man hired a certain house in the RUE PLUMET, including a building in the rear, with a passage which ran out to the RUE DE BABYLONE. He had the secret openings of the two doors of this passage repaired, and finally came and installed himself with a young girl and an aged servant, without any noise, rather like somebody stealing in than like a man who enters his own house. There were no neighbors to gossip about it.

This tenant was Jean Valjean; the young girl was Cosette. The servant was an old spinster named Toussaint, whom Jean Valjean had saved from the hospital and misery. He hired the house under the name of Monsieur Fauchelevent, gentleman.

Why had Jean Valjean left the convent of the Petit Picpus? He saw Cosette every day, he felt paternity springing up and developing within him more and more. But this child, he said to himself, would certainly become a nun, being every day gently led on toward it; he would grow old there and she would grow up there; she would grow old there and he would die there. He believed this child had a right to know what life was before renouncing it; that to cut her off, in advance, and without consulting her, from all pleasure, under pretense of saving her from all trial, to take advantage of her ignorance and isolation to give her an artificial vocation, was to outrage a human creature and to lie to God. And who knew but, thinking over all this some day, and being a nun with regret, Cosette might come to hate him—a final thought, which was almost selfish and less heroic than the others, but which was insupportable to him. He resolved to leave the convent.

He might return tranquilly among men. He had grown old, and all had changed. Who would recognize him now? And then, to look at the worst, there was no danger save for himself, and he had no right to condemn Cosette to the cloister for the reason that he had been condemned to the galleys. Cosette's education was almost finished and complete.

His determination once formed, he awaited an opportunity. It was not slow to present itself. Old Fauchelevent died. Jean Valjean asked an audience of the reverend prioress and told her that having received a small inheritance on the death of his brother, which enabled him to live henceforth without labor, he would leave the service of the convent and take away his daughter; but as it was not fitting that Cosette, not taking her vows, should have been educated gratuitously, he humbly begged the reverend prioress to allow him to offer the community, as indemnity for the five years which Cosette had passed there, the sum of five thousand francs.

Thus Jean Valjean left the convent of the Petit Picpus. He nevertheless did not appear again in the open city without deep misgivings. He discovered the house in the RUE PLUMET and buried himself in it. He was henceforth in possession of the name of Ultimus Fauchelevent. At the same time he hired two other lodgings in Paris in order to attract less attention than if he always remained in the same quartier, to be able to change his abode on occasion, at the slightest anxiety which he might feel, and finally, that he might not again find himself in such a strait as on the night when he had so miraculously escaped from Javert.

Every day Jean Valjean took Cosette's arm, and went with her to the least frequented walk of the Luxembourg, and every Sunday to Mass, always at Saint Jacques du Haut Pas, because it was quite distant. As that is a very poor quarter, he gave many alms there, and the unfortunate surrounded him in the church. He was fond of taking Cosette to visit the needy and the sick.

M. Fauchelevent belonged to the National Guard*: he had not been able to escape the close meshes of the enrollment of 1831.

Three or four times a year, Jean Valjean donned the old man's uniform and very willingly performed his duties. It was a good disguise for him, which associated him with everybody else while leaving him solitary. Jean Valjean had completed his sixtieth year, the age of legal exemption, but he did not appear more than fifty. He had no civil standing; he was concealing his name, he was concealing his identity, he was concealing his age, he was concealing everything; and was very willingly a National Guard. To resemble the crowd who pay their taxes, this was his whole ambition.

When Jean Valjean went out with Cosette, he dressed as we have seen, and had much the air of an old officer. When he went out alone—and this was most usually in the evening—he was always clad in the waistcoat and trousers of a workingman and wore a cap which hid his face.

Neither Jean Valjean, nor Cosette, nor Toussaint ever came in or went out except by the gate on the RUE DE BABYLONE. Unless one had seen them through the grated gate of the garden, it would have been difficult to guess that they lived in the RUE PLUMET. This gate always remained closed. Jean Valjean had left the garden uncultivated, that it might not attract attention.

In this he deceived himself, perhaps.

It seemed as if this garden had been rendered fit for the shelter of chaste mysteries. There was a magnificent disheveled obscurity falling like a veil upon all sides. There was also in this solitude a heart which was all ready. Love had only to show himself; there was a temple there composed of verdure, of grass, of moss, of the sighs of birds, of soft shade, of agitated branches, and a soul made up of gentleness, of faith, of candor, of hope, of aspiration, and of illusion.

Cosette had left the convent, still almost a child; she was a little more than fourteen years old. Cosette could have found nothing more exhilarating and more dangerous than the house on the RUE PLUMET. It was the continuation of solitude with the beginning of liberty; an enclosed garden, but a sharp, rich, voluptuous, and odorous nature; the same dreams as in the convent, but with glimpses of young men; a grating, but upon the street.

Cosette had but vague remembrance of her childhood. She prayed morning and evening for her mother, whom she had never known. The Thénardiers had remained to her like two hideous faces of some dream. She remembered that she had been one day into a wood after water. It seemed to her that she had commenced life in an abyss, and that Jean Valjean had drawn her out of it. When she was dozing at night, before going to sleep—as she had no very clear idea of being Jean Valjean's daughter, and that he was her father—she imagined that her mother's soul had passed into this good man and come to live with her. She did not even know her mother's name. Whenever she happened to ask Jean Valjean what it was, he was silent. If she repeated her question, he answered by a smile. Once she insisted; the smile ended with a tear.

While Cosette was a little girl, Jean Valjean had been fond of talking with her about her mother; when she was a young maiden, this was impossible for him. It seemed to him that he no longer dared. Was this on account of Cosette? Was it on account of Fantine? He felt a sort of religious horror at introducing that shade into Cosette's thoughts. He thought of Fantine and felt overwhelmed with silence. He saw dimly in the darkness something which resembled a finger on a mouth. Had all that modesty which had once been Fantine's and which, during her life, had been forced out of her by violence, returned after her death to take its place over her, to watch, indignant, over the peace of the dead woman, and to guard her fiercely in her tomb? Did Jean Valjean, without knowing it, feel its influence?

One day Cosette said to him, "Father, I saw my mother in a dream last night. She had two great wings. My mother must have attained to sanctity in her life."

"Through martyrdom," answered Jean Valjean.

It was at this period that Marius, after the lapse of six months, saw her again at the Luxembourg. Cosette, in her seclusion, like Marius in his, was all ready to take fire. Destiny, with its mysterious and fatal patience, was slowly bringing these two beings near each other, fully charged and all languishing with the stormy electricities of passion—these two souls which held love as two clouds hold lightning, and which were to meet and mingle in a glance, like clouds in a flash.

Marius and Cosette were in the dark in regard to each other; they did not speak, they did not bow, they were not acquainted. They saw each other, and, like the stars in the sky separated by millions of leagues, they lived by gazing upon each other. Thus it was that Cosette gradually became a woman and, beautiful and loving, grew with the awareness of her beauty, ignorant of her love—coquettish withal, through innocence.

Chapter 48

All this did not escape Jean Valjean. He very soon saw that Cosette was beginning to show an interest in this strange young man. When he was convinced of it, he discontinued his walks in the Luxembourg. Cosette accepted the change without a word, but she grew sad and thoughtful. Jean Valjean also, with the fear of losing her gnawing at his soul, became almost morose. Even after their life had been saddened, however, they continued their habit of morning walks.

However, their life gradually darkened. There was left to them but one distraction, and this had formerly been a pleasure: that was to carry bread to those who were hungry and clothing to those who were cold. In these visits to the poor, in which Cosette often accompanied Jean Valjean, they found some remnant of their former lightheartedness; and, sometimes, when they had had a good day, when many sorrows had been relieved and many little children revived and made warm, Cosette, in the evening, was a little gay. It was at this period that they visited the Jondrette den.

The day after that visit, Jean Valjean appeared in the cottage in the morning with his ordinary calmness but with a large wound on his left arm, very much inflamed and very venomous, which resembled a burn, and which he explained in some fashion. This wound confined him within doors more than a month with fever. He would see no physician. Cosette dressed it night and morning with so divine a grace and so angelic a pleasure in being useful to him, that Jean Valjean felt all his old happiness return, his fears and his fretting dissipate.

Cosette, as her father was sick, spent almost all her time with him, and read to him the books which he liked, in general, books of travels. Jean Valjean was born anew; his happiness revived with inexpressible radiance.

At the convent, Sister Sainte Mechthilde had taught Cosette music. Cosette had the voice of a warbler with a soul, and sometimes in the evening, in the humble lodging of the wounded man, she sang plaintive songs which cheered Jean Valjean.

In the first fortnight in April, Jean Valjean went on a journey, as happened with him from time to time, at very long intervals. He remained absent one or two days at the most. Where did he go? Nobody knew, not even Cosette. It was generally when money was needed for the household expenses that Jean Valjean made these little journeys.

In the evening, Cosette was alone in the parlor. To amuse herself, she had opened her piano and begun to sing, playing

National Guard : a paramilitary unit established after the July Revolution in 1830 *

an accompaniment, the chorus from *Euryanthe**: hunters wandering in the woods! All at once it seemed to her that she heard a step in the garden.

It could not be her father—he was absent; it could not be Toussaint—she was in bed. It was ten o'clock at night. She went to the window shutter, which was closed, and put her ear to it. It appeared to her that it was a man's step, and that he was treading very softly. She ran immediately up to her room, opened a slide in her blind, and looked into the silent garden. The moon was full. She could see as plainly as in broad day. There was nobody there.

Cosette thought she had been mistaken. She had imagined she heard this noise. She thought no more about it.

Moreover, Cosette by nature was not easily startled. There was in her veins the blood of the gypsy and of the adventuress who goes barefoot. It must be remembered she was rather a lark than a dove. She was wild and brave at heart.

The next day, not so late, at nightfall, she was walking in the garden. In the midst of the confused thoughts which filled her mind, she thought she heard for a moment a sound like the sound of the evening before, as if somebody were walking in the darkness under the trees, not very far from her. Cosette stood still, terrified. By the side of her shadow, the moon marked out distinctly upon the sward another shadow singularly frightful and terrible, a shadow with a round hat. It was like the shadow of a man who might have been standing in the edge of the shrubbery, a few steps behind Cosette. For a moment she was unable to speak, or cry, or call, or stir, or turn her head. At last she summoned up all her courage and resolutely turned round.

There was nobody there. She looked upon the ground. The shadow had disappeared. She returned into the shrubbery, boldly hunted through the corners, went as far as the gate, and found nothing. She felt her blood run cold. Was this also a hallucination? One hallucination may pass, but two hallucinations? What made her most anxious was that the shadow was certainly not a phantom. Phantoms never wear round hats.

The next day Jean Valjean returned. Cosette narrated to him what she thought she had heard and seen. Jean Valjean became worried. He went into the garden, and she saw him examining the gate very closely. In the night she awoke; now she was certain; she distinctly heard somebody walking very near the steps under her window. She ran to her slide and opened it. There was in fact a man in the garden with a big club in his hand. Just as she was about to cry out, the moon lighted up the man's face. It was her father.

Jean Valjean passed that night in the garden and the two nights following. Cosette saw him through the hole in her shutter. The third night the moon was smaller and rose later. It might have been one o'clock in the morning, when she heard a loud burst of laughter and her father's voice calling her, "Cosette!"

She sprang out of bed, threw on her dressing gown, and opened her window. Her father was below on the grass plot.

"I woke you up to show you," said he. "Look, here is your shadow in a round hat."

And he pointed to a shadow on the sward made by the moon, which really bore a close resemblance to the appearance of a man in a round hat. It was a figure produced by a sheet iron stovepipe with a cap, which rose above a neighboring roof. Cosette also began to laugh, all her gloomy suppositions fell to the ground, and the next day she made merry over the mysterious garden haunted by shadows of stovepipes.

Jean Valjean became entirely calm again. A few days afterward, however, a new incident occurred.

In the garden, near the grated gate, on the street, there was a stone seat protected from the gaze of the curious by a hedge, but which, nevertheless, by an effort, the arm of a passer could reach through the grating and the hedge. One evening in this same month of April, Jean Valjean had gone out; Cosette, after sunset, had sat down on this seat, musing.

Cosette rose, slowly made the round of the garden, and then returned to the seat. Just as she was sitting down, she noticed, in the place she had left, a stone of considerable size which evidently was not there the moment before.

Suddenly the idea that this stone did not come upon the seat of itself, that somebody had put it there, came to her and made her afraid. It was a genuine fear this time. She did not touch it, fled without daring to look behind her, and took refuge in the house. All night she saw the stone, big as a mountain and full of caves.

At sunrise, Cosette, on waking, dressed herself, went down to the garden, ran to the bench, and felt a cold sweat. The stone was there.

But this was only for a moment. What is fright by night is curiosity by day. She raised the stone. There was something underneath which resembled a letter. Cosette seized it; there was no address. She examined it. There was no more fright; there was a beginning of anxious interest.

Cosette took out of the envelope a quire* of paper, each page of which was numbered and contained a few lines written in a rather pretty handwriting. Cosette looked for a name, there was none; a signature, there was none. To whom was it addressed? To her probably, since a hand had placed the packet upon her seat. From whom did it come? She looked at the sky, the street, the acacias all steeped in light, some pigeons which were flying about a neighboring roof, then all at once, her eye eagerly sought the manuscript.

Cosette did not hesitate for a moment. One single man. He!

When evening came, Jean Valjean went out. Cosette dressed herself; she arranged her hair in the manner which best became her. At dusk, she went down to the garden and reached the seat. The stone was still there. She sat down and laid her soft white hand upon that stone as if she would caress it and thank it.

All at once, she had that indefinable impression that there was somebody standing behind her. She turned her head and arose. It was he.

He was bareheaded. He appeared pale and thin. She hardly discerned his black clothing. The twilight dimmed his fine forehead and covered his eyes with darkness. He had, under a veil of incomparable sweetness, something of death, and of night. His face was lighted by the light of a dying day, and by the thought of a departing soul.

Cosette, ready to faint, did not utter a cry. She drew back slowly; he did not stir. Through the sad and ineffable something which enwrapped him, she felt the look of his eyes, which she did not see. Then she heard his voice, that voice which she had never really heard, hardly rising above the rustling of the leaves, and murmuring,

"Pardon me, I am here. I could not live as I was; I have come. Have you read what I placed there, on this seat? Do

Euryanthe: a German opera by Carl Maria von Weber. Act 3, scene 5 includes a hunter's chorus (*Jägerchor*) about the joys of hunting in the forest in the fresh morning.

quire : twenty-five sheets of paper *

you recognize me at all? Do not be afraid of me. It is a long time now; do you remember the day when you looked upon me? It was at the Luxembourg, near the Gladiator. And the day when you passed before me? It will soon be a year. For a very long time now, I have not seen you at all. You lived in the RUE DE L'OUEST, on the third floor front, in a new house. I followed you. What was I to do? And then you disappeared. At night, I come here. Do not be afraid; nobody sees me. I come for a near look at your windows. I walk very softly that you may not hear, for perhaps you would be afraid. The other evening I was behind you; you turned round; I fled. Once I heard you sing. I was happy. See, you are my angel; let me come sometimes. If you but knew! I adore you! Pardon me, I am talking to you—I do not know what I am saying to you; perhaps I annoy you. Do I annoy you?"

She sank down upon herself as if she were dying. He caught her in his arms; he grasped her tightly, unconscious of what he was doing. He supported her even while tottering himself. He felt as if his head were enveloped in smoke; flashes of light passed through his eyelids; his ideas vanished; it seemed to him that he was performing a religious act; he was lost in love.

She took his hand and laid it on her heart. He felt the paper there, and stammered, "You love me, then?"

She answered in a voice so low that it was no more than a breath which could scarcely be heard. "Hush! You know it!" And she hid her blushing head in the bosom of the proud and intoxicated young man.

He fell upon the seat, she by his side. There were no more words. The stars were beginning to shine. How was it that their lips met? How is it that the rose opens, that the dawn whitens behind the black trees on the shivering summit of the hills? One kiss, and that was all.

Both trembled, and they looked at each other in the darkness. They felt neither the fresh night, nor the cold stone, nor the damp ground, nor the wet grass; they looked at each other, and their hearts were full of thought. They had clasped hands without knowing it.

Gradually they began to talk. Overflow succeeded to silence, which is fullness. The night was serene and splendid above their heads. These two beings, pure as spirits, told each other all their dreams, their frenzies, their ecstasies, their chimeras, their despondencies, how they had adored each other from afar, how they had longed for each other, their despair when they had ceased to see each other. These two hearts poured themselves out into each other, so that at the end of an hour, it was the young man who had the young girl's soul and the young girl who had the soul of the young man. They interpenetrated, they enchanted, they dazzled each other.

When they had finished, when they had told each other everything, she laid her head upon his shoulder and asked him, "What is your name?"

"My name is Marius," said he. "And yours?"

"My name is Cosette."

Chapter 49

While Marius and Cosette were sitting together in the garden, they little realized that forces of evil were at work, and that plans had already been made for an attack upon this house in the RUE PLUMET. The band that was working and planning was none other than Thénardier's, for he and his companions had succeeded in escaping from La Force.

Éponine, whose task it was to play the scout to this band, was sent by her father to make a reconnaissance of the place and its inhabitants, and to report what she could find out. When she discovered that it was where Cosette lived, she began by diverting the bandits from their intention and conducting Marius to the garden.

Her reports did not satisfy her father, so he carried on some investigations on his own account, which made him arrive at conclusions far different from those that Éponine had hoped for. He tried to keep to himself these secret expeditions, but it was impossible for him to deceive his daughter. She knew something was in the wind, so every night she hid herself near the wall and watched.

One night after Marius had left, six men, who were walking separately and at some distance from each other along the wall, entered the RUE PLUMET. The first to arrive at the grating of the garden stopped and waited for the others; in a second they were all six together. These men began to talk in a low voice.

"The grating is old," said one.

"So much the better," said another. "It will not be so hard to cut."

The sixth began to examine the grating as Éponine had done an hour before, grasping each bar successively and shaking it carefully. He came to one which Marius had loosened. Just as he was about to lay hold of this bar, a hand, starting abruptly from the shadow, fell upon his arm; he felt himself pushed sharply back by the middle of his breast, and a roughened voice said to him without crying out, "There is a dog."

He saw a pale girl standing before him. He bristled up; he recoiled and stammered, "What is this creature?"

"Your daughter." It was indeed Éponine who was speaking to Thénardier.

On the appearance of Éponine, the five others approached without a sound, without haste, without saying a word, with the ominous slowness peculiar to these men of the night. In their hands might be distinguished some strangely hideous tools.

"What are you doing here?" exclaimed Thénardier in a whisper. "Why do you come and hinder us in our work?"

Éponine sprang to his neck.

"I am here, my darling father, because I am here. It is you who shouldn't be here. I told you so. There is nothing to do here."

Thénardier tried to free himself from Éponine's arms and muttered, "Now, be off."

But Éponine did not loose her hold and redoubled her caresses.

Thénardier answered, "Let me alone. I tell you to be off."

"I don't want to go away just now," said Éponine, and she caught her father again by the neck and turned toward the five bandits and continued, "You know very well that I am not a fool. Ordinarily you believe me. I have done you service on occasion. Well, I have learned all about this; you would expose yourselves uselessly; do you see? I swear to you that there is nothing to be done in that house. The people have moved away."

"The candles have not, anyhow!" said her father, and he showed Éponine, through the top of the trees, a light in the garret of the cottage.

Éponine made a final effort. "Well," said she, "they are very poor people, and it is a shanty where there isn't a sou."

"Go to the devil!" cried Thénardier. "When we have turned the house over, and when we have put the cellar at the top and the garret at the bottom, we will tell you what there is inside." And he pushed her to pass by.

But she placed her back against the grating, faced the six bandits who were armed to the teeth and to whom the night gave faces of demons, and said in a low and firm voice, "Well, I won't have it."

They stopped, astounded. She resumed, "Friends! Listen to me. If you go into the garden, if you touch this grating, I shall cry out; I shall wake everybody up; I shall have all six of you arrested, beginning with my father!"

Thénardier approached.

"Not so near!" said she.

He drew back, muttering between his teeth.

She began to laugh in a terrible way. "You shall not go in. There are six of you; what is that to me? You are men. Now, I am a woman. I am not afraid of you, not a bit. I tell you that you shall not go into this house, because it does not please me. If you approach, I shall cry out. Go where you like, but don't come here. I forbid it!"

She kept her eye fixed upon Thénardier and said, "What is it to me whether somebody picks me up tomorrow on the pavement, beaten to death with a club by my father, or whether they find me in a year in the ditches of Saint Cloud, among the old rotten rubbish and the dead dogs?"

She was obliged to stop; a dry cough seized her, and her breath came like a rattle from her narrow and feeble chest. "I have but to cry out, and they come, bang! You are six, but I am everybody!"

The six cutthroats, sullen and abashed at being held in check by a girl, went under the protecting shade of the lantern and held counsel. She watched them the while with a quiet yet indomitable air. In a few minutes they went away.

Éponine rose and began to creep along the walls and houses behind them. She followed them as far as the boulevard. There, they separated, and she saw these men slink away in obscurity.

The next evening Marius found Cosette sad; she had been weeping. She sat down on the seat near the stairs, and as he took his place all trembling beside her, she said, "My father told me this morning to hold myself in readiness, that he had business, and that perhaps we should go away."

Marius shuddered from head to foot. For six weeks Marius, gradually, slowly, by degrees, had been each day taking possession of Cosette. He felt Cosette living within him. To have Cosette, to possess Cosette, this to him was not separable from breathing. Into the midst of this faith, of this intoxication, of this virginal possession, marvelous and absolute, of this sovereignty, these words, "*We are going away,*" fell all at once, and the sharp voice of reality cried to him, "Cosette is not yours!"

Marius awoke. For six weeks Marius had lived, as we have said, outside of life; these words, *going away*, brought him roughly back to it.

She resumed, "This morning my father told me to arrange all my little affairs and to be ready, that he would give me his clothes to pack, that he was obliged to take a journey, that we were going away, that we must have a large trunk for me and a small one for him, to get all that ready within a week from now, and that we should go perhaps to England."

He asked in a feeble voice, "And when should you start?"

"He didn't say when."

"And when should you return?"

"He didn't say when."

Marius arose and said coldly, "Cosette, will you go?"

Cosette turned upon him her beautiful eyes full of anguish and answered with a sort of bewilderment, "Marius, I have an idea. Come and join me where I am!"

Marius was now a man entirely awakened. He had fallen back into reality. He cried to Cosette, "Go with you? It takes money, and I have none. Go to England? Cosette, I am a miserable wretch. You only see me at night, and you give me your love; if you should see me by day, you would give me a sou! Go to England? Ah! I have not the means to pay for a passport!"

He threw himself on the seat and remained there for a long time sunk in thought. Cosette was weeping. All of a sudden he had an idea; he jumped up. "Listen," said he, "do not expect me till the day after tomorrow!"

"Why not?"

"You will see."

"A day without seeing you! Why, that is impossible."

"Let us sacrifice one day to gain perhaps a whole life."

She took his head in both her hands, rising on tiptoe to reach his height and striving to see his hope in his eyes.

Marius continued: "It occurs to me that you should know my address; something may happen. I live with that friend named Courfeyrac, RUE DE LA VERRERIE, number 16."

He put his hand in his pocket, took out a penknife, and wrote with the blade upon the plastering of the wall: *16, Rue de la Verrerie.*

Cosette, meanwhile, began to look into his eyes again. "Tell me your idea. Marius, you have an idea. Oh! Tell me, so that I may pass a good night!"

"My idea is this: that it is impossible that God should wish to separate us. Expect me day after tomorrow."

And, moved by the same thought, drawn on by those electric currents which put two lovers in continual communication, both intoxicated with pleasure even in their grief, they fell into each other's arms, without perceiving that their lips were joined, while their uplifted eyes, overflowing with ecstasy and full of tears, were fixed upon the stars.

Chapter 50

Grandfather Gillenormand was now ninety-one. He still lived with Mademoiselle Gillenormand in that old house which belonged to him. He was, as we remember, one of those antique old men who await death still erect, whom age loads without making them stoop, and whom grief itself does not bend. Four years he had been waiting for Marius with his foot down—that is just the word—in the conviction that the naughty little scapegrace would ring at his door some day or other. Now he had come, in certain gloomy hours, to say to himself that it was not death that was insupportable to him; it was the idea that perhaps he should never see Marius again. That notion had not, even for an instant, entered into his thought until this day; now this idea began to appear to him, and it chilled him. Absence had only increased this grandfather's love for the ungrateful child who had gone away.

In the deepest of this reverie, his old domestic, Basque, came in and asked, "Can monsieur receive Monsieur Marius?"

The old man straightened up, pallid and like a corpse; all his blood had flown back to his heart. He faltered. "Monsieur Marius! What? Show him in."

The door opened. Marius stopped at the door as if waiting to be asked to come in. His almost-wretched dress was not noticed. Only his face, calm and grave, but strangely sad, could be distinguished.

M. Gillenormand, as if congested with astonishment

and joy, sat for some moments without seeing anything but a light, as when one is in the presence of an apparition. He was almost fainting; he perceived Marius through a blinding haze. It was indeed Marius!

But there came forth a harsh word. He said abruptly, "What is it you come here for?"

Marius answered with embarrassment: "Monsieur—"

M. Gillenormand would have had Marius throw himself into his arms. He was displeased with Marius and with himself, to feel himself so tender and so much in tears within, while he could only be harsh without. He interrupted Marius with a sharp tone. "What do you come for? Do you come to ask my pardon? Have you seen your fault?"

"No, monsieur."

This violent method of pushing the grandson to tenderness produced only silence on the part of Marius. M. Gillenormand folded his arms, a posture which with him was particularly imperious.

"Let us make an end of it. You have come to ask something of me. Well, what? What is it? Speak!"

"Monsieur," said Marius, "I come to ask your permission to marry."

Grandfather Gillenormand returned and stood with his back to the fireplace. "You marry! At twenty-one! You have arranged that! You have nothing but a permission to ask! A formality. Sit down, monsieur. So you want to marry? Whom? Can the question be asked without indiscretion?"

He stopped, and, before Marius had time to answer, he added violently, "Come now, you have a business? Your fortune made? How much do you earn at your lawyer's trade?"

"Nothing," said Marius, with a firmness and resolution which were almost savage.

"Nothing? You have nothing to live on but the twelve hundred livres which I send you?"

Marius made no answer.

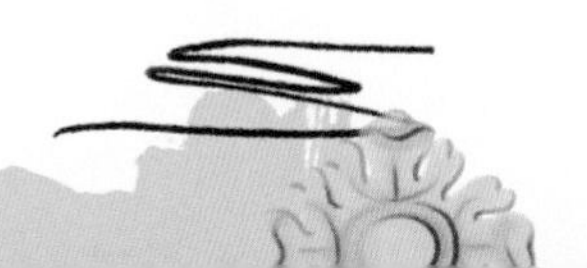

M. Gillenormand continued, "Then I understand the girl is rich?"

"As I am."

"What! No dowry?"

"No."

"Some expectations?"

"I believe not."

The old man burst into a shrill, dreary laugh.

"Father!"

"Never!"

It was that single word, *Father*, dropped by Marius, which had caused this revolution. The young man sat down, smiling. "Father," resumed Marius, "my good father, if you knew. I loved her the first time that I saw her. Now I see her every day at her own house; her father does not know it, but we see each other in the garden in the evening. Now her father wants to take her to England, so I said to myself, 'I will go and see my grandfather and tell him about it.' I should go crazy in the first place; I should die; I should throw myself into the river. I must marry her. That is the whole truth; I do not believe that I have forgotten anything. She lives in the RUE PLUMET."

Grandfather Gillenormand, radiant with joy, had sat down by Marius's side. At those words, *Rue Plumet*, he let his snuff fall on his knee.

"RUE PLUMET! You say RUE PLUMET? Are there not some barracks down there? Why yes, your cousin Théodule—the lancer, the officer—has told me about her. A lassie, my good friend, a lassie! RUE PLUMET, it comes back to me now. I have heard tell about this little girl of the RUE PLUMET. Your taste is not bad. They say she is nice; make her your mistress."

Marius turned pale. Marius understood and saw it as a deadly insult to Cosette. That phrase, *"Make her your mistress,"* entered the heart of the chaste young man like a sword.

He rose, picked up his hat, which was on the floor, and walked toward the door with a firm and assured step. There he turned, bowed profoundly before his grandfather, raised his head again, and said, "Five years ago you slandered my father; today you have slandered my wife. I ask nothing more of you, monsieur. Adieu."

Grandfather Gillenormand, astounded, opened his mouth, stretched out his arms, attempted to rise, but before he could utter a word, the door closed and Marius had disappeared. The old man was for a few moments motionless, and as it were thunderstruck, unable to speak or breathe. At last he tore himself from his chair, ran to the door as fast as a man who is ninety-one can run, opened it, and cried, "Help!"

His daughter appeared, then the servants. He continued with a pitiful rattle in his voice, "Run after him! Catch him! What have I done to him! He is mad! He is going away! Oh! This time he will not come back!"

He went to the window which looked upon the street, opened it with his tremulous old hands, hung more than half his body outside, and cried, "Marius! Marius!"

But Marius was already out of hearing. The nonagenarian lifted his hands to his temples two or three times with an expression of anguish, drew back tottering, and sank into an armchair, pulseless, voiceless, tearless, shaking his head, having now nothing in his eyes or in his heart but something deep and mournful, which resembled night.

Chapter 51

That very day, toward four o'clock in the afternoon, Jean Valjean was sitting alone upon a solitary embankment of the Champ de Mars. He wore his workingman's trousers and his cap with the long visor. He was now calm and happy in regard to Cosette; what had for some time alarmed and disturbed him was dissipated; but within a week or two anxieties of a different nature had come upon him. One day, when walking on the boulevard, he had seen Thénardier; thanks to his disguise, Thénardier had not recognized him. But since then Jean Valjean had seen him again several times, and he was now certain that Thénardier was prowling about the quarter. This was sufficient to make him take a serious step.

Paris was not quiet. The political troubles had this inconvenience for him who had anything in his life to conceal, that the police had become very active, and very secret. Jean Valjean had decided to leave Paris, and even France, and to pass over to England. He had told Cosette. In less than a week he wished to be gone. He was revolving all manner of thoughts in his mind: Thénardier, the police, the journey, and the difficulty of procuring a passport. On all these points he was fretful. Finally, an inexplicable circumstance had added to his alarm. Rising early one day, being the only one up in the house and walking in the garden before Cosette's shutters were open, he had suddenly come upon this line scratched upon the wall, probably with a nail: *16, Rue de la Verrerie*.

It was quite recent; the lines were white in the old black mortar. It had probably been written during the night. What was it? An address? A signal for others? A warning for him? At all events, it was evident that the garden had been violated, and that some persons unknown had penetrated into it. He recalled the strange incidents which had already alarmed the house. He took good care not to speak to Cosette of the line written on the wall, for fear of frightening her.

In the midst of these meditations, he perceived, by a shadow which the sun projected, that somebody had just stopped upon the crest of the embankment immediately behind him. He was about to turn round, when a folded paper fell upon his knees, as if a hand had dropped it from above his head. He took the paper, unfolded it, and read on it this word, written in large letters with a pencil: *REMOVE.*

Jean Valjean rose hastily; there was no longer anybody on the embankment. He returned home immediately, full of thought.

Chapter 52

Marius had left M. Gillenormand's desolate. He had entered with a very small hope; he came out with an immense despair. He began to walk the streets, the consolation of those who suffer. He returned to Courfeyrac's and threw himself, dressed as he was, upon his mattress. It was broad sunlight when he fell asleep. When he awoke, he saw standing in the room, their hats upon their heads, all ready to go out, and very busy, Courfeyrac, Enjolras, and Combeferre.

Courfeyrac said to him, "Are you going to the funeral of General Lamarque*?"

Marius paid no attention to what he said. He went out some time after them. He put into his pocket the pistols which Javert had confided to him at the time of the adventure of the third of February and which had remained in his hands.

These pistols were still loaded. He rambled about all day without knowing where; it rained at intervals, but he did not perceive it; for his dinner he bought a penny roll at a baker's, put it in his pocket, and forgot it. At intervals, while walking along the most deserted boulevards, he seemed to hear strange sounds in Paris. He roused himself from his reverie, and said, "Are they fighting?"

At nightfall, at precisely nine o'clock, as he had promised Cosette, he was in the RUE PLUMET. When he approached the grating, he forgot everything else. It was forty-eight hours since he had seen Cosette; he was going to see her again; every other thought faded away, and he felt now only a deep and wonderful joy. Those minutes in which we live centuries always have this sovereign and wonderful peculiarity, that for the moment while they are passing, they entirely fill the heart.

Marius displaced the grating and sprang into the garden. Cosette was not at the place where she usually waited for him. He raised his eyes and saw that the shutters of the house were closed. He took a turn around the garden and found it deserted.

Marius fixed his despairing eyes upon that dismal house, as black, as silent, and more empty than a tomb. He looked at the stone seat where he had passed so many hours with Cosette. Then he sat down upon the steps, his heart full of tenderness and resolution. He blessed his love in the depths of his thought, and he said to himself that since Cosette was gone, there was nothing more for him but to die.

Suddenly he heard a voice which appeared to come from the street, and which cried through the trees, "Monsieur Marius!"

He arose.

"Your friends are expecting you at the barricade, in the RUE DE LA CHANVRERIE."

This voice was not entirely unknown to him. It resembled the harsh and roughened voice of Éponine. Marius ran to the grating, pushed aside the movable bar, passed his head through, and saw somebody who appeared to him to be a young man, rapidly disappearing in the twilight.

The next dawn, Marius's friend Father Mabeuf, the churchwarden, was seated on the stone post in the garden, and he might have been seen from over the hedge all the morning motionless, his head bowed down, his eye vaguely fixed upon the withered beds. At intervals he wept; the old man did not seem to perceive it. In the afternoon, extraordinary sounds broke out in Paris. They resembled musket shots. Father Mabeuf raised his head. He saw a gardener going by, and asked, "What is that?"

General Lamarque : Lamarque was an outspoken political figure known as a defender of the people, and his death in 1832 was a contributing factor to the June 1832 uprising. *

PONT DE L'ARCHEVÊCHÉ, PARIS • UNKNOWN ARTIST • 1848

The gardener answered in the most quiet tone, his spade upon his shoulder. "They are fighting."

Father Mabeuf went into the house, took his hat, and went away with a bewildered air.

Chapter 53

In 1832, Paris had for a long time been ready for a commotion. The great city resembles a piece of artillery; when it is loaded, the falling of a spark is enough. In June 1832, the spark was the death of General Lamarque.

Lamarque was a man of renown and of action. He had successively, under the empire and under the Restoration, demonstrated the two braveries necessary to the two epochs—the bravery of the battlefield and the bravery of the rostrum*. He was as eloquent as he had been valiant. After having upheld command, he upheld liberty. His death, which had been looked for, was dreaded by the people as a loss and by the government as an opportunity. This death was a mourning. Like everything which is bitter, mourning may turn into revolt.

The eve and the morning of the fifth of June, the day fixed for the funeral of Lamarque, in the quarter of Saint Antoine, men armed themselves as they could. The procession of General Lamarque passed through Paris with official military pomp, somewhat increased by way of precaution. Two battalions, drums muffled, muskets reversed, and ten thousand National Guards, their sabers at their sides, with their batteries of artillery escorted the coffin. The hearse was drawn by young men. The officers of the Invalides* followed immediately, bearing branches of laurel*. Then came a countless multitude, strange and agitated, children waving green branches, stonecutters and carpenters who were on strike, printers walking two by two, uttering cries, almost all brandishing clubs, a few swords, without order, and yet with a single soul. On the cross alleys of the boulevards, in the branches of the trees, on the balconies, at the windows, on the roofs, were swarms of heads, men, women, children; their eyes were full of anxiety. An armed multitude was passing by; a terrified multitude was looking on.

The government also was observing, with its hand upon the hilt of the sword. Anxious authority held suspended over the threatening multitude twenty-four thousand soldiers in the city and thirty thousand in the banlieue*.

The cortège* made its way, with a feverish slowness, from the house of death, along the boulevards as far as the Bastille*. It rained from time to time. At the Bastille, long and formidable files of the curious from the quarter of Saint Antoine made their junction with the cortège, and a certain terrible ebullition began to upheave the multitude.

The hearse passed the Bastille, followed the canal, crossed the little bridge, and reached the esplanade* of the bridge of

Austerlitz. There it stopped. The vast assemblage became silent. Lafayette* spoke and bade farewell to Lamarque. It was a touching and august moment; all heads were uncovered; all hearts throbbed. Suddenly a man on horseback, dressed in black, appeared in the midst of the throng with a red flag*!

Meanwhile, on the left bank, the municipal cavalry was in motion. The dragoons* were advancing at a walk, in silence, their pistols in their holsters, their sabers in their sheaths, their muskets in their rests, with an air of gloomy expectation.

At two hundred paces from the little bridge, they halted. Then the dragoons and the multitude came together. The women fled in terror.

What took place in that fatal moment? Nobody could tell. It was the dark moment when two clouds mingle. There are no more words, the tempest breaks loose, stones fall like hail, musketry bursts forth, a barricade is planned out, the young men crowd back, pass the bridge of Austerlitz with the hearse at a run, and charge on the municipal guard, the mass scatters in every direction, a rumor of war flies to the four corners of Paris, men cry, "To arms!" They run, they fly, they resist. Wrath sweeps them along as the wind sweeps along a fire.

It was this noise and commotion that Father Mabeuf, the churchwarden, heard, and he rushed toward its source. It was this, too, that Marius heard in the afternoon; but with his mind filled with Cosette, he heeded nothing. It was only when he found her gone, and in desperation was about to commit suicide, that the voice of Éponine called him back.

Enjolras and his friends were on the BOULEVARD BOURDON, near the warehouses, at the moment the dragoons charged. Enjolras, Courfeyrac, and Combeferre were among those who ran crying, "To the barricades!" Little Gavroche, who was of course in the crowd, ran with them.

In the RUE LESDIGUIÈRES they met an old man trudging along, walking zigzag, as if he were drunk. Courfeyrac recognized Marius's friend Father Mabeuf. He knew him from having seen him many times accompanying Marius to his door. Knowing the peaceful and timid habits of the old churchwarden, and astounded at seeing him in the midst of this tumult, walking among the bullets, he went up to him and exchanged this dialogue:

"Monsieur Mabeuf, go home."

"What for?"

"There is going to be a row."

"Very well."

"Saber strokes, musket shots, cannon shots, Monsieur Mabeuf."

"Very well. Where are you going, you boys?"

"We are going to pitch the government over."

"Very well." And he followed them. From that moment he did not utter a word. His step suddenly became firm.

"What a desperate goodman!" murmured the students.

rostrum : a raised platform on which a person stands to make a public speech

Invalides (Hôtel des Invalides) : a complex of buildings in Paris that housed military officers and was a retirement home for war veterans

branches of laurel : a symbol of triumph dating back to Greek mythology

banlieue : a suburb of a French city, especially Paris; an outlying housing development in a French city

cortège : a solemn procession, especially for a funeral

Bastille (Bastille Saint-Antoine) : a fortress in Paris used as a prison by the kings of France; it was stormed by a crowd on 14 July 1789 and came to symbolize the French Republican movement

esplanade : an open, level space separating a fortress from a town

Lafayette : The Marquis de Lafayette was a French aristocrat and military officer who fought in the American Revolutionary War and was a key figure in the French Revolution of 1789 and the 1830 July Revolution.

red flag : In the military, unofficially a red flag would be lifted to show the enemy they would be given no quarter.

dragoon : an infantryman mounted on horseback

The rumor ran through the assemblage that he was an ancient conventionist*, an old regicide*. The company had turned into the RUE DE LA VERRERIE. Little Gavroche marched on singing with all his might.

The band increased at every moment. Toward the RUE DES BILLETTES a tall man, who was turning gray, whose rough and bold mien Courfeyrac, Enjolras, and Combeferre noticed, but whom none of them knew, joined them. Gavroche, busy singing, paid no attention to this man.

It happened that in the RUE DE LA VERRERIE, they passed by Courfeyrac's door. The portress hailed him. "Monsieur Courfeyrac, there is someone who wishes to speak to you. He has been waiting more than an hour for you to come home."

At the same time, a sort of young workingman, thin, pale, small, freckled, dressed in a torn blouse and patched pantaloons of ribbed velvet, and who had rather the appearance of a girl in boy's clothes than of a man, came out of the lodge and said to Courfeyrac in a voice which, to be sure, was not the least in the world a woman's voice, "Monsieur Marius, if you please?"

"He is not in."

"Will he be in this evening?"

"I don't know anything about it. I am going to the barricades."

"Do you want me to go with you?"

"If you like," answered Courfeyrac. "The road is free; the streets belong to everybody." And he ran off to rejoin his friends. It was not until a quarter of an hour afterward that he perceived that the young man had in fact followed them.

A mob does not go precisely where it wishes; a gust of wind carries it along. They found themselves, without really knowing how, in the RUE SAINT DENIS.

CHAPTER 54

The RUE DE LA CHANVRERIE, which led from the RUE SAINT DENIS, was a short street which gradually narrowed away like an elongated funnel, but with two black openings on the right and on the left. At the corner of the opening on the right might be seen a house only two stories high, in which had been festively installed for three hundred years an illustrious wineshop known as Corinth. The landlord was Father Hucheloup. A basement room housing the counter, a room on the first floor with a billiard table, a spiral wooden staircase piercing the ceiling, wine on the tables, smoke on the walls, candles in broad day—such was the wineshop. A stairway with a trapdoor in the basement led to the cellar.

Corinth was one of the meeting places, if not rallying places, of Courfeyrac and his friends.

On the fifth of June, Bossuet and two other young men, friends of Courfeyrac and Enjolras, were breakfasting at Corinth. They had decided not to attend the funeral of General Lamarque. Suddenly they heard a tumult, hurried steps, cries to arms! They rushed to the window and saw in the RUE SAINT DENIS, at the end of the RUE DE LA CHANVRERIE, Enjolras passing, carbine in hand, and Gavroche with his pistol, Courfeyrac with his sword, Combeferre with his musket, and all the armed and stormy gathering which followed them.

Bossuet improvised a speaking trumpet with his two hands and shouted, "Courfeyrac! Ahoy! Where are you going?"

"To make a barricade," answered Courfeyrac.

"Well, this is a good place! Make it here!"

"That is true," said Courfeyrac. And at a sign from Courfeyrac, the band rushed into the RUE DE LA CHANVRERIE.

The place was indeed admirably chosen, the entrance of

the street wide, the further end contracted and like a cul-de-sac, Corinth throttling it, easy to bar at the right and left, no attack possible except from the RUE SAINT DENIS, that is from the front, and without cover.

At the eruption of the mob, dismay seized the whole street. Shutters were closed from the ground to the roofs; one frightened old woman fixed a mattress before her window as a shield against the musketry. The wineshop was the only house which remained open, because the band had rushed into it.

In a few minutes, twenty iron bars had been wrested from the grated front of the wineshop, twenty yards of pavement had been torn up; Gavroche had seized and tipped over a dray* which contained three barrels full of lime*, which they had placed under the piles of paving stones; Enjolras had opened the trapdoor of the cellar, and all Hucheloup's empty casks had gone to flank the lime barrels. Some timbers had been pulled down from the front of a neighboring house and laid upon the casks. Half the street was already barred by a rampart higher than a man. An omnibus* with two white horses that passed at the end of the street was seized and a moment later, lying on its side, completed the barring of the street.

The rain had ceased. Recruits had arrived. Some working-men had brought under their blouses a keg of powder and a hamper containing bottles of vitriol*. Enjolras, Combeferre, and Courfeyrac directed everything. Two barricades were now being built at the same time, both resting on the house of Corinth and making a right angle; the larger one closed the RUE DE LA CHANVRERIE, while the other closed the opening on the right, constructed only of casks and paving stones. There were about fifty laborers there, some thirty armed with muskets.

Nothing could be more fantastic and more motley than this band. All were hurrying as they talked about the chances that Paris would rise.

A fire had been kindled in the kitchen, and they were melting pitchers, dishes, forks, all the pewter ware of the wineshop, into bullets. They drank through it all. The man of tall stature whom Courfeyrac, Combeferre, and Enjolras had noticed at the moment he joined the company at the corner of the RUE DES BILLETTES was working on the little barricade and making himself useful there. Gavroche worked on the large one. As for the young man who had waited for Courfeyrac at his house and had asked him for Monsieur Marius, he had disappeared.

Gavroche, completely carried away and radiant, had charged himself with making all ready—filling the air, being everywhere at once. He vexed the loungers, excited the idle, reanimated the weary, provoked the thoughtful; he kept some in cheerfulness, others in wrath, others in anger, all in motion. There was an interval of about twenty yards between the great barricade and the tall houses which formed the end of the street. All was accomplished without hindrance in less than an hour by this handful of bold men. The two barricades were finished and the red flag run up; a table was dragged out of the wineshop. Enjolras brought a square box filled with cartridges.

Courfeyrac distributed them with a smile. Each one received thirty cartridges. Many had powder and set about making more cartridges with the balls which they were molding. As for the keg of powder, it was on a table by itself near the door. They loaded their muskets and their carbines all together with a solemn gravity. The barricades built, and the posts assigned, the muskets loaded, alone in these fearful

conventionist : a member of the French National Convention (1792–95), which had sentenced King Louis XVI to death in January 1793

regicide : a person who kills a king

dray : a truck or cart for delivering beer barrels or other heavy loads, especially a low one without sides

lime : a highly caustic powder used in cement and mortar

omnibus : a long horse-drawn passenger-carrying vehicle that transported people along the main thoroughfares of Paris

vitriol : sulfuric acid

streets in which there were now no passers; surrounded by these dumb and dead houses, which throbbed with no human motion; enwrapped by the deepening shadows of the twilight, which was beginning to fall, and this silence, through which they felt the advance of something inexpressibly terrifying; isolated, armed, determined, tranquil, they waited.

CHAPTER 55

It was now a quiet night; nothing came. This prolonged respite was a sign that the government was taking its time and massing its forces. These fifty men were awaiting sixty thousand.

Enjolras went to find Gavroche, who had set himself to making cartridges in the basement room. Gavroche at this moment was very much engaged, not exactly with his cartridges. The man from the RUE DES BILLETTES, had just entered the basement room and had taken a seat at the table which was least lighted. When he came in, Gavroche mechanically followed him with his eyes, admiring his musket; then, suddenly, when the man had sat down, the gamin arose. The man had fallen into a kind of meditation. The gamin approached this thoughtful personage and began to turn about him.

It was in the deepest of this examination that Enjolras accosted him.

"You are small," said Enjolras. "Nobody will see you. Go out of the barricades, glide along by the houses, look about the streets a little, and come and tell me what is going on."

Gavroche straightened himself up. "I will go! Meantime, trust the little folks; distrust the big—" And Gavroche, raising his head and lowering his voice, added, pointing to the man of the RUE DES BILLETTES, "He is a spy."

"You are sure?"

"It isn't a fortnight since he pulled me by the ear off the cornice of the Pont Royal."

Enjolras hastily left the gamin and murmured a few words very low to a workingman who was there. The workingman went out of the room and returned almost immediately, accompanied by three others. The four men, four broad-shouldered porters, placed themselves discreetly behind the table on which the man of the RUE DES BILLETTES was leaning.

Then Enjolras approached the man and asked him, "Who are you?"

At this abrupt question, the man gave a start. He smiled disdainfully and resolutely, and answered with a haughty gravity, "I am an officer of the government."

"Your name is?"

"Javert."

Enjolras made a sign to the four men. In a twinkling, before Javert had had time to turn around, he was collared, thrown down, bound, searched. They found upon him a little round card bearing on one side the arms of France, engraved with the legend *Surveillance et vigilance*, and on the other side this endorsement: *JAVERT, inspector of police, aged fifty-two*, and the signature of the prefect of police of the time. He had besides his watch and his purse, which contained a few pieces of money. They left him his purse and his watch.

The search finished, they raised Javert, tied his arms behind his back, and fastened him standing backed up against a post in the middle of the basement room. Gavroche, who had witnessed the whole scene and approved it all by silent nods of his head, approached Javert and said to him, "The mouse has caught the cat."

All this was executed rapidly, and Javert had not uttered a cry. He was so surrounded with ropes that he could make no movement. He held up his head with the intrepid serenity of the man who has never lied.

"It is a spy," said Enjolras to Courfeyrac and Combeferre,

who had run in. And turning toward Javert, "You will be shot ten minutes before the barricade is taken."

Javert replied in his most imperious tone, "Why not immediately?"

"We are economizing powder."

"Then do it with a knife."

"Spy," said the handsome Enjolras, "we are judges, not murderers."

Then he called to Gavroche, "Do what I told you."

"I am going," cried Gavroche.

The gamin made a military salute and sprang gaily through the opening in the large barricade.

Courfeyrac again saw along the barricade the small young man who in the morning had called at his house for Marius. This boy, who had a bold and reckless air, had come at night to rejoin the insurgents.

Chapter 56

The clock of Saint Merri had struck ten. Enjolras and Combeferre had sat down, carbines in hand, near the opening of the great barricade, listening. Suddenly, in the midst of this dismal calm, a clear young voice, which seemed to come from the RUE SAINT DENIS, arose and began to sing distinctly an old popular air. They grasped each other by the hand.

"It is Gavroche," said Enjolras.

"He is warning us," said Combeferre.

A headlong run startled the empty street; they saw a creature nimbler than a clown climb over the omnibus, and Gavroche bounded into the barricade all breathless, brandishing the cartridges. "Here they are."

An electric thrill ran through the whole barricade. Every man had taken his post for the combat. Forty-three insurgents, among them Enjolras, Combeferre, Courfeyrac, Bossuet, and Gavroche, were on their knees behind the great barricade, the barrels of their muskets and their carbines pointed, watchful, silent, ready to fire, six stationed in the windows of the two upper stories of Corinth.

A few moments more elapsed, then a sound of steps, measured, heavy, numerous, was distinctly heard. It approached still nearer and stopped. They could see nothing but then discovered in that dense obscurity a multitude of metallic threads, as fine as needles, which moved about. They were bayonets and musket barrels dimly lighted up by the distant reflection of the torch. There was still a pause, as if on both sides they were awaiting something.

Suddenly, from the depth of that shadow, a voice, so much the more ominous because nobody could be seen, cried, "Who is there?"

At the same time they heard the click of the leveled muskets.

Enjolras answered in a lofty and ringing tone, "The French Revolution!"

"Fire!" said the voice.

A flash empurpled all the facades on the street, as if the door of a furnace were opened and suddenly closed. A fearful explosion burst over the barricade. The red flag fell. The volley had been so heavy and so dense that it had cut the staff. Some balls, which ricocheted from the cornices of the houses, entered the barricade and wounded several men.

The impression produced by this first charge was freezing; it was evident that they faced a whole regiment at least.

"Comrades," cried Courfeyrac, "don't waste the powder. Let us wait to reply till they come into the street."

"And, first of all," said Enjolras, "let us hoist the flag again."

He picked up the flag which had fallen just at his feet. They heard from without the rattling of the ramrods in the muskets; the troops were reloading.

Enjolras continued, "Who is there here who has courage? Who replants the flag on the barricade?"

Nobody answered. To mount the barricade at the moment when without doubt it was aimed at anew was simply death. The bravest hesitated to sentence himself; Enjolras himself felt a shudder. He repeated, "Nobody volunteers?"

Chapter 57

Since they had arrived at Corinth and had commenced building the barricade, hardly any attention had been paid to Father Mabeuf. He had entered the ground floor of the wineshop and sat down; he no longer seemed to look or to think. Courfeyrac and others had accosted him two or three times, warning him of the danger, entreating him to withdraw, but he had appeared not to hear them. When everybody had gone to take his place for the combat, there remained in the basement room only Javert tied to the post, an insurgent with drawn saber watching Javert, and Mabeuf. At the moment of the attack, at the discharge, the physical shock reached him and, as it were, awakened him; he rose suddenly, crossed the room, and at the instant when Enjolras repeated his appeal, "Nobody volunteers?" they saw the old man appear in the doorway of the wineshop.

His presence produced some commotion in the group. A cry arose. "It is the representative of the people!"

He walked straight to Enjolras; the insurgents fell back before him with a religious awe; he snatched the flag from Enjolras and then, with shaking head but firm foot, began to climb slowly up the stairway of paving stones built into the barricade. At each step it was frightful; his white hair, his large forehead bald and wrinkled, his hollow eyes, his old arm raising the red banner surged up out of the shadow and grew grand in

the bloody light of the torch, and they seemed to see the ghost of '93* rising out of the earth, the flag of terror in its hand.

When he was on the top of the last step, when this trembling and terrible phantom, standing upon that mound of rubbish before twelve hundred invisible muskets, rose up, in the face of death and as if he were stronger than it, the whole barricade had in the darkness a supernatural and colossal appearance.

In the midst of this silence the old man waved the red flag and cried, "*Vive la révolution! Vive la république!* Fraternity! Equality! And death!"

Then the same ringing voice which had cried, "Who is there?" cried, "Disperse!"

M. Mabeuf, pallid, haggard, his eyes illumined by the mournful fires of insanity, raised the flag above his head and repeated, "*Vive la république!*"

ghost of '93 : In 1793, during the French Revolution, King Louis XVI, Marie Antoinette, and many other French nobles were executed. *

"Fire!" said the voice.

A second discharge, like a shower of grape*, beat against the barricade. The old man fell upon his knees, then rose up, let the flag drop, and fell backward upon the pavement within, like a log, at full length, with his arms crossed.

Enjolras stooped down, raised the old man's head, and timidly kissed him on the forehead; then, separating his arms and handling the dead with a tender care, as if he feared to hurt him, he took off his coat, showed the bleeding holes to all, and said, "There now is our flag!"

They threw a long black shawl over Father Mabeuf. Six men made a litter* of their muskets; they laid the corpse upon it and bore it, bareheaded, with a solemn slowness, to the large table in the basement room.

During this time little Gavroche, who alone had not left his post and had remained on the watch, thought he saw some men approaching the barricade with a stealthy step. Suddenly he cried, "Take care!"

Courfeyrac, Enjolras, Combeferre, Bossuet, all sprang tumultuously from the wineshop. There was hardly a moment to spare. They perceived a sparkling breadth of bayonets undulating above the barricade. Municipal guards of tall stature were penetrating, some by climbing over the omnibus, others by the opening, pushing before them the gamin, who fell back but did not fly. The moment was critical. It was that first fearful instant of the inundation; a second more, and the barricade had been breached.

The first municipal guard who entered fell at the very muzzle of a carbine; the second killed the first defender with his bayonet. Another guard had already prostrated Courfeyrac. The largest of all marched upon Gavroche with fixed bayonet. The gamin took Javert's enormous musket in his little arms, aimed it resolutely at the giant, and pulled the trigger. Nothing went off. Javert had not loaded his musket. The municipal guard burst into a laugh and raised his bayonet over the child.

Before the bayonet touched Gavroche, the musket dropped from the soldier's hands. A ball had struck the municipal guard in the middle of the forehead, and he fell on his back. A second ball struck the other guard, who had assailed Courfeyrac, full in the breast, and threw him upon the pavement.

It was Marius who had just entered the barricade. That voice which through the twilight had called Marius to the barricade of the RUE DE LA CHANVRERIE sounded to him like the voice of destiny. Armed with Javert's pistols, he wished to die, and the opportunity had presented itself.

Marius now threw away his discharged pistols, but he noticed the keg of powder near the door. As he turned half round, looking in that direction, a soldier aimed at him. At the moment the soldier aimed at Marius, a hand was laid upon the muzzle of the musket and stopped it. It was somebody who had sprung forward, the young workingman with velvet pantaloons. The shot went off, passed through the hand, and perhaps also through the workingman, for he fell, but the ball did not reach Marius. Marius hardly noticed it. Still he had caught a dim glimpse of that musket directed at him and that hand which had stopped it, and he had heard the shot.

The insurgents, surprised but not dismayed, had rallied. Most of them had gone up to the window of the second story and to the dormer windows. The most determined, with Enjolras, Courfeyrac, and Combeferre, openly faced the ranks of soldiers and guards which crowded the barricade and were taking aim, the muzzles of the guns almost touching.

An officer with huge epaulets extended his sword and said, "Take aim!"

"Fire!" said Enjolras.

The two explosions were simultaneous, and everything disappeared in the smoke. When the smoke cleared away, on both sides the combatants were seen, thinned out but still in the same places, and reloading their pieces in silence.

Suddenly a thundering voice was heard, crying, "Begone, or I'll blow up the barricade!"

All turned in the direction whence the voice came. Marius had taken the keg of powder and, in the smoke of obscure fog which filled the entrenched enclosure, had glided along the barricade as far as that cage of paving stones in which the torch was fixed. To pull out the torch, to put the keg of powder in its place, to push the pile of paving stones upon the keg—all this had been for Marius the work of stooping down and rising up; and now all—National Guards, municipal guards, officers, soldiers, grouped at the other extremity of the barricade—beheld him with horror, his foot upon the stones, the torch in his hand. And he lowered the torch toward the keg of powder.

But there was no longer anybody on the wall. The assailants, leaving their dead and wounded, fled pell-mell and in disorder toward the end of the street, and were again lost in the night. It was a rout. The barricade was redeemed.

All flocked round Marius. Courfeyrac sprang to his neck. Marius inquired, "Where is the chief?"

"You are the chief," said Enjolras.

Chapter 58

A few minutes later, Marius heard his name faintly pronounced in the obscurity. He shuddered, for he recognized the voice which had called him two hours before, through the grating in the RUE PLUMET. Only this voice now seemed to be but a breath.

He looked about him and saw nobody. He started to leave the barricade.

"Monsieur Marius!" repeated the voice. "At your feet."

He stooped and saw a form in the shadow, which was dragging itself toward him. The torch enabled him to distinguish a blouse, a pair of torn pantaloons of coarse velvet, bare feet, and something which resembled a pool of blood.

Marius caught a glimpse of a pale face which rose toward him and said to him, "You do not know me?"

"No."

"Éponine."

Marius bent down quickly. It was indeed that unhappy girl. She was dressed as a man.

"How came you here? What are you doing there?"

"I am dying," said she.

"You are wounded! Wait, I will carry you into the room! They will dress your wounds!" And he tried to pass his arm under her to lift her.

In lifting her, he touched her hand. She uttered a feeble cry.

"Have I hurt you?" asked Marius.

"A little."

She raised her hand into Marius's sight, and Marius saw in the center of that hand a black hole.

"What is the matter with your hand?" said he.

"It is pierced."

"How?"

"Did you see a musket aimed at you?"

"Yes, and a hand which stopped it."

"That was mine."

"What madness! Poor child! But that is not so bad—if that is all, it is nothing. Let me carry you to a bed. They will care for you."

She murmured, "The ball passed through my hand, but it went out through my back. It is useless to take me from here!

grape : a type of shot composed of a mass of small metal balls or slugs packed tightly into a canvas bag, resembling a cluster of grapes. When fired, the balls spread out with an effect similar to that of a giant shotgun.

litter : a device (such as a stretcher) for carrying a sick or injured person

I will tell you how you can care for me, better than a surgeon. Sit down by me on that stone."

He obeyed; she laid her head on Marius's knees, and without looking at him she said, "Oh! How good it is! How kind he is! That is it! I don't suffer anymore!"

She remained a moment in silence; then she turned her head with effort and looked at Marius. "Do you know, Monsieur Marius? It worried me that you should go into that garden."

She continued. "See, you are lost! Nobody will get out of the barricade now. It was I who led you into this, it was! You are going to die, I am sure. And still when I saw him aiming at you, I put up my hand upon the muzzle of the musket. How absurd it is! But it was because I wanted to die before you. When I got this ball, I dragged myself here, nobody saw me, nobody picked me up. I waited for you. Oh! If you knew, I bit my blouse, I suffered so much! Now I am well. Don't go away! It will not be long now!"

She was sitting almost upright, but her voice was very low and broken by coughs. At intervals the death rattle interrupted her. She brought her face as near as she could to Marius's face. She added, "Listen, I don't want to deceive you. I have a letter in my pocket for you. Since yesterday. I was told to put it in the post. I kept it. I didn't want it to reach you. But you would not like it of me, perhaps, when we meet again so soon. Take your letter."

She grasped Marius's hand convulsively with her wounded hand, but she seemed no longer to feel the pain. She put Marius's hand into the pocket of her blouse. Marius took the letter.

She made a sign of satisfaction and of consent. "Now, promise me—" And she hesitated.

"What?" asked Marius.

"Promise to kiss me on the forehead when I am dead. I shall feel it."

She let her head fall back upon Marius's knees, and her eyelids closed. Éponine lay motionless, but just when Marius supposed her forever asleep, she slowly opened her eyes in which the gloomy deepness of death appeared, and said to him with an accent the sweetness of which already seemed to come from another world, "And then, do you know, Monsieur Marius, I believe I was a little in love with you."

She essayed to smile again and expired. Marius kept his promise. He kissed her forehead. This was not an infidelity to Cosette; it was a thoughtful and gentle farewell to an unhappy soul.

Not without a tremor had he taken the letter Éponine had given him. He was impatient to read it. He laid her gently upon the ground and went away. Something told him that he could not read that letter in sight of this corpse. He went to a candle in the basement room. It was a little note; the address was in a woman's hand. He broke the seal and read,

> *My beloved, alas! My father wishes to start immediately. We shall be tonight in the Rue de l'Homme Armé, no. 7. In a week we shall be in London. —COSETTE. June 4th.*

What happened may be told in a few words. Éponine had done it all. It was she who, in the Champ de Mars, had given Jean Valjean the expressive warning *REMOVE.* Jean Valjean returned home and said to Cosette, "We start tonight, and we are going to the RUE DE L'HOMME ARMÉ with Toussaint. Next week we shall be in London."

Cosette, prostrated by this unexpected blow, had hastily written two lines to Marius. But how should she get the letter to the post? In this anxiety, Cosette saw, through the grating, Éponine in men's clothes, and handed her five francs and the letter, saying to her, "Carry this letter to its address right away." Éponine put the letter in her pocket.

Marius had a pocketbook with him. He tore out a leaf and wrote with a pencil these few lines,

Our marriage was impossible. I have asked my grandfather; he has refused. I am without fortune, and you also. I ran to your house; I did not find you. You know the promise that I gave you? I keep it, I die, I love you. When you read this, my soul will be near you, and will smile upon you.

He folded the paper, and wrote upon it the address:

To Mademoiselle Cosette Fauchelevent, at M. Fauchelevent's, Rue de l'Homme Armé, no. 7.

The letter folded, he remained a moment in thought, took his pocketbook again, opened it, and wrote these lines on the first page with the same pencil:

My name is Marius Pontmercy. Carry my corpse to my grandfather's, M. Gillenormand, Rue des Filles du Calvaire, no. 6, in the Marais.

He put the book into his coat pocket; then he called Gavroche. "Will you do something for me?"

"Anything," said Gavroche. "Without you, I should have been cooked."

"You see this letter? Take it. Go out of the barricade immediately, and tomorrow morning you will carry it to its address, to Mademoiselle Cosette, at M. Fauchelevent's, RUE DE L'HOMME ARMÉ, number seven. Go, right away!"

Gavroche stood there, undecided. Suddenly, with one of his birdlike motions, he took the letter.

"All right," said he. And he started off at a run.

Gavroche had an idea which decided him: *It is hardly midnight; the* RUE DE L'HOMME ARMÉ *is not far. I will carry the letter right away, and I shall get back in time.*

Chapter 59

On the eve of that same day, June 5, Jean Valjean, accompanied by Cosette and Toussaint, had installed himself in the RUE DE L'HOMME ARMÉ. Cosette had not left the RUE PLUMET without an attempt at resistance. For the first time since they had lived together, Cosette's will and Jean Valjean's will had shown themselves distinct, and had been, if not conflicting, at least contradictory. There was objection on one side and inflexibility on the other. Cosette had to yield.

They both arrived at the RUE DE L'HOMME ARMÉ without saying a word, Jean Valjean so fretful that he did not perceive Cosette's sadness, Cosette so sad that she did not perceive Jean Valjean's anxiety. Jean Valjean had brought Toussaint, which he had never done in his preceding visits.

In this departure from the RUE PLUMET, which was almost a flight, Jean Valjean carried nothing but his little valise, christened by Cosette "the inseparable." Cosette herself carried only her writing desk and her blotter. Jean Valjean, to increase the solitude and mystery of this disappearance, had arranged to leave the cottage on the RUE PLUMET at the close of the day, which left Cosette time to write her note to Marius. They arrived in the RUE DE L'HOMME ARMÉ after nightfall. They went silently to bed.

The next morning, while walking up and down with slow steps, Jean Valjean suddenly met something strange. In the inclined mirror which hung above the sideboard, he distinctly read the lines which follow:

My beloved, alas! My father wishes to start immediately. We shall be tonight in the Rue de l'Homme Armé, no. 7. In a week we shall be in London. —COSETTE. June 4th.

Jean Valjean stood aghast.

Cosette, on arriving, had laid her blotter on the sideboard before the mirror and, wholly absorbed in her sorrowful anguish, had forgotten it there. Jean Valjean went to the mirror. He read the lines again, but he did not believe it. Little by little his perception became more precise; he looked at Cosette's blotter, and the consciousness of the real fact returned to him.

Jean Valjean tottered and sank down into the old armchair by the sideboard. Poor old Jean Valjean did not, certainly, love Cosette otherwise than as a father; but, as we have already mentioned, into this paternity the very bereavement of his life had introduced every love; he loved Cosette as his daughter, and he loved her as his mother, and he loved her as his sister; and, as he had never had either sweetheart or wife, that sentiment, also, the most indestructible of all, was mingled with the others, pure.

He put together certain circumstances, certain dates, and he said to himself, "It is he." With his first conjecture, he hit Marius. He did not know the name, but he found the man at once.

After he had fully determined that that young man was at the bottom of this state of affairs, and that it all came from him, he, Jean Valjean, the regenerated man, the man who had labored so much upon his soul, the man who had made so many efforts to resolve all life, all misery, and all misfortune into love, looked within himself, and there saw a specter, a vision of hatred.

Five minutes afterward found him in the street. He was bareheaded, seated upon the stone block by the door of his house. He seemed to be listening. The night had come.

Suddenly he raised his eyes; somebody was walking in the street. Gavroche had just arrived in the RUE DE L'HOMME ARMÉ and appeared to be searching for something. He saw Jean Valjean.

"Could you show me number seven?"

"What do you want with number seven?"

Here the boy stopped; he feared that he had said too much. An idea flashed across Jean Valjean's mind. He said to the child, "Have you brought the letter I am waiting for?"

"You?" said Gavroche. "You are not a woman."

"The letter is for Mademoiselle Cosette, isn't it?"

"Cosette?" muttered Gavroche. "Yes."

"Well," resumed Jean Valjean, "I am to deliver the letter to her. Give it to me."

"In that case you must know that I am sent from the barricade?"

"Of course," said Jean Valjean.

Gavroche thrust his hand into his pocket, drew out a folded paper, and handed it to Jean Valjean.

Jean Valjean went in with Marius's letter and read it. In the note he saw only these words: *I die. . . . When you read this, my soul will be near you.* Jean Valjean felt that he was delivered. He would then find himself once more alone with Cosette. He had only to keep the note in his pocket. Cosette would never know what had become of Marius. "If he is not dead yet, it is certain that he will die."

All this said within himself, he became gloomy. About an hour afterward, Jean Valjean went out in the full dress of a National Guard, and armed. He had a loaded musket and a cartridge box full of cartridges. He went in the direction of the markets.

Meanwhile, the insurgents, under the eye of Enjolras, for Marius no longer looked to anything, turned the night to advantage. The barricade was not only repaired but made larger. They raised it two feet. They cleared up the basement room, took the kitchen for a hospital, completed the dressing of the wounds, gathered up the powder scattered over the floor and the tables, cast bullets, made cartridges, distributed the arms of the fallen, cleaned the interior of the redoubt, picked up the fragments, carried away the corpses.

Most of the wounded could and would still fight. There were, upon a straw mattress in the kitchen, five men severely wounded, four of whom were municipal guards. Nothing now remained in the basement room but Mabeuf, under his black cloth, and Javert bound to the post.

About two o'clock in the morning, they took a count. There were left thirty-seven of them. The insurgents were full of hope. They awaited the attack and smiled at it. They had no more doubt of their success than of their cause. Moreover, help was evidently about to come. They counted on it.

All these hopes were communicated from one to another in a sort of cheerful yet terrible whisper. But soon Enjolras reappeared from making a reconnaissance. He listened for a moment to all this joy with folded arms; then, fresh and rosy in the growing whiteness of the morning, he said, "The whole army of Paris fights. A third of that army is pressing upon this barricade. As for the people, they were boiling yesterday, but this morning they do not stir. Nothing to expect, nothing to hope. You are abandoned."

These words fell upon the groups. There was a moment of inexpressible silence, when you might have heard the wings of death.

This moment was short. A voice from the most obscure depths of the group cried to Enjolras, "So be it. Let us make the barricade twenty feet high, and let us all stand by it. Citizens, let us offer the protest of corpses. Let us show that, if the people abandon the republicans, the republicans do not abandon the people."

Chapter 60

After the man of the people had spoken, from all lips arose a strangely satisfied and terrible cry, funereal in meaning and triumphant in tone: "Long live death! Let us all stay!"

"Why all?" said Enjolras.

"All! All!"

Enjolras resumed, "The position is good; the barricade is fine. Thirty men are enough. Why sacrifice forty?"

Marius raised his voice. "Enjolras is right," said he. "No useless sacrifice. I add my voice to his, and we must hasten. There are among you some who have families, mothers, sisters, wives, children. Let those leave the ranks."

Nobody stirred.

"Make haste," said Courfeyrac. "In a quarter of an hour it will be too late."

"Citizens," continued Enjolras, "this is the republic, and universal suffrage reigns. Designate yourselves those who ought to go."

They obeyed. In a few minutes five were unanimously designated and left the ranks.

"There are five!" exclaimed Marius. "But there are only the four uniforms of the wounded guards."

At this moment a fifth uniform dropped, as if from heaven, upon the four others. The fifth man was saved.

Jean Valjean had just entered the barricade.

At the moment he entered the redoubt, nobody had noticed him, all eyes being fixed upon the five chosen ones and upon the four uniforms. Jean Valjean himself saw and understood. He silently stripped off his coat and threw it upon the pile with the others. The commotion was indescribable.

"Who is this man?" asked Bossuet.

"He is," answered Combeferre, "a man who saves others."

Marius added in a grave voice, "I know him."

This assurance was enough for all.

Enjolras turned toward Jean Valjean. "Citizen, you are welcome." And he added, "You know that we are going to die?"

Jean Valjean, without answering, helped the insurgent whom he saved to put on his uniform.

When the five men sent away into life had gone, Enjolras thought of the one condemned to death. He went into the basement room. Javert, tied to the pillar, was thinking.

LOVE EACH OTHER
DEARLY
ALWAYS.
THERE IS SCARCELY
ANYTHING ELSE IN THE WORLD
BUT THAT:
TO LOVE
ONE ANOTHER.
VICTOR HUGO

"Do you need anything?" Enjolras asked him.

"I am uncomfortable at this post," answered Javert. "It was inconsiderate to leave me to pass the night here. Tie me as you please, but you can surely lay me on a table. Like the other." And with a motion of his head he indicated M. Mabeuf's body.

There was, at the back of the room, a long, wide table, upon which they had cast balls and made cartridges. All the cartridges being made and all the powder used up, this table was free. While they were binding Javert to the table, a man at the threshold of the door gazed at him with singular attention. The shade which this man produced made Javert turn his head. He raised his eyes and recognized Jean Valjean. He did not even start; he haughtily dropped his eyelids and merely said, "It is very natural."

It was growing light rapidly. The extremity of the RUE DE LA CHANVRERIE opposite the barricade had been evacuated by the troops. The RUE SAINT DENIS was as silent as the grave.

They had not long to wait. Upon the mouth of the street a piece of artillery appeared. The gunners pushed forward the piece; it was already loaded; the smoke of the burning match was seen.

"Fire!" cried Enjolras.

The whole barricade flashed fire. The explosion was terrible; an avalanche of smoke covered and effaced the gun and the men; in a few seconds the cloud dissipated, and the cannon and the men reappeared; those in charge of the piece placed it in position in front of the barricade, slowly, correctly, and without haste. Not a man had been touched. Then the gunner, bearing his weight on the breech to elevate the range, began to point the cannon with the gravity of an astronomer adjusting a telescope. There was intense anxiety in the barricade. The gun went off; the detonation burst upon them.

"Present!" cried a cheerful voice. And at the same time as the ball, Gavroche tumbled into the barricade. Marius, in sending his letter, had two objects: to say farewell to Cosette and to save Gavroche. He was obliged to be content with half of what he intended.

The gun was about to be fired again. They could not hold out a quarter of an hour in that storm of grape. It was absolutely necessary to deaden the blows. Enjolras threw out his command. "We must put a mattress there."

"We have none," said Combeferre. "The wounded are on them."

There was a mattress, fallen into the street in front of the barricade, in full view between the besieged and the besiegers. Jean Valjean went out, entered the street, passed through the storm of balls, went to the mattress, picked it up, put it on his back, and returned to the barricade. He put the mattress into the opening himself. He fixed it against the wall in such a way that the artillerymen did not see it. This done, they awaited the charge of grape.

They had not long to wait. The cannon vomited its package of shot with a roar. But there was no ricochet. The grape miscarried upon the mattress. The desired effect was obtained. The barricade was preserved. "Citizen," said Enjolras to Jean Valjean, "the republic thanks you."

"This goes well," said Bossuet to Enjolras.

Enjolras shook his head and answered, "A quarter of an hour more of this success, and there will not be ten cartridges in the barricade."

It would seem that Gavroche heard this remark, so he took a basket from the wineshop, went out, and was quietly occupied in emptying into his basket the full cartridge boxes of the National Guards who had been killed on the slope of the redoubt. Some twenty dead lay scattered along the whole length of the street on the pavement. Twenty cartridge boxes for Gavroche, a supply of cartridges for the barricade!

The smoke in the street was like a fog. Under the folds of this veil of smoke, and thanks to his small size, Gavroche could advance far into the street without being seen. He emptied the first seven or eight cartridge boxes without much danger. He crawled on his belly, ran on his hands and feet, took his basket in his teeth, twisted, glided, writhed, wormed his way from one body to another, and emptied a cartridge box as a monkey opens a nut. From the barricade, of which he was still within hearing, they dared not call to him to return, for fear of attracting attention to him.

Just as Gavroche was relieving a sergeant who lay near a stone block of his cartridges, a ball struck the body. "The deuce!" said Gavroche. "So they are killing my dead for me."

A second ball splintered the pavement beside him. A third upset his basket. He rose up straight, on his feet, his hair in the wind, his hands upon his hips, his eye fixed upon the National Guards who were firing. Then he picked up his basket, put into it the cartridges which had fallen out, without losing a single one, and, advancing toward the fusillade, began to empty another cartridge box. There, a fourth ball just missed him again.

The sight was appalling and fascinating. Gavroche, fired at, mocked the firing. He appeared to be very much amused. The insurgents, breathless with anxiety, followed him with their eyes. The barricade was trembling; he was singing.

One bullet, however, better aimed or more treacherous than the others, reached the will-o'-the-wisp child. They saw Gavroche totter; then he fell. The whole barricade gave a cry. Gavroche had fallen only to rise again. He sat up; a long stream of blood rolled down his face; he raised both arms in the air, looked in the direction whence the shot came, and began to sing.

He did not finish. A second ball from the same marksman cut him short. This time he fell with his face upon the pavement and did not stir again. That little great soul had taken flight.

Marius sprang out of the barricade. Combeferre followed him, but it was too late. Gavroche was dead. Combeferre brought back the basket of cartridges; Marius brought back the child.

Alas! thought he. What the father had done for his father he was returning to the son; only Thénardier had brought back his father living, while he brought back the child dead.

When Marius reentered the barricade with Gavroche in his arms, his face, like the child's, was covered with blood. Just as he had stooped down to pick up Gavroche, a ball grazed his skull.

They laid Gavroche on the same table as Mabeuf, and they stretched the black shawl over the two bodies. It was large enough for the old man and the child. Combeferre distributed the cartridges from the basket which he had brought back. This gave each man fifteen shots.

Suddenly between two discharges they heard the distant sound of a clock striking. "It is noon," said Combeferre.

The twelfth stroke had not sounded when Enjolras sprang to his feet and flung down from the top of the barricade this thundering shout: "Carry some paving stones into the house. Fortify the windows with them. Half the men to the muskets; the other half to the stones. Not a minute to lose."

A platoon of sappers*, their axes on their shoulders, had just appeared in order of battle at the end of the street. It was their duty to demolish the barricade preceding the soldiers who were to scale it.

Enjolras's order was executed with haste; in less than a minute, the fortress was complete. He gave his last instructions in the basement room in a quick but deep and calm voice.

The dispositions made, he turned toward Javert and said to him, "I won't forget you." And, laying a pistol on the table, he added, "The last man to leave this room will blow out the spy's brains!"

"Here?" inquired a voice.

"No, do not leave this corpse with ours. You can climb over the little barricade. The man is well tied. You will take him and execute him there."

Here Jean Valjean appeared. He was in the throng of insurgents. He stepped forward and said to Enjolras, "You thanked me just now."

"In the name of the republic. The barricade has two saviors: Marius Pontmercy and you."

"Do you think that I deserve a reward?"

"Certainly."

"Well, I ask one. To blow out that man's brains myself."

Javert raised his head, saw Jean Valjean, made an imperceptible movement, and said, "That is appropriate."

As for Enjolras, he had begun to reload his carbine. He cast his eyes about him and, turning toward Jean Valjean, said, "Take the spy."

Almost at the same moment, they heard a flourish of trumpets.

When Jean Valjean was alone with Javert, he untied the rope that held the prisoner by the middle of the body. Then he motioned to him to get up. Javert obeyed with that indefinable smile of his. Jean Valjean took Javert as you would take a beast of burden, by a strap, and, drawing Javert after him, went out of the wineshop slowly, for Javert, with his legs fettered, could take only very short steps. Jean Valjean had the pistol in his hand.

When they had climbed over the wall of the RUE MONDÉTOUR, they found themselves alone in the little street. Nobody saw them now. Jean Valjean put the pistol under his arm and fixed upon Javert a look which had no need of words to say, *Javert, it is I.*

Javert answered, "Take your revenge."

Jean Valjean took a knife out of his pocket and opened it.

"You are right," exclaimed Javert. "That suits you better."

Jean Valjean cut the strap which Javert had about his neck; then he cut the ropes which he had on his wrists; then, stooping down, he cut the cord which he had on his feet; and, rising, he said to him, "You are free."

Javert was not easily astonished. Still, complete master as he was of himself, he stood aghast and motionless.

Jean Valjean continued, "I don't expect to leave this place. Still, if by chance I should, I live under the name of Fauchelevent in the RUE DE L'HOMME ARMÉ, number seven. Go."

Javert buttoned his coat, restored the military stiffness between his shoulders, turned half round, folded his arms, and walked off in the direction of the markets. Jean Valjean followed him with his eyes.

After a few steps, Javert turned back and cried to Jean Valjean, "Kill me rather."

Javert did not notice that his tone was more respectful toward Jean Valjean.

"Go away," said Jean Valjean.

Javert receded with slow steps. A moment afterward, he turned the corner. When Javert was gone, Jean Valjean fired the pistol in the air.

Marius sprang up at the moment they heard the pistol shot. Jean Valjean reappeared and cried, "It is done."

"What was that man's name?"

"Javert."

A dreary chill passed through the heart of Marius.

Chapter 61

Suddenly the drum beat the charge. The attack was a hurricane. The army rushed upon the barricade; a powerful column of infantry of the line, supported by deep masses heard but unseen, came straight upon the barricade. The wall held well.

There was assault after assault. The horror continued to increase. Bossuet was killed; Courfeyrac was killed; Combeferre, pierced by three bayonet thrusts in the breast, just as he was lifting a wounded soldier, had only time to look to

sapper : a soldier responsible for tasks such as building and repairing roads and bridges, laying and clearing mines, etc. *

heaven, and expired. Marius, still fighting, was so hacked with wounds, particularly about his head, that his countenance was lost in blood. Enjolras alone was untouched.

When there were none of the chiefs alive save Enjolras and Marius, who were at the extremities of the barricade, the center gave way. A final assault was now attempted, and this assault succeeded. But Enjolras and Marius, with seven or eight who had been rallied about them, sprang forward. Enjolras, keeping the door of the wineshop open, cried to the despairing, "There is but one door open. This one." And, covering them with his body, he made them pass in behind him. All rushed in.

Marius remained without.

A ball had broken his shoulder blade; he felt that he was fainting and that he was falling. At that moment, his eyes already closed; he experienced the shock of a vigorous hand seizing him, and his fainting fit, in which he lost consciousness, left him this thought, mingled with the last memory of Cosette: *I am taken prisoner. I shall be shot.*

When the cartridges ran out in the wineshop, the soldiers rushed in. A hand-to-hand struggle followed. The revolutionists fought with savage might, but they could do nothing. They were all killed, Enjolras the last. Then silence. The barricade was taken.

Marius was in fact a prisoner. But the hand which had seized him from behind at the moment he was falling was the hand of Jean Valjean.

Jean Valjean had taken no other part in the combat than to expose himself. Save for him, in that supreme phase of the death struggle, nobody would have thought of the wounded. Thanks to him, everywhere present in the carnage like a providence, those who fell were taken up and carried into the basement room, and their wounds were dressed. In the intervals, he repaired the barricade. But nothing which could resemble a blow, an attack, or even a personal defense came from his hands. He was silent, and gave aid.

When a shot struck down Marius, Jean Valjean bounded with the agility of a tiger, dropped upon him as upon prey, and carried him away.

In the whirlwind of the attack nobody saw Jean Valjean cross the unpaved field of the barricade, holding the senseless Marius in his arms, and disappear behind the corner of the house of Corinth. There Jean Valjean stopped; he let Marius slide to the ground, set his back to the wall, and cast his eyes about him. What should he do?

Jean Valjean looked at the house in front of him; he looked at the barricade by the side of him; then he looked upon the ground, and something vaguely outlined itself and took form at his feet. He perceived a few steps from him, under some fallen paving stones which partly hid it, an iron grating laid flat and level with the ground. The stone frame which held it had been torn up. Through the bars a glimpse could be caught of an obscure opening, something like the flue of a chimney or the main of a cistern. Jean Valjean sprang forward. His old science of escape mounted to his brain like a flash. To remove the stones, to lift the grating, to load Marius, who was as inert as a dead body, upon his shoulders, to descend with that burden upon his back, by the aid of his elbows and knees, into this kind of well—fortunately not very deep—to let fall over his head the heavy iron trapdoor upon which the stones were shaken back again, to find a foothold upon a flagged surface ten feet below the ground—this was executed with the strength of a giant and the rapidity of an eagle.

Jean Valjean found himself, with Marius still senseless, in the sewer of Paris—a sort of long underground passage. There, deep peace, absolute silence, night. The impression which he had formerly felt in falling from the street into the convent came back to him. Only, what he was now carrying away was not Cosette; it was Marius. He could now hardly hear above him, like a vague murmur, the fearful tumult of the wineshop taken by assault.

The wounded man did not stir, and Jean Valjean did not know whether what he was carrying away in this grave was alive or dead.

When he had turned the corner of the gallery, the distant gleam of the airhole disappeared, the curtain of obscurity fell back over him, and he became blind. He went forward nonetheless, and as rapidly as he could. Marius's arms were passed about his neck, and his feet hung behind him. He held both arms with one hand and groped for the wall with the other. Marius's cheek touched his and stuck to it, being bloody. He felt a moist warmth at his ear, which indicated respiration, and consequently life.

All at once he saw his shadow before him. In amazement he turned round. Behind him, in the portion of the passage through which he had passed, at a distance which appeared to him immense, flamed, throwing its rays into the dense obscurity, a sort of horrible star which appeared to be looking at him. It was the gloomy star of the police which was rising in the sewer. Behind this star were, moving without order, eight or ten black forms.

During the day, a patrol of the sewers had been ordered. It was feared that they would be taken as a refuge by the vanquished. Three platoons of officers and sewer men explored the subterranean streets of Paris.

Luckily, if he saw the lantern well, the lantern saw him badly. It was light and he was shadow. He was far off, and he merged into the blackness of the place. He drew close to the side of the wall and stopped. Jean Valjean saw these goblins form a kind of circle. The sergeant gave the order to file left toward the descent to the Seine.

Jean Valjean resumed his advance and was not stopped again. This advance became more and more laborious. Jean Valjean tore up his shirt, bandaged Marius's wounds as well as he could, and stanched the flowing blood.

In opening Marius's clothes, he found the lines written by Marius:

My name is Marius Pontmercy. Carry my corpse to my grandfather's, M. Gillenormand, Rue des Filles du Calvaire, no. 6, in the Marais.

He replaced the pocketbook in Marius's pocket. His strength had returned to him. He took Marius on his back again, laid his head carefully upon his right shoulder, and began to descend the sewer.

This obscurity suddenly became terrible. He felt that he was entering the water, and that he had under his feet pavement no longer, but mud.

Jean Valjean found himself in the presence of a slough*, caused by the showers of the previous day and a damming of the rainwater. The floor had disappeared in the mire. He sank still deeper; he threw his face back to escape the water and to be able to breathe. He who might have seen him in this obscurity would have thought he saw a mask floating upon the

slough : an area of soft, muddy ground; a swamp

darkness. Jean Valjean dimly perceived Marius's drooping head and livid face above him; he made a desperate effort and thrust his foot forward and found a support.

Jean Valjean ascended this inclined plane and reached the other side of the quagmire. On coming out of the water, he struck against a stone and fell upon his knees. He rose, shivering, chilled, infected, bending beneath this dying man, whom he was dragging on, all dripping with slime, his soul filled with a strange light.

He walked with desperation, almost with rapidity, for a hundred paces, without raising his head, almost without breathing, and suddenly struck against the wall. He raised his eyes, and at the extremity of the passage, down there before him, far, very far away, he perceived a light. This time, it was not the terrible light; it was the good and white light. It was the light of day. Jean Valjean saw the outlet and felt exhaustion no more. He felt Marius's weight no longer; he found again his knees of steel; he ran rather than walked. Jean Valjean reached the outlet.

There he stopped. The outlet did not let him out. The arch was closed by a strong grating, which, according to all appearances, rarely turned upon its rusty hinges and was held in its stone frame by a stout lock, red with rust.

Jean Valjean laid Marius along the wall on the dry part of the floor, then walked to the grating and clenched the bars with both hands; the grating did not stir. The obstacle was invincible. No means of opening the door.

Must he then perish there? What should he do? All the outlets were undoubtedly closed in this way. He had only succeeded in escaping into a prison.

It was over. All that Jean Valjean had done was useless. He turned his back to the grating and dropped upon the pavement beside the yet-motionless Marius, and his head sank between his knees. This was the last drop of anguish. Of whom did he think in this overwhelming dejection? Neither of himself nor of Marius. He thought of Cosette.

CHAPTER 62

In the midst of this devastation, a hand was laid upon his shoulder, and a voice which spoke low said to him, "Go halves."

A man was before him, dressed in a blouse; he was barefooted; he held his shoes in his left hand; he had evidently taken them off to be able to reach Jean Valjean without being heard.

Jean Valjean had not a moment's hesitation. Unforeseen as was the encounter, this man was known to him. This man was Thénardier.

There was a moment of delay. Jean Valjean perceived immediately that Thénardier did not recognize him.

"Go halves."

"What do you mean?"

"You have killed the man; very well. For my part, I have the key."

Thénardier pointed to Marius. He went on, "I don't know you, but I would like to help you. You must be a friend."

Jean Valjean began to understand. Thénardier took him for a murderer.

Thénardier resumed, "Listen, comrade. You haven't killed that man without looking to what he had in his pockets. Give me my half. I will open the door for you." And he drew a big key half out from under his blouse. "Now, let us finish the business. Let us divide. You have seen my key; show me your money."

Jean Valjean felt in his pockets. It was, as will be remembered, his custom always to have money about him. This time, however, he was caught unprovided. On putting on his National Guard's uniform the evening before, he had forgotten to take his pocketbook with him. He had only some coins in his waistcoat pocket. He turned out his pocket and displayed upon the curb of the sewer a louis d'or and five or six big sous.

Thénardier thrust out his underlip with a significant twist of the neck, and then began to handle, in all familiarity, the pockets of Jean Valjean and Marius. Jean Valjean, principally concerned in keeping his back to the light, did not interfere with him. While he was feeling Marius's coat, Thénardier, with the dexterity of a juggler, found means, without attracting Jean Valjean's attention, to tear off a strip, which he hid under his blouse, probably thinking that this scrap of cloth might assist him afterward to identify the victim and the killer. He found, however, nothing more than the thirty francs.

"It is true," said he, "both together, you have no more than that." And he took the whole. This done, he took the key from under his blouse anew. "Now, friend, you must go out. You have paid; go out."

Thénardier helped Jean Valjean to replace Marius upon his shoulders; then he went toward the grating upon the points of his bare feet, beckoning to Jean Valjean to follow him; he looked outside, and put the key into the lock. The bolt slid and the door turned.

Thénardier half opened the door, left just a passage for Jean Valjean, closed the grating again, turned the key twice in the lock, and plunged back into the obscurity. Jean Valjean found himself outside.

Chapter 63

Jean Valjean was plunging his hand into the river when suddenly he felt an indescribable uneasiness. He turned round.

Somebody was indeed behind him. A man of tall stature, wrapped in a long overcoat, with folded arms, and holding in his right hand a club, the leaden knob of which could be seen, stood erect a few steps behind Jean Valjean, who was stooping over Marius. Jean Valjean recognized Javert.

Javert did not recognize Jean Valjean, who no longer resembled himself. He said in a quick and calm voice, "Who are you?"

"Jean Valjean."

Javert put the club between his teeth, bent his knees, inclined his body, laid his two powerful hands upon Jean Valjean's shoulders, examined him, and recognized him. Their faces almost touched. Javert's look was terrible.

"Inspector Javert," said Jean Valjean, "you have got me. Besides, since this morning, I have considered myself your prisoner. I did not give you my address to try to escape you. Take me. Only grant me one thing."

Javert seemed not to hear. He rested his fixed eye upon Jean Valjean. At last, he let go of Jean Valjean, rose up, took his club firmly in his grasp, and, as if in a dream, murmured rather than pronounced, "What are you doing here? And who is this man?"

Jean Valjean answered, and the sound of his voice appeared to awaken Javert. "It is precisely of him that I wished to speak. Dispose of me as you please, but help me first to carry him home. I only ask that of you."

He stooped down again, took a handkerchief from his pocket, which he dipped in the water, and wiped Marius's bloodstained forehead.

"This man was at the barricade," said he in an undertone. "This is he whom they called Marius. He is wounded."

"He is dead," said Javert.

Jean Valjean answered, "No. Not yet."

"You have brought him, then, from the barricade here?" observed Javert.

Jean Valjean, for his part, seemed to have but one idea. He resumed, "He lives in the Marais, on RUE DES FILLES DU CALVAIRE, at his grandfather's—I forget the name."

Jean Valjean felt in Marius's coat, took out the pocket-book, opened it at the page penciled by Marius, and handed it to Javert.

There was still enough light floating in the air to enable one to read. Javert deciphered the few lines written by Marius. Then he cried, "Driver!"

There was a carriage waiting near at hand. A moment later, the carriage, descending by the slope of the watering place, was on the beach. Marius was laid upon the back seat, and Javert sat down by the side of Jean Valjean on the front seat.

It was after nightfall when the fiacre arrived at number six in the RUE DES FILLES DU CALVAIRE. They carried Marius up to the first story, and while Basque went for a doctor and Nicolette, the maid, was opening the linen closets, Jean Valjean felt Javert touch him on the shoulder. He understood, and went downstairs, having behind him Javert's following steps. They got into the fiacre again, and the driver mounted upon his box.

"Inspector Javert," said Jean Valjean, "grant me one thing more."

"What?" asked Javert roughly.

"Let me go home a moment. Then you shall do with me what you will."

Javert remained silent for a few seconds, his chin drawn back into the collar of his overcoat; then he let down the window in front and directed the driver to proceed.

They did not open their mouths again for the whole distance.

What did Jean Valjean desire? To finish what he had begun, to inform Cosette, to tell her where Marius was, to give her perhaps some other useful information, to make, if he could, certain final dispositions. As to himself, as to what concerned him personally, it was all over.

Near the entrance of the RUE DE L'HOMME ARMÉ, Javert ordered the fiacre to stop. Javert and Jean Valjean got out, and Javert paid the driver and sent him on his way. They walked to the entrance of the RUE DE L'HOMME ARMÉ. It was, as usual, empty. Javert followed Jean Valjean. They reached number seven. Jean Valjean rapped. The door opened.

"Very well," said Javert. "Go up." He added with a strange expression and as if he were making an effort in speaking in such a way, "I will wait here for you."

Jean Valjean looked at Javert. This manner of proceeding was little in accordance with Javert's habits. He opened the door, went into the house. On reaching the first story, he paused. Jean Valjean, either to take breath or mechanically, looked out the window. He leaned over the street. Javert was gone.

Javert made his way with slow steps from the RUE DE L'HOMME ARMÉ. He walked with his head down for the first time in his life. He plunged into the silent streets and followed one direction. He took the shortest route toward the Seine and stopped at a little distance from the post of the Place du Châtelet, at the corner of the Pont Notre-Dame. This point of the Seine is dreaded by mariners. Men who fall in there, one never sees again; the best swimmers are drowned.

Javert leaned both elbows on the parapet, with his chin in his hands. Javert was suffering frightfully. One thing had astonished him, that Jean Valjean had spared him, and one thing had petrified him, that he, Javert, had spared Jean Valjean.

What should he do now? Turn in Jean Valjean—that was wrong. Leave Jean Valjean free—that was wrong. In every course which was open to him, there was a fall. His reflections gradually became terrible. This could not last. Twenty times, while he was in that carriage face-to-face with Jean Valjean, the legal tiger had roared within him. Twenty times he had been tempted to throw himself upon Jean Valjean, to seize him and to arrest him. But he had heard a voice, a strange voice crying to him, *"Very well. Give up your savior. Then have Pontius Pilate's basin brought, and wash your claws."*

Could that be endurable? No. Unnatural state, if ever there was one. There were only two ways to get out of it. One, to go resolutely to Jean Valjean and to return the man of the galleys to the dungeon. The other—

Javert bent his head and looked. All was black. He remained for some minutes motionless, gazing into that opening of darkness. Suddenly he took off his hat and set it on the edge of the quay. A moment afterward, a tall and black form appeared standing on the parapet, bent toward the Seine, then sprang up and fell straight into the darkness. There was a dull splash, and the obscure form disappeared under the water.

Chapter 64

They carried Marius into the parlor, still motionless, when the doctor arrived. The body had not received any interior lesion; a ball, deadened by the pocketbook, had turned aside, with a hideous gash, but not deep, and consequently not dangerous. The long walk underground had completed the dislocation of the broken shoulder blade, and there were serious difficulties there. There were sword cuts on the arms. No scar disfigured his face; the head, however, was as it were covered with deep cuts; did they stop at the scalp? Did they affect the skull? That could not yet be told.

The physician seemed to be reflecting sadly. From time to time he shook his head. At the moment he was wiping the face and touching the still-closed eyelids lightly with his finger, a door opened at the rear end of the parlor, and a long, pale figure approached. It was the grandfather.

"Monsieur," said Basque, "monsieur has just been brought home. He has been to the barricade, and—"

"He is dead!" cried the old man in a terrible voice. "He is dead, isn't he?"

At this moment, Marius slowly raised his lids.

"Marius!" cried the old man. "Marius! My child! My dear son! You are opening your eyes, you are looking at me, you are alive!" And he fell fainting.

Marius had for several weeks a fever accompanied by delirium. He repeated the name of Cosette during entire nights. As long as there was danger, M. Gillenormand, in despair at the bedside of his grandson, was, like Marius, neither dead nor alive. Every day, and sometimes twice a day, a very well-dressed gentleman with white hair came to inquire after the wounded man.

At last, on October 7, four months after the sorrowful night they had brought him home dying to his grandfather,

the physician declared him out of danger. Convalescence began. Marius was, however, obliged still to remain for more than two months stretched on a long chair, on account of the accidents resulting from the fracture of the shoulder blade. Marius was left in peace.

M. Gillenormand passed first through every anguish, and then every ecstasy. On the day the physician announced to him that Marius was out of danger, the good man was in delirium.

As for Marius, while he let them dress his wounds and care for him, he had one fixed idea: Cosette. Since the fever and the delirium had left him, he had not uttered that name, and they might have supposed that he no longer thought of it. He held his peace precisely because his soul was in it.

He did not know what had become of Cosette; he understood nothing in regard to his own life: he knew neither how nor by whom he had been saved, and nobody around him knew.

One day M. Gillenormand bent over Marius. Marius, nearly all of whose strength had returned, gathered it together, sat up in bed, looked his grandfather in the face, and said, "I wish to marry."

"You shall have her, your lassie."

Marius, astounded, trembled in every limb. M. Gillenormand continued, "Yes, you shall have her, your handsome, pretty little girl. She comes every day in the shape of an old gentleman to inquire after you. Since you were wounded, she has passed her time in weeping and making bandages. She lives in the RUE DE L'HOMME ARMÉ, number seven. Ah, we are ready! Ah! You want her! Well, you shall have her. Listen. I have made inquiries, too; she is charming, she is modest, she is a jewel, she worships you. If you had died, there would have been three of us; her bier* would have accompanied mine. I had a strong notion, as soon as you were better, to plant her square at your bedside, but it is only in romances that they introduce young girls unceremoniously to the side of the couch of the pretty wounded men who interest them. Take her. Be happy, my dear child." This said, the old man burst into sobs.

"Father!" exclaimed Marius.

The old man stammered, "The ice is broken. He has called me 'Father.'"

Marius said softly, "But, Father, now that I am well, it seems to me that I could see her."

"You have called me 'Father'; it is well worth that. I will see to it. She shall be brought to you."

Cosette and Marius saw each other again. She appeared on the threshold; it seemed as if she were in a cloud. With Cosette and behind her had entered a man with white hair, grave, smiling nevertheless, but with a vague and poignant smile. This was Jean Valjean. He had under his arm a package, wrapped in paper.

After the two had greeted each other, Father Gillenormand formally asked for Cosette's hand.

Jean Valjean, assenting, said in a grave and tranquil voice, "Mademoiselle Euphrasie Fauchelevent has nearly six hundred thousand francs." And he laid on the table the package which looked like a book.

Jean Valjean opened the package himself; it was a bundle of banknotes.

Marius and Cosette paid little attention to this incident.

All the preparations were made for the marriage. The physician being consulted said that it might take place in February. This was in December. Jean Valjean did all, smoothed all, conciliated all, made all easy. He hastened toward Cosette's happiness with as much eagerness, and apparently as much joy, as Cosette herself. As he had been a mayor, he knew how to solve a delicate problem, a secret he alone knew: Cosette's civil state. A notary's act was drawn up. Cosette became before the law Mademoiselle Euphrasie Fauchelevent. She was declared an orphan. Jean Valjean arranged matters in such a way as to be designated, under the name of Fauchelevent, as Cosette's guardian, with M. Gillenormand as overseeing guardian. As for the 584,000 francs, that was a legacy left to Cosette by a dead person who had desired to remain unknown.

Cosette learned that she was not the daughter of that old man whom she had so long called Father. She had Marius. The young man came, the old man faded away; such is life. She continued, however, to say "Father" to Jean Valjean.

Marius surrounded this M. Fauchelevent, who was to him simply benevolent and cold, with all sorts of silent questions. There came to him at intervals doubts about his own recollections. He was led to ask himself if it were really true that he had seen M. Fauchelevent, such a man, so serious and so calm, at the barricade. At moments, Marius covered his face with his hands, and the vague past tumultuously traversed the twilight which filled his brain. He saw Mabeuf fall again; he heard Gavroche singing beneath the grape; he felt upon his lip the chill of Éponine's forehead; Enjolras, Courfeyrac, Combeferre, Bossuet, all his friends, rose up before him, then dissipated. He interrogated himself; he groped within himself. Where were they all then? Was it indeed true that all were dead? A fall into the darkness had carried off all, except himself. It all seemed to him to have disappeared as if behind a curtain at a theatre. There are such curtains which drop down in life. God is passing to the next act.

And himself, was he really the same man? He, the poor, was rich; he, the despairing, was marrying Cosette. It seemed to him that he had passed through a tomb, that he had gone in black and that he had come out white. And in this tomb, the others had remained.

M. Fauchelevent almost had a place among these vanished beings. Marius hesitated to believe that the Fauchelevent of the barricade was the same as this Fauchelevent in flesh and blood, so gravely seated near Cosette. Moreover, their two natures showing a steep front to each other, no question was possible from Marius to M. Fauchelevent.

The enchantment, great as it was, did not efface other preoccupations from Marius's mind. During the preparations for the marriage, and while waiting for the time fixed upon, he had some difficult and careful retrospective researches made. He owed gratitude on several sides: he owed some on his father's account, and he owed some on his own. There was Thénardier; there was the unknown man who had brought him to M. Gillenormand's.

None of the various agents whom Marius employed succeeded in finding Thénardier's track. The Thénardiess had died in prison. Thénardier and his daughter Azelma, the two who alone remained of that woeful group, had plunged back into the shadow.

As for the other, the unknown man who had saved Marius, the researches at first had some results, then stopped short. They succeeded in finding the fiacre which had brought Marius on the evening of the sixth of June. The driver declared that they went first to the RUE DES FILLES DU CALVAIRE; that they left the dead man there; that they then got into his carriage again; that he had been called to stop; that there, in the street, he had been paid and left, and that the officer took away the other man; that he knew nothing more, as the night was very dark.

In the hope of deriving aid in his researches from them, Marius had preserved the bloody clothes which he wore when he was brought back to his grandfather's. On examining the coat, it was noticed that one skirt was oddly torn. A piece was missing.

One evening Marius spoke before Cosette and Jean Valjean of all this singular adventure, of the numberless inquiries which he had made, and of the uselessness of his efforts. He exclaimed, "That man, whoever he may be, was a hero. He intervened like the archangel. And his life, he did not risk it once, but twenty times! And each step was a

bier : a movable frame on which a coffin or a corpse is placed before burial or cremation or on which it is carried to the grave danger. The proof is that on coming out of the sewer, he was arrested. And he could expect no recompense. What was I? An insurgent, a vanquished man. Oh! If Cosette's six hundred thousand francs were mine—"

"They are yours," interrupted Jean Valjean.

"Well," resumed Marius, "I would give them to find that man!"

Jean Valjean kept silence.

CHAPTER 65

The night of 16 February 1833 was a blessed night. Above its shade the heavens were opened. It was the wedding night of Marius and Cosette.

On the previous evening, Jean Valjean had handed to Marius, in the presence of M. Gillenorm and, the 584,000 francs.

As for Jean Valjean, there was a beautiful room in the Gillenormand house furnished expressly for him, and Cosette had said to him so irresistibly, "Father, I pray you," and made him almost promise that he would occupy it.

A few days before the marriage, an accident happened to Jean Valjean; he slightly bruised the thumb of his right hand. It was not serious, and he had allowed nobody to take any trouble about it, nor to dress it. It compelled him, however, to muffle his hand in a bandage and to carry his arm in a sling, and prevented his signing anything. M. Gillenormand, as Cosette's overseeing guardian, took his place.

On the way to the church, the party ran into a company of maskers*, one of whom happened to be Thénardier. He recognized Jean Valjean.

After the ceremony, when they had returned to the house, Jean Valjean sat in a chair in the parlor, behind the door. A few moments before they took their seats at the table, Cosette came, as if from a sudden impulse, and made him a low curtsy.

"Father, are you pleased?"

"Yes," said Jean Valjean, "I am pleased."

"Well, then, laugh."

Jean Valjean began to laugh.

Immediately after having laughed, nobody observing him, Jean Valjean left his seat, got up, and, unperceived, reached the antechamber. It was that same room which eight months before he had entered, black with mire, blood, and powder, bringing the grandson home to the grandfather. He listened. He heard the loud words of the grandfather, the clatter of the plates and glasses, the bursts of laughter, and through all that gay uproar he distinguished Cosette's sweet, joyous voice.

He left the RUE DES FILLES DU CALVAIRE and returned to the RUE DE L'HOMME ARMÉ, his home. He lighted his candle and went upstairs. The apartment was empty. He went into Cosette's room. All the little feminine objects to which Cosette clung were gone; there remained only the heavy furniture and the four walls. A single bed was made and seemed waiting for somebody; that was Jean Valjean's.

He approached his bed, and his eye fell upon the valise and the little trunk which never left him. He had placed the valise upon a candle stand at the head of his bed. He went to this stand, took a key from his pocket, and opened the valise.

He took out slowly the black garments in which, ten years before, Cosette had left Montfermeil. As he took them out of the valise, he laid them on the bed. He remembered it was in winter, a very cold December, her poor little feet all red in her wooden shoes. He thought of that forest of Montfermeil; they had crossed it together, Cosette and he. He arranged the little things upon the bed; then his venerable white head fell upon the bed, his old heart broke, his face was swallowed up in Cosette's garments, and anybody who had passed along the staircase at the moment would have heard fearful sobs.

Chapter 66

The day after a wedding is solitary. But that morning, a little before noon, Basque heard a light rap at the door. He opened it and saw M. Fauchelevent.

"Has your master risen?" inquired Jean Valjean.

"Monsieur the baron?" asked Basque. "I will tell him that Monsieur Fauchelevent is here."

"No. Do not tell him that it is I. Tell him that somebody asks to speak with him in private, and do not give him any name."

Jean Valjean remained alone. A few minutes elapsed. Jean Valjean was motionless in the spot where Basque had left him. He was very pale. There was a noise at the door; he raised his eyes. Marius entered, his head erect, smiling.

"How glad I am to see you! If you knew how we missed you yesterday! Good morning, Father. How is your hand? Better, is it not?"

"Monsieur," said Jean Valjean, "I have one thing to tell you. I am an old convict."

Jean Valjean untied the black cravat which supported his right arm, took off the cloth wound about his hand, laid his thumb bare, and showed it to Marius.

"There is nothing the matter with my hand," said he. "There has never been anything the matter with it. It was best that I should be absent from your marriage. I absented myself as much as I could. I feigned this wound so as not to commit a forgery."

Marius stammered out, "What does this mean?"

"It means," answered Jean Valjean, "that I have been in the galleys. Monsieur Pontmercy, I was nineteen years in the galleys. For robbery. Then I was sentenced for life. For robbery. For a second offense. At this hour I am an outlaw."

It was useless for Marius to recoil before the reality, to refuse the evidence; he was compelled to yield. He began to comprehend. He caught a glimpse in the future of a hideous destiny for himself.

"Tell all!" cried he.

Jean Valjean raised his head with majesty. "It is necessary that you believe me in this."

Here he made a pause; then, with a sort of sovereign and sepulchral authority, he added, "Monsieur Baron Pontmercy, I am a peasant of Faverolles. I earned my living by pruning trees. My name is not Fauchelevent; it is Jean Valjean."

Marius faltered, "Who proves it to me?"

"I. Since I say so."

Marius looked at this man. No lie could come out of such a calmness. "I believe you," said Marius.

Jean Valjean inclined his head as if making an oath and continued, "What am I to Cosette? A passer. Ten years ago, I did not know that she existed. I love her; a child whom one has seen when little, being himself already old, he loves. Today Cosette leaves my life; our two roads separate. Her protector is changed. And Cosette gains by the change. As for the six hundred thousand francs, you have not spoken of them to me, but I anticipate your thought; that is a trust. I make over the trust. Nothing more can be asked of me. I complete the restitution by telling my real name. I desire that you should know who I am."

And Jean Valjean looked Marius in the face.

"But after all," exclaimed Marius, "why do you tell me all this? What compels you to? You could have kept the secret to yourself. Finish it. There is something else. In connection with what do you make this avowal? From what motive?"

masker : one who appears in disguise at a masquerade or wears a mask in a ritual *

"From what motive?" answered Jean Valjean, in a voice so low and so hollow that one would have said it was to himself he was speaking. "Well, it is from honor. Yes, my misfortune is a cord which I have here in my heart and which holds me fast. I have tried to break this cord; I have pulled upon it; it held firmly; it did not snap; I was tearing my heart out with it. Then I said I cannot live away from here. I must stay. But you are right; I am a fool; why not just simply stay? You offer me a room in the house—we will have but one roof, but one table, but one fire, we will live as one family. One family! No. I am of no family. I am not of yours. I am not of the family of men. In houses where people are at home, I am an encumbrance. There are families, but they are not for me. I am the unfortunate; I am outside. You ask why I speak? I am neither informed against, nor pursued, nor hunted, say you. Yes! I am informed against! Yes! I am pursued! Yes! I am hunted! When one has such a horror over him, he has no right to make others share it without their knowledge. To live, once I stole a loaf of bread; today, to live, I will not steal a name."

Marius crossed the parlor slowly and, when he was near Jean Valjean, extended him his hand. But Marius had to take that hand which did not offer itself.

"My grandfather has friends. I will procure your pardon."

"It is useless," answered Jean Valjean. "They think me dead; that is enough."

"Poor Cosette!" murmured Marius. "When she knows—"

At these words, Jean Valjean trembled in every limb. He sank into an armchair and hid his face in both hands, and Marius heard him murmur, "Oh! Would that I could die!"

"Be calm," said Marius. "I will keep your secret for myself alone."

"I thank you, monsieur," answered Jean Valjean gently.

He remained thoughtful a moment; then he raised his voice. "It is all nearly finished. There is one thing left. Now that you know, do you think, monsieur, you who are the master, that I ought not to see Cosette again?"

"You will come every evening," said Marius, "and Cosette will expect you."

"You are kind, monsieur," said Jean Valjean.

Marius bowed to Jean Valjean, and these two men separated.

Chapter 67

The next evening, at nightfall, Jean Valjean knocked at the Gillenormand porte-cochère*. The porter addressed him. "Monsieur the baron told me to ask monsieur whether he desires to go upstairs or to remain below?"

"To remain below," answered Jean Valjean.

Basque, who was absolutely respectful, opened the door of the basement room and said, "I will inform madame."

The room which Jean Valjean entered was an arched and damp basement, used as a cellar when necessary, looking upon the street, paved with red tiles, and dimly lighted by a window with an iron grating. But a fire was kindled, which indicated that somebody had anticipated Jean Valjean's answer: *"To remain below."* Two armchairs were placed at the corners of the fireplace.

Jean Valjean was fatigued. For some days he had neither eaten nor slept. He let himself fall into one of the armchairs. Suddenly Cosette was behind him. He turned. She was adorably beautiful. But what he looked upon with that deep look was not her beauty but her soul.

"Ah!" exclaimed Cosette. "Father, Marius tells me that it is you who wish me to receive you here."

"Yes, it is I."

"But why? You choose the ugliest room in the house to see me in. It is horrible here."

"You know, madame, I am peculiar."

"Not to me, Father."

"Don't call me Father anymore."

"What?"

"Call me Monsieur Jean. Jean, if you will. You have no more need of a father; you have a husband."

Cosette, growing suddenly serious, looked at Jean Valjean and added, "You don't like it that I am happy?"

Jean Valjean grew pale. For a moment he did not answer; then he murmured, "Her happiness was the aim of my life. Now God may beckon me away. Cosette, you are happy; my time is full."

"Ah, you have called me Cosette!" exclaimed she. And she sprang upon his neck.

Jean Valjean, in desperation, clasped her to his breast wildly. It seemed to him almost as if he were taking her back.

"Thank you, Father!" said Cosette to him.

The transport was becoming poignant to Jean Valjean. He gently put away Cosette's arms and took his hat.

Every succeeding morrow brought Jean Valjean at the same hour. He came every day. Marius made his arrangements so as to be absent at the hours when Jean Valjean came. The house became accustomed to M. Fauchelevent's new mode of life.

Several weeks passed thus. A new life gradually took possession of Cosette. The disappearance of familiarity, the "madame," the "Monsieur Jean," all this made him different to Cosette. The care which he had taken to detach her from him succeeded with her. She became more and more cheerful and less and less affectionate. However, she still loved him very much, and he felt it.

One day she suddenly said to him, "You were my father, you are no longer my father; you were my uncle, you are no longer my uncle; you were Monsieur Fauchelevent, you are Jean. Who are you, then? If I did not know you were so good, I should be afraid of you."

The next day there was a fire. But the two armchairs were placed at the other end of the room, near the door. He went for the armchairs and put them back in their usual place near the chimney. This fire being kindled again encouraged him, however. He continued the conversation still longer than usual.

As he was getting up to go away, Cosette said to him, "My husband said a funny thing to me yesterday. He said, 'Cosette, we have an income of thirty thousand francs. Twenty-seven that you have; three that my grandfather allows me.' I answered, 'That makes thirty.' 'Would you have the courage to live on three thousand?' I answered, 'Yes, on nothing. Provided it be with you.'"

Jean Valjean did not say a word. He went back to the RUE DE L'HOMME ARMÉ. His mind was racked with conjectures. It was evident that Marius had doubts in regard to the origin of these six hundred thousand francs, that he feared some impure source. Besides, vaguely, Jean Valjean began to feel that the door was shown him.

The next day he received, on entering the basement room, something like a shock. The armchairs had disappeared. There was not even a chair of any kind.

"Ah," exclaimed Cosette as she came in, "no chairs!"

"They are gone," answered Jean Valjean. "I told Basque to take them away."

"And what for?"

"I shall stay only a few minutes today. I believe that Basque needed some armchairs for the parlor."

"What for?"

"You doubtless have company this evening."

Jean Valjean could not say a word more.

porte-cochère : a covered entrance large enough for vehicles to pass through, typically opening into a courtyard *

Chapter 68

It would be unjust to blame Marius. Before his marriage, he had put no questions to M. Fauchelevent, and, since, he had feared to put any to Jean Valjean. He had regretted the promise into which he had allowed himself to be led.

Marius did what he deemed necessary and just. He believed at that very time that he had a solemn duty to perform, the restitution of the six hundred thousand francs to somebody whom he was seeking as cautiously as possible. In the meantime, he abstained from using that money.

One day Jean Valjean went downstairs, took three steps into the street, and sat down upon a stone block. He remained there a few minutes, then went upstairs again. The next day, he did not leave his room. The day after, he did not leave his bed.

His portress, who prepared his frugal meal, looked into the brown earthen plate and exclaimed, "Why, you didn't eat anything yesterday, poor dear man!"

"I will eat tomorrow."

Jean Valjean scarcely ever saw any other human being than this good woman. While he still went out, he had bought of a brazier for a few sous a little copper crucifix, which he had hung upon a nail before his bed.

A week elapsed, and Jean Valjean had not taken a step in his room. He was still in bed. The portress saw a physician of the quarter passing at the end of the street; she took it upon herself to beg him to go up. The physician saw Jean Valjean and spoke with him. When he came down, the portress questioned him.

"Your sick man is very sick," he said.

"What is the matter with him?"

"Everything and nothing. He is a man who, to all appearance, has lost some dear friend. People die of that."

"Will you come again, Doctor?"

"Yes," answered the physician.

One evening Jean Valjean had difficulty in raising himself up on his elbow; he felt his wrist and found no pulse; his breathing was short, and stopped at intervals; he realized that he was weaker than he had been before. Then he made an effort, sat up in bed, and dressed himself. He put on his old workingman's garb. He opened the valise and took out Cosette's garment. He spread it out upon his bed.

The bishop's candlesticks were in their place on the mantel. He took two wax tapers from a drawer and put them into the candlesticks. Then, although it was still broad daylight, he lighted them. Each step that he took in going from one piece of furniture to another exhausted him, and he was obliged to sit down. Then he fainted. When he regained consciousness, he shivered, he felt that the chill was coming; he leaned upon the table which was lighted by the bishop's candlesticks and took the pen. His hand trembled. He slowly wrote the few lines which follow:

> _Cosette, I bless you. I am going to make an explanation to you. Your husband is very good. Always love him well when I am dead. This is what I want to tell you. The money is really your own. This is the whole story: The white jet* comes from Norway; the black jet* comes from England; the black glass imitation comes from Germany. We can make imitations in France as well as in Germany. Spain purchases many of them. This is the country of jet—_

Here he stopped; the pen fell from his fingers; he gave way to one of those despairing sobs which rose at times from the depths of his being. The poor man clasped his head with both hands.

"Oh!" exclaimed he within himself. "It is all over. I shall never see her more. She is a smile which has passed over me. I am going to enter into the night without even seeing her again.

It is nothing to die, but it is dreadful to die without seeing her. It is over, forever. Here I am, all alone. I shall never see her again."

At this moment there was a rap at his door.

Chapter 69

That very evening, just as Marius left the table and retired into his office, having a bundle of papers to study over, Basque handed him a letter, saying, "The person who wrote the letter is in the antechamber."

Marius took it. It smelled of tobacco. The recognition of the tobacco made him recognize the handwriting. The Jondrette garret appeared before him. He broke the seal eagerly and read,

> *Monsieur Baron, I am in possession of a secret concerning an individual. This individual concerns you. I hold the secret at your disposition, desiring to have the honor of being useful to you.*

The letter was signed *THÉNARD*. The signature was not a false one. It was only a little abridged.

The emotion of Marius was deep. Let him now find the other man whom he sought, the man who had saved him, and he would have nothing more to wish.

"Show him in," said Marius.

Marius examined the man from head to foot, while the personage bowed without measure, and asked the visitor in a sharp tone, "What do you want?"

"I would like to go and establish myself in America. The voyage is long and dear. I must have a little money."

"How does that concern me?" inquired Marius.

"Then monsieur the baron has not read my letter?"

"Explain."

"Certainly. I have a secret to sell you."

"What is this secret?"

Marius examined the man more and more closely while listening to him.

"I commence gratis," said the stranger. "You will see that I am interesting."

"Go on."

"Monsieur Baron, you have in your house a robber and a murderer."

Marius shuddered.

The stranger continued, "Murderer and robber. Observe, Monsieur Baron, that I do not speak here of acts old, bygone, and withered. I speak of recent acts, present acts, acts yet unknown to justice at this hour. This man has glided into your confidence, and almost into your family, under a false name. I am going to tell you his true name. And to tell it to you for nothing."

"I am listening."

"His name is Jean Valjean."

"I know it."

"I am going to tell you, also for nothing, who he is. He is an old convict."

"I know it."

The stranger resumed with a smile, "I do not permit myself to contradict monsieur the baron. At all events, you must see that I am informed. Now, what I have to acquaint you with is known to myself alone. It concerns the fortune of madame the baroness. It is an extraordinary secret. It is for sale, cheap. Twenty thousand francs."

white jet : an ivory-like stone that, when carefully cut, produces a dazzling effect

black jet : a compact velvet-black coal that takes a good polish and is often used for jewelry

YOU WHO

LOVE THE LORD,

HATE EVIL!

HE PROTECTS THE LIVES

OF HIS GODLY PEOPLE AND

RESCUES

THEM FROM THE POWER OF

THE WICKED.

PSALM 97:10

"I know your extraordinary secret, just as I knew Jean Valjean's name, just as I know your name."

"That is not difficult, Monsieur Baron. I have had the honor of writing it to you and telling it to you. Thénard."

"Thénardier," Marius replied. "You are also the workingman Jondrette, and you have kept a chophouse at Montfermeil, and you are Thénardier."

"Thanks!" Then bluntly, "Well, so be it, I am Thénardier."

Marius interrupted, "Thénardier, I have told you your name. Now your secret, what you came to make known to me—do you want me to tell you that? I, too, have my means of information. You shall see that I know more about it than you do. Jean Valjean, as you have said, is a murderer and a robber. A robber, because he robbed a rich manufacturer, M. Madeleine, whose ruin he caused. A murderer, because he slew the police officer Javert."

"I don't understand, Monsieur Baron," said Thénardier.

"I will make myself understood. Listen. There was, in 1822, a man who had had some old difficulty with justice, and who, under the name of M. Madeleine, had reformed and reestablished himself. He had become in the full force of the term an upright man. By means of the manufacture of black glass trinkets, he had made the fortune of an entire city. He was the foster father of the poor. He founded hospitals, opened schools, visited the sick. He had been appointed mayor. A liberated convict knew the secret of a penalty once incurred by this man; he informed against him, had him arrested, and took advantage of the arrest to come to Paris and draw from the banker Laffitte—I have the fact from the cashier himself—by means of a false signature, a sum of more than half a million francs which belonged to M. Madeleine. This convict who robbed M. Madeleine is Jean Valjean. As to the other act, you have just as little to tell me. Jean Valjean killed the officer Javert; he killed him with a pistol. I, who am now speaking to you, was present."

Thénardier merely said to Marius, "Monsieur Baron, we are on the wrong track. Monsieur Baron, Jean Valjean never robbed Monsieur Madeleine, and Jean Valjean never killed Javert. For two reasons. The first is this: he did not rob Monsieur Madeleine since it is Jean Valjean himself who was Monsieur Madeleine. And the second is this: he did not kill Javert, since Javert committed suicide."

"Prove it! Prove it!" cried Marius, beside himself.

Thénardier took from his pocket a large envelope of gray paper, which seemed to contain folded sheets of different sizes. "I have my documents," said he, with calmness.

While speaking, Thénardier took out of the envelope two newspapers, yellow, faded, and strongly saturated with tobacco. "Two facts, two proofs," said Thénardier. And unfolding the two papers, he handed them to Marius.

One, the oldest, a copy of *Le Drapeau blanc**, of 25 July 1823, established the identity of M. Madeleine and Jean Valjean. The other, a *Moniteur* of 15 June 1832, verified the suicide of Javert, adding that it appeared from a verbal report made by Javert to the prefect that, taken prisoner in the barricade of the RUE DE LA CHANVRERIE, he had owed his life to the magnanimity of an insurgent who, though he had him at the muzzle of his pistol, instead of blowing out his brains, had fired into the air.

Marius could not doubt. The information derived from the cashier was false, and he himself was mistaken. Jean Valjean, suddenly growing grand, arose from the cloud. Marius could not restrain a cry of joy. "Well, then, this unhappy man is a wonderful man. All that fortune was really his own! He is Madeleine, the providence of a whole region! He is Jean Valjean, the savior of Javert! He is a hero! He is a saint!"

"He is not a saint, and he is not a hero," said Thénardier. "He is a murderer and a robber. Jean Valjean did not rob Madeleine, but he is a robber. He did not kill Javert, but he is a murderer. What I have to reveal to you is absolutely unknown.

Le Drapeau blanc: translates *The White Flag*, a Paris newspaper in publication from 1819 to 1827 *

It belongs to the unpublished. Monsieur Baron, on the sixth of June, 1832, about a year ago, a man was in the Grand Sewer of Paris, near where the sewer empties into the Seine, between the Pont des Invalides and the Pont d'Iéna. This man, compelled to conceal himself, had taken the sewer for his dwelling and had a key to it. It was, I repeat it, the sixth of June; it might have been eight o'clock in the evening. The man heard a noise in the sewer. Strange to say, there was another man in the sewer beside him. This man was carrying something on his back. He walked bent over. The man who was walking was an old convict, and what he was carrying upon his shoulders was a corpse. As for the robbery, it follows of course. This convict was going to throw this corpse into the river. It is a noteworthy fact that, before reaching the grating of the outlet, this convict, who came from a distance in the sewer, had been compelled to pass through a horrible quagmire in which it would seem that he might have left the corpse, but the sewer men working upon the quagmire might, the very next day, have found the slain man. He preferred to go through the quagmire with his load, and his efforts must have been terrible; it is impossible to put one's life in greater peril; I do not understand how he came out of it alive. This brute said, 'You see what I have on my back. I must get out; you have the key; give it to me.' This convict was a man of terrible strength. There was no refusing him. Still he who had the key parleyed, merely to gain time. He examined the dead man, but he could see nothing, except that he was young, well dressed, apparently a rich man, and all disfigured with blood. While he was talking, he found means to cut and tear off from behind, without the killer perceiving it, a piece of the murdered man's coat. He put this piece of evidence in his pocket. After which he opened the grating, let the man out with his encumbrance on his back, shut the grating again, and escaped. You understand now. He who was carrying the corpse was Jean Valjean; he who had the key is now speaking to you, and the piece of the coat—"

Thénardier finished the phrase by drawing from his pocket and holding up, on a level with his eyes, between his thumbs and his forefingers, a strip of ragged black cloth covered with dark stains.

Marius had risen, his eye fixed upon the scrap of black cloth.

Without losing sight of this rag, he retreated to the wall and opened a closet near the chimney, without removing his startled eyes from the fragment that Thénardier held up.

Meanwhile Thénardier continued, "Monsieur Baron, I have the strongest reasons to believe that the murdered young man was an opulent stranger drawn into a snare by Jean Valjean."

"The young man was myself, and there is the coat!" cried Marius, and he threw an old black coat covered with blood upon the carpet. Then, snatching the fragment from Thénardier's hands, he bent down over the coat and applied the piece to the cut skirt. The edges fitted exactly, and the strip completed the coat. Marius rose up, quivering, desperate, flashing. He felt in his pocket, and walked, furious, toward

Thénardier, offering him and almost pushing into his face his fist full of five-hundred-franc notes.

"You are a wretch! You are a liar, a slanderer, a scoundrel. You came to accuse this man; you have justified him. You wanted to destroy him; you have succeeded only in glorifying him. And it is you who are a robber! And it is you who are a murderer! I saw you, Thénardier, Jondrette, in that den on the BOULEVARD DE L'HÔPITAL. I know enough about you to send you to the galleys, and further even, if I wished. Take this money, and leave this place! Waterloo protects you."

"Waterloo!" muttered Thénardier, pocketing the notes.

"Yes, murderer! You saved the life of a colonel there—"

"Of a general," said Thénardier, raising his head.

"Of a colonel!" replied Marius with a burst of passion. "I would not give a sou for a general. Go! Out of my sight! Ah! Monster! There are three thousand francs more. Take them. You will start tomorrow for America, with your daughter. I will see to your departure, bandit, and I will count out to you then twenty thousand francs. Go and get hanged elsewhere!"

And Thénardier went out.

As soon as Thénardier was out of doors, Marius ran to the garden where Cosette was still walking. "Cosette! Come quick! Oh! It was he who saved my life! Let us not lose a minute!"

In a moment, a fiacre was at the door. Marius helped Cosette in and sprang in himself.

"Driver," said he, "RUE DE L'HOMME ARMÉ, number seven."

"Oh! What happiness!" said Cosette. "We are going to see Monsieur Jean."

"Your father! Cosette, your father more than ever. Cosette, I see it. You told me that you never received the letter which I sent you by Gavroche. It must have fallen into his hands. Cosette, he went to the barricade to save me. On the way, he saved others; he saved Javert. He snatched me out of that gulf to give me to you. He carried me on his back in that frightful sewer. Cosette, after having been your providence, he was mine!"

Meanwhile the fiacre rolled on.

Chapter 70

At the knock on his door, Jean Valjean turned his head. "Come in," said he feebly.

Cosette and Marius appeared. Cosette rushed into the room. Marius remained upon the threshold.

"Cosette!" said Jean Valjean, and he rose in his chair, his arms stretched out and trembling.

Cosette, stifled with emotion, fell upon Jean Valjean's breast.

"Father!" said she.

Jean Valjean stammered, "Cosette! Oh, you forgive me then!"

Marius stepped forward and murmured, "Father!"

"And you, too, you forgive me!" said Jean Valjean.

Marius could not utter a word, and Jean Valjean added, "Thank you."

Cosette, seating herself upon the old man's knees, stroked away his white hair and kissed his forehead. Jean Valjean, bewildered, offered no resistance. For a moment he could not speak; then he continued, "I really needed to see Cosette a little while from time to time. Monsieur Pontmercy, let me call her Cosette. It will not be very long."

At these words which Jean Valjean now said, all that was swelling in Marius's heart broke forth. "Cosette, do you hear? He begs my pardon, and do you know what he has done for me, Cosette? He has saved my life. He has done more. He has given you to me. And, after having saved me, and after having given you to me, Cosette, what did he do with himself? He sacrificed himself. And to me the ungrateful, to me the forgetful, he says, 'Thanks!' Cosette, my whole life passed at the feet of this man would be too little. That barricade, that sewer, he went through everything for me, for you, Cosette! He bore me through death in every form, which he put aside from me, and which he accepted for himself. All courage, all virtue, all heroism, all sanctity, he has it all, Cosette. That man is an angel!"

"I told the truth," answered Jean Valjean.

"No," replied Marius, "the truth is the whole truth. You were Monsieur Madeleine; why not have said so? You saved Javert; why not have said so? I owe my life to you; why not have said so?"

"Because I thought as you did. I felt that you were right. It was necessary that I should go away."

"Do you suppose you are going to stay here?" replied Marius. "We are going to carry you back. You are a part of us. You are her father and mine. You shall not spend another day in this house. Do not imagine that you will be here tomorrow."

"Tomorrow," said Jean Valjean, "I shall not be here, but I shall not be at your house."

"What do you mean?" replied Marius.

"I shall die in a few minutes."

"Die!" exclaimed Marius.

"Yes, but that is nothing," said Jean Valjean.

Cosette uttered a cry. "Father! You shall live."

"Oh! Yes, forbid me to die. Who knows? I shall obey, perhaps. I was just dying when you came. That stopped me; it seemed to me that I was born again."

There was a noise at the door. It was the physician coming in.

"Good day and good-bye, Doctor," said Jean Valjean. "Here are my poor children."

Marius approached the physician. There was a silence. Jean Valjean turned toward Cosette. He began to gaze at her as if he would take a look which should endure through eternity.

The physician felt his pulse. "Ah! It was you he needed!" murmured he, looking at Cosette and Marius. And, bending toward Marius's ear, he added very low, "Too late."

Jean Valjean turned upon Marius and the physician a look of serenity. They heard these almost-inarticulate words come from his lips: "It is nothing to die; it is frightful not to live."

Suddenly he arose. These returns of strength are sometimes a sign also of the death struggle. He walked with a firm step to the wall, put aside Marius and the physician, who offered to assist him, took down from the wall the little copper crucifix which hung there, came back, and sat down with all the freedom of motion of perfect health, and said in a loud voice, laying the crucifix on the table, "Behold the great martyr."

Then his breast sank in and his head wavered, as if the dizziness of the tomb seized him.

Jean Valjean gathered strength and became almost completely lucid once more. He took a fold of Cosette's sleeve and kissed it.

"He is reviving! Doctor, he is reviving!" cried Marius.

"You are both kind," said Jean Valjean.

The portress had come up and was looking through the half-open door. "Do you want a priest?" she said.

"I have one," answered Jean Valjean.

And, with his finger, he seemed to designate a point above his head, where, you would have said, he saw someone. It is probable that the bishop was indeed a witness of this death.

From moment to moment, Jean Valjean grew weaker. He was sinking; he was approaching the dark horizon. His breath had become intermittent; it was interrupted by a slight rattle. He had difficulty in moving his wrist; his feet had lost all motion, but all the majesty of the soul rose and displayed itself upon his forehead. The light of the unknown world was already visible in his eye. His face grew pale, and at the same time smiled.

He motioned to Cosette to approach, then to Marius; it was evidently the last minute of the last hour, and he began to speak to them in a voice so faint it seemed to come from afar:

"Come closer, both of you. I love you dearly. You, too, love me, my Cosette. You will weep for me a little, will you not? Not too much. I do not wish you to have any deep grief.

I was writing just now to Cosette. To her, I bequeath the two candlesticks which are on the mantel. They change the candles which are put into them into consecrated tapers. I do not know whether he who gave them to me is satisfied with me in heaven. I have done what I could. My children, you will not forget that I am a poor man; you will have me buried in the most convenient piece of ground under a stone to mark the spot. That is my wish. No name on the stone. If Cosette will come for a little while sometimes, it will give me pleasure. You too, Monsieur Pontmercy. It was only ten years ago. How time passes! It is over. My children, do not weep. I am not going very far; I shall see you from there. You will only have to look when it is night; you will see me smile. Cosette, the time has come to tell you the name of your mother. Her name was Fantine. Remember that name: Fantine. Fall on your knees whenever you pronounce it. She suffered much. And loved you much. Her measure of unhappiness was as full as yours of happiness. Such are the distributions of God. He is on high, he sees us all, and he knows what he does in the midst of his great stars. So I am going away, my children. Love each other dearly always. There is scarcely anything else in the world but that: to love one another."

Cosette and Marius fell on their knees, choked with tears, each grasping one of Jean Valjean's hands. He had fallen backward; the light from the candlesticks fell upon him; his white face looked up toward heaven; he was dead.

The night was starless and very dark. Without doubt, in the gloom some mighty angel was standing with outstretched wings, awaiting the soul.

Chapter 71

There is, in the cemetery of Père Lachaise, in the neighborhood of the potter's field, far from the elegant quarter of that city of sepulchers, in a deserted corner, among the dog grass and the mosses, a stone. This stone is exempt no more than the rest from the leprosy of time. The air turns it black, the water green. It is near no path, and people do not go in that direction. When there is a little sunshine, the lizards come out. There is, all about, a rustling of wild oats. In the spring, the linnets sing in the tree.

No name can be read there.

Three things
will last forever—
faith, hope, and
love—and the greatest
of these is love.

1 CORINTHIANS 13:13

You who suffer
because you love,
love still more.
To die of love,
is to live by it.

VICTOR HUGO

NÔTRE DAME, PARIS • DAVID ROBERTS • 1828

VICTOR HUGO

Victor Hugo was a reformer, and like most reformers was intense, undaunted, insatiable, experiencing fierce but fleeting joys with keen and bitter suffering, receiving his due tribute only after living and dying for his conviction. His aim was twofold: in literature, he fought for truth; in politics, for the cause of the people; in both he was a radical.

He was born in Besançon, France, 26 February 1802. His father was a military officer of the empire, and a strong supporter of Napoleon. Victor's childhood was unsettled; he was taken hither and thither, from station to station, to Elba, Corsica, Switzerland, and Italy, and the dramatic scenes and episodes of travel and army life gave a meditative trend to his thoughts while yet a child. When his father was in Italy under Joseph Bonaparte, then king of Naples, his mother made a home for her children in Paris. He was put under the instruction of an old priest, along with his elder brother, Eugène, and a young girl, Adèle Foucher, whom he afterward married. Madame Hugo was a royalist. Her teaching and that of the priest influenced his first works, which show marked monarchical and Roman Catholic tendencies. His ode dedicated to the consecration of Charles X was a tribute to the vanishing monarchy. At the same time, the dramatic aspects of Napoleon's career appealed to this poetic youth, and he dwelt on the glorious victories and overwhelming tragedy of the great emperor. Later, however, moved by the sorrows of the people who were crushed by arbitrary despots, he became fiercely democratic and anticlerical.

In 1811, General Hugo followed Joseph Bonaparte to Spain, and Victor entered the Seminary of Nobles in Madrid, with the intention of becoming a page of King Joseph. With the fall of the empire, the family left Spain, and Victor's parents separated. Victor remained in his father's care and was preparing to enter the École Polytechnique, which would lead to government employment, but he inclined so strongly toward a literary life, and his first poem gave such promise, that his father relinquished his plan and allowed Victor to devote himself to writing. While still a boy he composed several poems and won three prizes. In 1819, he and his brother started a paper called *Le Conservateur littéraire*, which lasted about a year, and in 1822 he published the first volume of *Odes et ballades*. His style at this time was classical and not especially individual, but it brought him into prominence and gave him something to live on. For a while before this, he had existed on practically nothing, as did his character Marius.

At this time he married Adèle Foucher. Their home was delightfully free from restraint and became the center of poetic spirits, who contemplated a new school of literature in France, unhampered by classic form and arbitrary laws—laws of an ancient world become artificial and devoid of grace. This little coterie formed a society called Le Cénacle, publishing a periodical, *La Muse française*. In 1827, Hugo's *Cromwell*, a romantic drama, was presented as an example of the reforms of this new school of Romanticism. It was a bold step in advancing a new language for poetry, and it aroused a tremendous clamor of protest. The strife between the two schools became more and more bitter and reached a climax when *Hernani* was presented in 1830. It was hissed in the theatre, and crowds attended intending to ridicule it; but Hugo persisted in having it played through the whole engagement of forty-five nights, and thus established the position of romantic drama on the French stage, and eminence for himself.

From this time on, he published a deluge of dramas, poems, and letters. *Notre-Dame de Paris* came out in 1831 and secured his position as a prose writer. He wrote in a vehement style, often crude, caring not at all for conventional form or even accuracy, exaggerating sometimes, but sketching life always. He was not yet thirty when he reached the height of his career. Byron, Scott, Chateaubriand, and Goethe were failing, leaving Hugo to take first place in European literature, a position which he held until his death. Though the old school opposed it, he was elected to the French Academy; he had already been made an officer of the Legion of Honor. Favored as he was, he seemed quite untouched by success. It is impossible to comprehend his inmost nature, so full is it. He studied the poets, he loved the book of Isaiah, and he took for his model the Oriental. Such works as "Les Feuilles d'automne" ("Autumn Leaves") and "Les Chants du crépuscule" ("Songs of the Twilight") suggest a brooding melancholy, and the background of *Notre-Dame de Paris* is gloom. His love of flowers and children tells us of his tenderness. He was devoted to his own children, and they no doubt inspired *Le Livre des mères* (*The Mothers' Book*) and later poems on childhood. But one design pervades his work, and later his policies: a groping for truth. Its frequent uncouthness and constant unconventionality aroused derision. He but shrugged at scorn; bent on reform, he suffered the fate of reformers. *Notre-Dame de Paris* was his last published work of fiction for thirty years. He began to take an interest in the politics of the time. He became a peer of France in 1845, and in 1848 he was elected a deputy to the Constituent Assembly. At first he showed conservative tendencies, but he was an opportunist and marched with the times. On reelection he became orator of the democratic party, denouncing President Louis Napoleon and his secret proceedings. When Napoleon proclaimed himself king, Hugo asserted the rights of the people and the constitution. His enemies secured his proscription, and he fled to Belgium. But he was too flagrant in his partisanship and was driven from there to take refuge on the Isle of Jersey. Here again he made trouble and was banished for violating the popular feeling of sympathy with France. He fled to the Isle of Guernsey, under English protection. There he lived in the famous Hauteville House, where his taste for luxury and richness in decoration found its extravagant expression, and where, high up, in a little glass-enclosed attic room overlooking the sea, he wrote the masterpiece of his later life. He meditated upon the misery and contradictions of the world, and *Les Misérables*, begun in 1848, was published in 1862. The long period of its growth accounts for the many digressions and additions.

His pride prevented him from taking advantage of the amnesty proclamation, and not until after the fall of Napoleon did he return to France. He was reelected to the national assembly in 1871, but he opposed so violently the peace treaty between France and Germany, and aroused such animosity during his speech, that he left the tribune and resigned his seat. During the insurrection of the commune he protested against violence, and was obliged to flee to Belgium again, where he was threatened by a mob. He escaped to London, and there remained until his enemies were condemned. He had become too vehement for practical politics; his passionate convictions carried him beyond reason.

In his old age he lived with the wife of one of his sons, to whose children he was devoted. *L'Art d'être grand-père* (*The Art of Being a Grandfather*) throws an interesting light on his many-sided character. His wife had died, his two sons as well; his favorite daughter, Léopoldine, had drowned with her young husband years before while on a pleasure trip, and his younger daughter was mentally ill. But despite all adversity, old age scarcely touched him; he remained active and a keen observer until the end. He wrote tirelessly—poems, letters, satires—and, strangely enough, exhibited a hopeful, prophetic character contrary to the melancholy tone of his early writing.

His death occurred on 22 May 1885, when he was eighty-three years of age. His last wishes were expressed in a memorandum written a few months before: "I give fifty thousand francs to the poor. I wish to be taken to the grave in their hearse. I refuse the prayers of all churches. I ask for a prayer from every human soul. I believe in God."

SELECTED ARTISTIC WORKS BY VICTOR HUGO

SOUVENIR OF A CASTLE IN VOSGES, 1857

CHÂTEAU DE WALZIN, 1863

EVACUATION OF AN ISLAND, 1870

MY DESTINY, 1867

VIANDEN, THE HOUSE I LIVED IN AT THE CORNER OF THE BRIDGE, DATE UNKNOWN

CASTLE ON A HILL, 1847

OLD CASTLE IN A STORM, 1837

SCHENGEN CASTLE, 1871

GRAPHITE ARTWORK BY MARGARET FERREC

Artwork created by artist specifically for this book

PAINTINGS BY CHIARA FEDELE

Artwork created by artist specifically for this book

LETTERING PAINTINGS BY JILL DE HAAN

Artwork created by artist specifically for this book

Jill's artwork for this book also includes the cover, all chapter opener borders, artistic borders, and other painted embellishments throughout the book.

Find victory and peace as you take a *Visual Journey*™ through Hannah Hurnard's classic allegory.

AVAILABLE WHEREVER BOOKS ARE SOLD

Hinds' Feet on High Places: An Engaging Visual Journey by Hannah Hurnard

978-1-4964-2467-9 | $15.99

LivingExpressionsCollection.com

TYNDALE, Tyndale's quill logo, *Living Expressions*, and the Living Expressions logo are registered trademarks of Tyndale House Ministries.

LIVING EXPRESSIONS COLLECTION

CP1643